Salvation

Hall

Also by this author

<u>The Lancefield Mysteries</u>

The Redemption

Hemlock Row

<u>The Rose Bennett Mysteries</u>

Dead on Account

Dead Ringer

Death Duties

Death Benefit

Dead & Buried

Salvation Hall

A Lancefield Mystery

MARIAH KINGDOM

~ Perceda Press ~

This novel is entirely a work of fiction. Any resemblance to actual persons, living or dead, or to events, locations or premises is purely coincidental. Salvation Hall, the Lancefield family, the Woodlands Plantation and the village of Penwithen do not and have not ever existed, except in the author's imagination.

First published in digital form 2018 by WL Fowler

Copyright © Mariah Kingdom 2018

This paperback edition Perceda Press 2022

Mariah Kingdom asserts the moral right to be identified as the author of this work.

A catalogue record for this publication is available from the British Library

All rights reserved. No part of this publication may be reproduced, stored in a retrieval system or transmitted in any form or by any means, electronic, mechanical, photocopying, recording or otherwise, without the written permission of the author and/or publisher.

ISBN 978-1-8380834-5-8

Cover design by www.ebooklaunch.com

'Swan flocks of lilies shoreward lying, In sweetness, not in music, dying'

John Greenleaf Whittier

1

Salvation Hall.

Viewed by day, the house never fails to impress. Viewed in the early evening, one can only ever be enchanted. Mullioned windows reflect a Cornish moon, stone gables stand erect despite their age, a gentle stream of smoke escapes from the chimney above the drawing room, the fire always lit, even when the room rests unoccupied.

In the fading light of a mid-September evening, the house looks warm, the rose-gold stone of its walls glowing with the heat of a late summer's day. Here and there a modest light illuminates an occasional window to the front of the house, a standard lamp in the grand hall to the right of the main doorway, a large table lamp atop a bookcase in the snug, a pair of spotlights glinting beneath a run of oak-framed cupboards in the kitchen. It is the habit here to make the house look lived in, even when there is no one within its walls.

Approaching the house from the front can often render an unsuspecting visitor silent, the perfect blend of gables and chimneys and stone-flanked bay windows a declaration of understated elegance. Those lucky enough to visit in the spring might find their breath taken away by a generous wisteria, its abundant flowers cascading down the west-facing walls from roof to ground like a passing shower of amethysts, happy with its situation despite a meagre ration of late afternoon sunlight. Now, as the days of summer give way to a warm and early autumn, three large and floriferous hydrangeas are found to provide the show, their blowsy lilac mopheads shifting gently in a constant Cornish breeze.

To the right of the house a gravel drive tapers to become a narrow path, skirting the walls and leading down a set of worn stone steps, through an arch of neatly trimmed yew, and down towards an ornamental lake. Turn back from this point in the evening and the outline of the rear of the house can just be made out in the moonlight: the bay windows of upper bedrooms, the roofline of an impressive conservatory, the sharp, rotating arrows of a pristine iron weather vane. Turn again to the water and the lake is always busy, its glassy surface spotted with a multitude of dozing water lilies, their glossy petals tightly closed against the evening chill, the lake's murky depths a bubbling cauldron of feeding carp, their silvery scales flashing in the moonlight between the floating lily leaves as they indulge their nightly appetites.

Tonight the evening ritual is disturbed. Two human eyes, open and unseeing, stare up from between the water lilies. An inquisitive carp comes close and nibbles at a lock of hair and, finding it unappetising, turns its back and flits towards the other end of the lake in search of something better. The human eyes do not move. Their lids do not flicker, the lashes do not flutter, and the pupils remain inert, untroubled by the carp's unwarranted attentions.

Tonight, beneath the moonlight, the carp are not alone. Tonight they have an unexpected guest.

2

Kathryn Clifton reached down and pulled her mobile phone from the handbag beneath her chair. A glance at the screen confirmed another incoming call from Moira to go with the three she'd already ignored that evening, and she calmly pressed the phone's off-button with her thumb and dropped the device back into the bag. She didn't have to take the call to know how the conversation would go.

Yes, she was fine. No, there was nothing for Moira to worry about. Yes, the drive from Cambridge to Penzance had been long and uneventful. Yes, she was tired. (How could you be anything else after a drive of three hundred and sixty miles?) Yes, she intended to proceed with the commission. And no, she wasn't planning to come back to Edinburgh any time soon.

Kathryn leaned back in her seat and blew out a sigh. Marrying Moira's brother hadn't been one of her finer decisions. But then again, she wouldn't be the first bride to be swept away on a wave of excitement so overwhelming that it had blinded her to all of the risks. Any marriage is a leap of faith, a dive into the unknown. For some that dive would lead to a lifetime of happiness. For others, like Kathryn…

She brushed the thought away and cast a glance around the room. The hotel lobby had been alive with guests when she'd first checked in, but now she was alone in the small and elegant dining room, waiting for a bouillabaisse that she wasn't really in the mood to eat. Even the hotel's owner – a one-man charm offensive who appeared to be receptionist, barman, waiter and bag-carrier – had disappeared from view. At least he'd left her with a decent glass of Chablis to pass the time until the meal arrived. She pulled the glass towards her and lifted it to her lips, sipping on the not-quite-icy wine. If the stew didn't appear soon, she thought, she would have to order another glass.

It must have been a telepathic thought. The restaurant door inched open and voices carried through from the hallway – a gaggle of German tourists making their way out into the night air, the hotel manager wishing them a most enjoyable evening. The gaggle gone, Ian Mitchell rolled around the door into the dining room and smiled at her with warm, grey, solicitous eyes. 'Kathryn, I feel I've neglected you. Can I get you another glass of Chablis?' He made his way to her table without waiting for an answer and took possession of her almost-empty glass.

She could feel his eyes on her face, the genuine concern of an attentive host for his guest and, under his gaze, she relaxed a little. 'Perhaps when the stew arrives?'

His brow furrowed but it was a practised manoeuvre and, beneath the furrow, the grey eyes were still smiling. 'Sorry it's taking a little time, but Ethan is a bit of a perfectionist. Everything from scratch, you know?' He took a step backwards. 'Why don't I freshen this up for you anyway? On the house.' Behind the bar, he pulled two clean glasses from a rack and set about filling them. 'You don't mind if I join you? I've had a hell of a day. It's the first time the hotel has been at full capacity for a couple of weeks, and I'm off the pace a bit.' He lifted the glasses, and made for Kathryn's table. 'If I'm honest, I'm quite pleased that you're our only dinner guest this evening. We had a full dining room last night, so Ethan is enjoying the chance to just cook for two and take his time.'

'For two?'

He was beside her now and set a glass down on the table. 'If he's going to cook bouillabaisse he might as well make it for two. I haven't had a treat like that for ages.' He sank onto a chair at the table adjacent to Kathryn's. 'Well, in truth he's making it for three, but he's going to eat his share in the kitchen.' Ian leaned across to her and lowered his voice. 'We'll be sitting at separate tables, of course. We don't have to speak to each other if you'd prefer it.'

'I'd be glad of the company, to be honest.' Kathryn turned towards him with a smile. 'You have a lovely hotel. Have you been here long?'

'Long enough to know better. I used to be a solicitor, in a partnership in Truro. This place belonged to an aunt and uncle on my mother's side, and we used to spend our holidays here when I was a kid. When they decided to retire to Brittany, I decided it was too good a chance to miss. My son Laurence had just graduated from university and gone off to work in the City, and I didn't want to spend the rest of my life chained up in a musty office. So I sold off my share of the practice, and just went for it.' His smile was wistful now. 'I've no regrets. I don't think anyone could regret living and working in Penzance.'

There was no mention of a wife, but that was no business of Kathryn's. 'I've never visited Penzance before, but I'm hoping to take a look around while I'm here. It all depends on how much free time I get.' She sipped on her wine. 'I'm here for professional reasons, not for a holiday.'

'So I understand.' Ian's face took on a knowing look. 'You're here to do some work for Richard Lancefield.'

*

Becca Smith glanced up as the kitchen clock chimed nine. She hated that damned clock, a hand-me-down from her grandmother's council flat in Hayle, one of those family treasures that no one but the original owner considered to be a treasure at all. And she hated the meaning behind those synthetic, clanging chimes. Philip should have been home by seven. He was already two hours late.

She pushed herself up from a shabby pine chair and leaned across the table to grasp at the dinner plate set in Philip's place. The plate was cold, the mixed grill prepared with so much care now greasily congealed against the cheap white porcelain beneath, and she muttered under her breath as she carried it over to the pedal bin. The lump in her throat was tightening now, and she swallowed against it as she scraped the wasted food into the bin and clattered the plate and cutlery into the stained ceramic sink beneath the window.

He had promised to be home by seven, promised to be there in time to put Frankie to bed. Becca snuffled back a tear and pursed her lips against a burgeoning sob. These days Philip's promises were only made for one reason. They were made to be broken.

There was a half-empty bottle of cheap Merlot on the worktop next to the sink, and she pulled the cork out with a curse and glugged most of the contents into an outsized, balloon-shaped wine glass. She'd already downed two glasses during the evening, another one wouldn't make much difference now, and she gulped at the wine, wincing as its vinegary flavours flowed over her tongue and her teeth, warming the inside of her cheeks.

Somewhere outside the cottage, a car door slammed in the darkness and she leaned over the sink, wine glass still in hand, and peered out through the window. But there was nothing to see other than the moonlight shining across the garden. Probably a car outside in the lane, then, and a malevolent breeze carrying the sound across the estate to taunt her.

She turned her eyes up towards the moon, clear and full, and the lump in her throat began to grow. When she and Philip were first together, he would take her down to the beach when the moon was full, and they would curl up on the sand, wrapped in a blanket, drinking red wine. They would feast on olives and figs and morsels of cheese – soft Cornish Blue or tangy, nettled Yarg. Sometimes they would paddle in the freezing cold water, and then wrap themselves back in the blanket and sip warming apple brandy from a hip flask, and talk of how they planned to spend their lives. They were free spirits, both. Philip loved the woods and the sky and sleeping outdoors, unfettered by the trappings of a mundane, everyday life. And Becca was a water baby who lived for the sea and the feel of salty Cornish breezes on her cheeks and neck, and through the tangle of her bleached-blonde, sun-streaked hair.

She swallowed hard against the lump and turned to glance around the kitchen, taking in the untidy worktops with their jumble of unwashed dishes, the growing pile of ironing in a basket on top of the washing machine, the clothes horse in the corner, the all-too-familiar rows of greying nappies draped across its bars. It was hard to be a free spirit with a child in tow. At least, for her.

After Frankie's birth there had been no more lying on the sand under the moon, no more al fresco feasts of wine and figs and olives and cheese. She had wanted Philip to take them both to the beach, to let Frankie lie in her Moses basket by the water's edge while her parents paddled together in the moonlight. The blanket was big enough to wrap all three of them together in a parcel of love, a woolly cocoon to bind them all until Frankie had sucked her fill of her father's love of the woods and the sky and her mother's love of the sea and the stars, and emerged into the world a free spirit on her own.

But Philip had other ideas.

Oh, he still cared for Becca, and he loved their child, and he had made a commitment of sorts, moving them into the tied cottage that came with his job at Salvation Hall. But it wasn't the sort of life that either of them had planned for.

There was something in Philip that just needed to be free, that needed to feel wild and untamed and at one with nature. Something that he could only share with another free spirit. And fettered by a mother's fears, hampered by a child's demands, Becca was no longer truly free. The passion was gone, and it hadn't taken long for Philip to find another free spirit to share his blanket on the beach.

Becca knew that there was someone else, and she knew who that someone was. Worse still, she knew that they were together now. The familiar thought hit her like an unexpected punch to the gut and the sob, once stifled, made its way out of her lips and punctuated the silence.

She knew who it was, and she knew where they were. And she knew that there was absolutely nothing that she could do to make it stop.

3

Despite a conspiracy of early morning traffic, a slow-moving tractor on the A394 and a wrong turn at Helston, the drive from the centre of Penzance to Salvation Hall, some fifteen miles to the east, had taken Kathryn barely thirty minutes. The house was on the approach to Penwithen village, and she found the entrance to the estate with ease and a sense of relief that the imposing wrought-iron gates were unlocked and standing open to welcome her as promised. She turned her car in slowly and trundled down the driveway with her foot barely on the accelerator, taking in the surroundings, and enjoying the tangle of foliage that ran rampant on either side of the road. Just a quarter of a mile in, the car rounded a bend and Kathryn drew in a breath as the jungle to her left gave way to a pristine, rolling lawn and a spectacular downhill view of the manor house itself.

A generous gravelled parking area flanked by clipped yew hedges lay at the end of the drive and she pulled the Volvo up against the left-hand hedge before alighting from the car and retrieving her bag from the boot. She had barely slammed the boot lid shut when Salvation Hall's heavy oak front door swung open and a sparky, wire-haired fox terrier scuttled out to greet her with a curious eye and an inquisitive bark.

'Kathryn Clifton?' Behind the dog, a gaunt and ageing figure in dishevelled country tweeds hovered in the doorway, a gnarled hand outstretched towards her in greeting. 'I'm Richard Lancefield. Welcome to Salvation Hall.' He took her hand and shook it warmly, and then nodded in the dog's direction. 'Don't mind Samson, he loves to meet a new friend.'

'As do I.' Kathryn offered him a smile.

'Then we'll all get on famously.' The old man turned back into the house and beckoned for her to follow him. 'Come on through to the library, it's just here across the hallway.' He led her briskly across polished parquet flooring and through a door at the end of the hall. The room beyond was light and airy, and he ushered her towards a small, damask-covered sofa before settling himself into the contours of a shabby, well-worn armchair opposite. The terrier had followed him, and he patted his knees with his hands and Samson responded with an enthusiastic leap into his lap.

Kathryn watched as the dog circled and then lowered himself into a curl, his chin resting on the old man's knee, his eyes focused on her with a keen, doggy interest. She returned the dog's gaze with an uncertain smile. 'I hope I'm not too early.'

'Not at all. There is much work to be done.' Richard smiled, not unpleasantly, his thin lips peeling back to reveal surprisingly well-preserved teeth. 'I do appreciate you travelling so far to work with me, Kathryn. I hope that Ian Mitchell has made you comfortable at the hotel? I've never been to the place myself, but I understand that it's a decent enough place to rest your head. They tell me that the chef is first rate.'

'I'm very happy there, thank you. And yes, the food is excellent.' Kathryn hesitated, and then ventured a question. 'Before we begin, could I just confirm my understanding of your instructions? You would like your family's history to be researched and recorded from original documents available here at the house? And there are a number of historical artefacts which require examination and curating?'

Richard placed a hand on Samson's neck and rubbed a bony finger into the animal's wiry coat. 'That is pretty much the size of it.' His rheumy eyes didn't leave

Kathryn's face as he spoke. 'The artefacts are curiosities that the family have acquired over the years, and I would appreciate your opinion on what best to do with them. As to the papers, the Lancefields have always been notorious hoarders. Most of the documents are up in the attic, but I will have them brought down to the library for you. You will understand that I would prefer them not to be taken away from the house, so I hope it will suit you to work with them here?'

'Of course. But you have no objection to my making copies so that I can also work on them at home?'

'No objection that I can think of, providing that you respect the family's privacy and keep the contents to yourself.' For a moment, a glint of mischief sparked in the pink-rimmed eyes. 'I think I explained in my letter to you that your name was given to me by the Ferguson family? I was up at Oxford with old Hugh Ferguson many years ago. I spent the New Year up at his place in Perth last year, and he told me of the work you did to document the history of his family. A very thorough and sensitive piece of work, he called it. An outstanding piece of work by a very diligent and discreet young woman. Those were his words, and that's a good enough recommendation for me.'

A blush rose to Kathryn's cheeks. 'It was kind of him to say so.'

'Kind, be damned. Ferguson's not the sort of fellow to waste words in empty flattery. No' – he shook his head – 'all I ask is that you do the same for me. I would like you to curate the documents, to write up the family's history from them for the family's private use, and to trace and document our genealogy from the family papers and any other sources at your disposal.' He frowned. 'I have not moved with the times, Kathryn, but I understand that there may be information available from public records which may supplement the documents we have here?'

'I'm sure there will be. If you wish, I can research online to fill in any gaps that remain after I've examined the documents, and there may also be papers at the county records office.'

'As you see fit.' He ran his tongue thoughtfully around the thin lips. 'The papers we have relate to the house and estate here, and also to our estates overseas. Some of the documents date back as far as the seventeenth century. And none of them have been shared outside of the family until now. I have been approached several times by academic institutions seeking access to the papers, but I have always considered it best to keep them private to the Lancefield family.' He paused to draw in a breath. 'As a young man, I inherited my father's whole estate outright. That is, Salvation Hall, all of the associated farmland acquired over many generations, and the majority of properties in the village of Penwithen, along with his various shares and investments. In addition, I inherited several properties on the Caribbean island of St Felix. My family were among the early settlers to the island, and I'm sure you will have already deduced that our connections – like those of the Ferguson family – are somewhat sensitive.'

'Your family owned a number of sugar plantations.'

The old man's frown morphed into a knowing smile. 'Amongst other things.' An inflection in his voice suggested that those other things might best remain unnamed. 'My son David has never attempted to hide his shame at the source of our family's wealth. He considers it an unfortunate birthright and has sought over many years to distance himself from it as far as he can. He lives in Edinburgh now – indeed he has lived there for many years – and he is not overjoyed at my proposal to document our family's heritage. And neither is my granddaughter Lucy.'

'Does Lucy share her father's views?'

The knowing smile took on a cynical twist. 'Lucy has a far more creative and self-seeking solution to deal with her heritage. She hopes to turn everything that she expects to inherit into a commercial enterprise, and thinks that everyone will eventually forget how her family came by it.' His frown returned. 'She has concocted a plan to turn Salvation Hall into some kind of hotel and health spa, and has enrolled her fiancé Marcus to work with her to deliver the plan.'

'Marcus Drake?' Kathryn had already heard the name. 'I met Ian Mitchell yesterday evening, and he mentioned that Marcus worked for him at The Zoological.'

'At the moment, yes. He's their business development manager. That's why we recommended that you use the hotel during your stay.' Richard's brow furrowed. 'Marcus is a decent enough chap, but I'm not sure that his talents will stretch to meet Lucy's lofty expectations. And even if they will, I think it's foolish of Lucy to believe that her plans will be sufficient to remove any stigma from her inheritance.'

'You don't agree with her.'

The old man's frown gave way to an enigmatic smile. 'It's not a question of my disagreeing with her, Kathryn. I simply don't believe that there is any stigma to be removed in the first place.'

*

'Philip hasn't been home all night.' Becca Smith leaned against the sleek kitchen counter. Her skin was pale and pallid, her cheeks sunken, and her eyes were swollen from hours of crying and sleeplessness. She was still wearing the previous day's clothes, and the faint odour of greasy food and stale Merlot hung about her. 'I want to see Lucy.'

The demand fell short of the mark. 'I've already told you, you can't see Lucy.' Nancy Woodlands, making coffee in a simple cafetiere, was just a few feet away from her. 'We're busy today with Richard's guest.' Her voice was gentle but firm. 'Are you going to do any work today? Because if not, you might as well go back to the cottage instead of cluttering up the house.'

'I know he's been with her, Nancy. He must be with her now. Please let me go and speak with them.'

Nancy turned on her heel and stepped away from the kitchen counter. She took hold of the girl's elbow and steered her firmly towards a large table at the end of the room. 'For heaven's sake, if you won't go home then at least please sit down. When I've taken Richard's coffee through to the library, I'll go up to Lucy's room and check for you. But I don't think they're up there. They never come into the house.' She leaned her face towards Becca's hair and gave an exploratory sniff. 'And then I think you should go home and shower. If Richard comes into the kitchen and finds you in this state, he won't be impressed. He doesn't pay you to mooch around after Philip. He pays you to keep the house clean and tidy. And you can't do that if you're not clean and tidy yourself.'

Becca ignored the reprimand. She lowered herself onto an upholstered chair and leaned her elbows on the table. 'He's been with that *bitch* all night.' She spat the words out, and a solitary tear escaped down her cheek. 'He won't stay away from her. I don't think I can take it much longer.' She rubbed at the cheek with the sleeve of her blouse. 'I've been calling and texting him all through the night, but he hasn't replied.'

'What have you done with Frankie?'

'I've taken her down to the village. She's with my mum. 'Becca chewed on her lip. 'How can Marcus bear it, Nancy? He does know, doesn't he, that his fiancée is sleeping with my man?'

Nancy blew out a breath, and then lowered herself slowly onto the chair beside Becca's. 'Look, there is no way that Lucy and Philip would spend the night together under this roof, not with Marcus in the same building.'

'I don't know why not. She's just a little slut.'

'For pity's sake.' Nancy gave Becca's chair an admonishing shove with her foot. 'Don't you think it would be a good idea for you to remember on which side your bread is buttered? Richard is your employer. Causing a scene isn't going to help matters. Lucy is just having her fun while she can.'

'She's having her fun with Philip. *My* Philip. My baby's father.'

Nancy let out a sigh. 'I know, honey.' She put up a hand to brush a strand of grubby blonde hair away from the girl's face, and her voice grew gentle. 'But this is life for us, Becca. You put up with Philip's behaviour because you don't want to lose him. Marcus puts up with Lucy's behaviour because he loves her. But they're just playing around. When Lucy and Marcus marry, things will change. They'll go back to how they used to be.'

'Is that what Marcus thinks?'

'I don't know what he thinks. He doesn't talk to me about it. I'm not even sure he does know what's going on. Or maybe he's in denial. Maybe he just hopes that if he ignores it, she'll get it out of her system and then, after the wedding, it will be different.'

'I don't think it will be different.'

'There's still no need to make a scene.' Nancy shook her head. 'Not in front of Richard's guest. Richard will be furious if you do, and things are bad enough. You know how private the family is. We can't let a stranger see what lies beneath the surface.'

Becca's mouth pushed forward into a pout. 'It's always about the Lancefields, isn't it?'

'Of course it's always about the Lancefields. We live in their world, at their behest. Why would it be any different?' Nancy took hold of Becca's hand and squeezed it. 'Now promise me that you'll sit here quietly until I get back.'

'Do I have a choice?' Becca withdrew her hand and slumped back in her seat. How few choices were left to her now – stay with Philip and tolerate his infidelity, or leave him and lose her job and her home into the bargain. Carry on being a fool, or carry the mantle of a martyr.

She didn't want to be a martyr. But then again, she

didn't know how much longer she could go on being a fool.

4

'Ah, here she is.' Richard Lancefield looked up as the door of the library opened and greeted the incomer with a smile. 'Here is my amanuensis.' He settled back into his seat. 'Nancy, come and meet Kathryn Clifton.'

The girl lowered her head with a modest smile and drifted across the room to place a neatly laid coffee tray onto a console table. She turned to Kathryn and held out a slim, manicured hand. 'I'm very pleased to meet you, Kathryn. And I'm Richard's *secretary*.' She cast a wry smile in his direction as Kathryn shook her hand. 'Richard is very pleased with himself for discovering that fancy word.'

The old man beamed. 'I'm told it derives from the Latin *servus a manu*.' He turned his eyes back to Nancy with a spark of mischief. 'And loosely translates as "a slave with secretarial duties".'

Nancy frowned at Kathryn. 'As I said, I'm his secretary.' She turned back to the console. 'I've brought you coffee and biscuits. I hope that will suffice for now. Becca is a little indisposed today, so if you need anything else I'll be in the kitchen.'

'Efficient as always.' He was watching the girl with an intensity that Kathryn found difficult to fathom. 'Is there any chance that Becca may become a little less indisposed? I was hoping that you would spend the day assisting Kathryn here in the library. I plan to take her for a tour of the house and gardens after we've had coffee, but then I think it might be appropriate to introduce her to our collection of secrets and delights.' He turned to Kathryn. 'Nancy is a most excellent assistant in such matters. We've already sorted out the first few boxes of papers for you to examine. I was hoping that you might work on them together.' The rheumy eyes looked expectant.

'Well, I would love to see the house and gardens, and then yes, if Nancy could give me some assistance it would be very much appreciated.'

'Appreciated? Now that would make a pleasant change in this household.' Nancy's tone was just the respectful side of teasing. She backed towards the door, her smile still turned to Richard. 'I will be back, but I'm just going to pop up to Lucy's room. I don't know if she's up yet, and Becca wanted to have a word with her.'

Richard's face grew solemn. 'My granddaughter keeps very odd hours, Kathryn. But you will eventually see her coming and going about the place. And her fiancé Marcus. They both have rooms on the first floor of the main house. And you will meet Becca at some point. When not indisposed, she is our part-time housekeeper. Her partner Philip you are less likely to meet unless we bump into him in the gardens. He is our head gardener.' He nodded to himself. 'A splendid fellow.' He turned again to Nancy. 'Marcus will have left for Penzance, but perhaps you could ask Lucy to come and introduce herself to Kathryn. I wouldn't want our guest to think the family lacks civility.' There was a stern edge to his words. He waited until Nancy had backed out of the room, and then he gently tipped Samson from his lap, pushed himself to his feet, and made his way slowly over to the console table. 'Black or white?' He grasped the handle of the cafetiere with arthritic fingers.

'White, please. With sugar.'

He smiled at her, the sternness gone. '"White, with sugar" could once have been the Lancefield family motto. It is, after all, the way we made our money.' He chuckled softly. 'I hope you're not too sensitive to my little jokes. I'm afraid political correctness is not my strong point.' He held a cup out towards her but inclined his head in the direction of the window. 'Would you stand here with me, to drink it? I do like to look out over the garden.' He looked pleased when she rose to her feet and took the cup from his hand.

The window of the library looked out across a paved terrace, beyond which a manicured lawn rolled down to the edge of a large, ornamental lake. Kathryn stirred absently at her coffee and gazed out across the view. It was undeniably beautiful.

Beside her, Richard had leaned against the window sill to steady himself. 'You can't see very well from here, but beyond the lake we have a fine collection of rhododendrons. It's the wrong time of year to see them flower, of course.' He blinked. 'I do believe we have one of the finest gardens in Cornwall, you know. But I won't open to the public.' He lifted his cup carefully to his lips and sipped. 'To the west of the house, we have a formal rose garden, built into what once was the walled vegetable garden. It's a fairly recent addition. Philip and I worked on it together.' There was a note of pride in his voice. 'And behind the Dower House – my own quarters, you know – I have an orchid house. Growing orchids is my particular pleasure. They remind me' – he gave a melancholy smile – 'of my island life. Of my time spent on St Felix as a young man.'

Kathryn smiled. 'Did you spend a long time there?'

'Several years. I went out there after coming down from Oxford and ran the estate for my father. Then I came home and married, so my enjoyment of the island was confined to annual visits.' His eyes clouded. 'My late wife didn't share my enthusiasm for the Caribbean. The climate, you know?' He was lost for a moment in distant thought, then he looked up again and pointed across the lake to the near horizon. 'If you look very closely, you will just make out the tower of the village church in the distance.'

Kathryn peered out through the glass. 'Yes, I can just about see it. A Norman tower?'

He looked pleased. 'It's a fine view.' His brow creased. 'Now who is that striding out across the lawn? I thought Becca was supposed to be indisposed.'

Kathryn leaned closer to the glass. A fair-haired girl in track-suit bottoms and a grey blouse was striding out towards the water's edge. She watched as the girl reached the lake and turned right to walk along the bank. 'Becca? That's your housekeeper, isn't it?'

He answered with a nod. 'A strange girl. I don't know what Philip sees in her. But they have a charming daughter, little Francesca.' He mumbled to himself. 'None of my business, I suppose. What does an old man like me know about it? Still, we have to look after them.' He turned back to Kathryn. 'Would you like more coffee?'

Kathryn didn't answer him. She was still gazing out of the window. The fair-haired girl had paused by the side of the lake and was looking down at something in the water. Then she seemed to hop, first on one leg and then the other, in a curious dance of consternation. Suddenly her arms began to flail around her head, and her movements became wild and convulsive.

And then she screamed.

It pierced the air like a whistle, a shrill, almost angry outpouring of emotion so loud they heard it through the window. Kathryn watched in alarm as the distant figure fell to its knees beside the lake and then somewhere to the left, just within her field of vision, another figure broke into the scene, running at speed down the smooth, grassy slope. It was Nancy. She threw herself onto the grass and wrapped her arms around the screaming girl then, having glanced down into the water, she turned her head back towards the library window.

'Something's wrong.' The old man's voice began to waver.

'You stay here. I'll go.'

'No. You'll take me with you.' His tone was commanding. He had already clattered his cup down onto the console table and was making for the door, the faithful Samson fretting at his heels.

Kathryn turned back and looked once more out of the window and, for a fleeting moment, the contents of her stomach churned. And then she was flying out of the library door, hot on Richard Lancefield's heels.

*

Becca was still on her knees when they reached the lake. She was staring into the water, her free arm held aloft, her left index finger pointing loosely down at something just below the surface. Nancy had risen to her feet, but her gaze was down towards the water, transfixed by something that from their present position neither Richard nor Kathryn could see.

Richard stepped slowly forward, and as he did so Kathryn laid a cautioning hand upon his arm. He tried to shake himself free but Kathryn, seeing the fear on Nancy's face, tightened her grip and tried to hold him back.

And then Nancy was beside him too, her arm gently draped around his shoulders, her face deliberately close to his, her dark eyes beseeching. 'Don't look, Richard. I don't want you to see.' For a moment he held her gaze, and then he shook himself free of Kathryn's grip and Nancy's gentle touch, to stand beside the water's edge and lower his eyes down into its murky, rippling depths.

Just below the surface, her blonde hair swirling around her face, a girl's lifeless body was drifting gently between the swathes of innocent water lilies. 'She looks like Ophelia, in Millais' painting.' Richard's voice was quiet and unnaturally calm. 'Ophelia lying peacefully in her watery grave.' His voice began to break. 'How beautiful she looks.'

There was a moment's ominous silence and then Nancy began to whimper, and as she did so a dreadful realisation began to creep across Richard's ashen face. He

wasn't looking down at a painting.
And it wasn't Ophelia lying cold and lifeless in the lake.

5

'Lucy Amelia Lancefield.' Detective Sergeant Tom Parkinson consulted his notebook and frowned at the illegibility of his own untidy script. 'She's Richard Lancefield's granddaughter, sir.' He turned his head and tilted it in the direction of the house, signifying the connection.

Detective Chief Inspector Ennor Price followed his signal and looked back across the gardens. An elderly man in country tweeds was huddled on a wooden bench on the terrace next to the house, watching the unfolding events. The distance between them was too far for Price to clearly read the man's expression, but he could guess. 'Is that Richard Lancefield the philanthropist?' He didn't really need to ask. He was already familiar with the name Lancefield. There had been Lancefields living at Salvation Hall for the better part of three hundred years. Their name was synonymous with that small part of Cornwall, their wealth interwoven with the scenery, their generosity visible in the naming of schools and hospital wings and bursaries for further education. But it wasn't a generosity always welcomed by the local community.

The policeman turned his attention back to the lake and gazed down again at the girl lying in the water. In life, he decided, she must have possessed an expensive, manufactured kind of beauty. Long blonde hair was gently eddying around her face, neck and shoulders, and her skin appeared to glow with an unnatural tan despite the water's early damage. She was wearing a long, fern-green sun dress which clung to the upper contours of her body, and a scarf of the same colour was wound around her neck. Her eyes were open and surprised, her face bloated, her lips parted, her head bent just so very slightly backwards as if the waters were unable to carry its weight. He didn't have much time for the overprivileged landed gentry as a rule, but this girl had surrendered her gentrification to a violent hand. He was in no doubt, even before the body had been examined, that she had been murdered, that her life had been taken from her. Victimhood was a leveller and, like all victims, she was deserving of his full attention and his best endeavours to deliver her some justice. He tilted his head towards the sergeant. 'What do we know so far?'

'She hadn't been seen by any member of the household since early yesterday evening, but that in itself wasn't a cause for concern. She had an active social life and was often out until late in the evening, and very often didn't surface until after ten in the morning. Nobody had missed her.'

'What were her plans for yesterday evening?'

'We don't know at this stage. There's a fiancé, Marcus Drake. He lives here, at Salvation Hall, but he went out to work in Penzance this morning at his usual time without speaking to any other member of the household.'

DCI Price raised an eyebrow. 'And he didn't notice that she was missing?'

'Apparently they don't share a room.'

'Who are the women with Richard Lancefield?' Price asked the question without looking back at the bench. At first sight he'd registered a slim, pale woman with long chestnut hair sitting to one side of Lancefield, and a smaller, dark-haired woman to the other. The brunette appeared to be clutching Lancefield's hand in hers.

'The one holding his hand is Nancy Woodlands. She's his secretary. The other is a visitor to the house, Kathryn Clifton. I'm not sure I fully understand what she's doing here. Something about the family's history.' Parkinson cleared his throat. 'There's another woman involved here, sir. Becca Smith. That's her sitting on the grass with

Halliwell.' He pointed across the lawn to where Becca was sitting on the ground, her knees drawn up under her chin, her arms hugging her knees. The comely WPC Halliwell had a comforting arm around the girl's shoulders and appeared to be offering words of comfort that were falling on deaf ears. 'It was Becca Smith who found the body.'

'And where does she fit in?'

'She's the housekeeper. She lives in a cottage on the estate, with her partner Philip McKeith. He's the gardener.' DS Parkinson flicked back through his notes. 'She came to the house this morning looking for Lucy Lancefield. She claims that McKeith has been missing all night and that he and Lucy Lancefield were lovers.'

Price raised an eyebrow. 'Has this Philip McKeith turned up yet?'

'No, sir. We're searching the house and grounds for him now.'

Price nodded, more to himself than to Parkinson. 'We need to get the body out of the water and nail down a cause of death. I think she was dead before she went into the lake.' It wasn't just his intuition. It was the placement of the body and the surprise in the eyes. 'I'm going to take Richard up to the house. Can you arrange for someone to notify the fiancé and bring him back here, and then take Becca Smith back to her cottage and talk to her again?' He frowned, thinking. 'Do we have a time for the pathologist?'

'In the next hour.' Parkinson flipped his notebook shut. 'I guess all we need to do now is find Philip McKeith.'

'Now, what have I told you about guessing?' Price gave a wry smile as he plunged his hands into the pockets of his jacket and then he turned away from the lake and strode out across the lawn towards the terrace. He didn't want to look at the body again just yet. It reminded him of a painting he'd seen in a gallery in London, an unexpected low point in an unhappy day of sightseeing.

He hadn't understood then, and he didn't understand

now, how anyone could see art and beauty in a corpse.

6

'She was just a little slut.' Becca looked away from DS Parkinson, her full lips curled in a show of disgust. 'And before you ask, no, I'm not sorry that she's dead.'

Tom Parkinson smiled to himself, and regarded the girl with a policeman's practised eye. There was a rough beauty beneath the smudged makeup and ill-fitting clothes, perhaps even a pretty smile if the self-righteous scowl could be cajoled from her face for long enough. He had brought her back from the lake to the tied cottage that she shared with McKeith, and now they were sitting at the cluttered kitchen table. The place was shabby rather than homely, grubby in a way that suggested her role as housekeeper with the Lancefields didn't leave her with enough time or energy to apply the same domestic rigours to the cottage.

He rested his forearms on the table and tried to look sympathetic. Grubby kitchen or not, she looked vulnerable to him, the shock of the morning's events still mirrored in her eyes. 'Well, I appreciate your honesty, Becca. But I have to ask you what Lucy Lancefield had done to deserve your damnation?'

Becca blinked back an angry tear. 'I already told you. The slut was sleeping with Philip. With *my* Philip.' She swallowed hard. 'I thought it would stop when she got engaged to Marcus, but it didn't.'

'When did it start?'

'When Frankie – Francesca – was born.'

'Francesca.' He repeated the name slowly. 'And how old is she?'

'She's almost two.'

'And how long were you and Philip together before Francesca was born?'

'About a year. He was mine then. But when Frankie was…' Becca's words trailed away and she looked up at the ceiling, fighting back a sob. 'It's not as if… they knew, both of them. They knew that *I* knew, and they knew how much it hurt me. And they still did it. They'd done it before. He knew her before he met me. He said he needed her, he needed the excitement. And he couldn't get that from me.'

Parkinson didn't respond. Witnesses in shock were apt to lack any sense of logical thought. His job was to make sense of the words as best he could. He thought for a moment, trying to decide on the best approach, then said quietly, 'I need to take you back to the beginning. I need to ask you about finding the body.'

Becca pulled a greying tissue from her pocket and dabbed at her eyes. 'I'd been up to the house looking for Lucy. Philip had been out all night, and I thought he was with her. I told Nancy I wanted to see her, and Nancy went up to her room to tell her. But the room was empty. Nancy said that the bed hadn't been slept in. I didn't believe her, but she wouldn't let me go up and look for myself.'

'And then what happened?'

'I came back out into the garden to look for Philip. I was going to walk up to the potting shed and see if he was up there, but as I walked along the edge of the lake I thought I saw something in the water.'

'And it was Lucy?'

'Yes.' Becca's face grew pale. 'I saw her dress first, a big patch of green amongst the water lilies. It was the wrong shade of green, brighter than the leaves, and I went to take a look'. She twisted the tissue between sticky, tear-stained fingers. 'She was just lying there in the water, almost submerged. I just froze. I think it was the shock. I don't know how long I stood there, and then I think I screamed.

I know Nancy came running from the house, and then I saw Richard and that Kathryn woman walking towards me.' What little composure Becca had left was beginning to crack, her face folding into a crumple of tears. 'Poor Richard.' She looked up at DS Parkinson through tear-soaked lashes. 'I mean, I hated the little bitch, but it's not Richard's fault she was like that.'

Parkinson gave her a moment to compose herself, and then quietly asked, 'Do you know where Philip is, Becca? Has he been in touch with you?'

'Of course not.' She spat the words out, angry again. 'Why do you think I was looking for him?'

'When did you last see him?'

'Yesterday teatime. He called in at the cottage to pick up a jumper. He said it was coming in cold.' She dabbed the tissue to her eyes. 'He said he had a job to do, a rose that needed digging out. He didn't want to leave it until today. He said he would be back by seven. He was going to put Frankie to bed.'

'And what was he wearing the last time you saw him?'

'Wearing? His work clothes. Jeans, and a pale green polo shirt. It's what he always wore for work, like a uniform.' Her face softened for a moment at the thought, and then a flicker of understanding lit up the swollen eyes. 'You have to look for him.' It was a statement, not a question. 'You don't think that he's been hurt too?'

'We don't know what's happened to him, Becca. But we have to find him.'

She was staring blankly at the detective now, silently piecing his questions together. 'You don't think he did this? You don't think he hurt Lucy? He wouldn't. He was too gentle.' Panic was beginning to rise in her voice. 'He wouldn't. He wouldn't hurt her. He wouldn't hurt anyone.'

Tom Parkinson put out a hand and rested it gently on her arm. 'Don't upset yourself. We don't think anything at this stage. The first thing is to find him, and I need your help with that. I'd like you to find me a photograph of

Philip, as recent as you can, something I can give to my colleagues so they know exactly who they're looking for. And then I'd like you to give me a list of the names of anyone who might know where he is. I need details of his family and his friends, close ones to begin with. The sooner we can find Philip, the sooner we can work out just what's been going on here.' He squeezed her arm. 'He might not even have been with Lucy last night.'

Becca looked unconvinced, but she pushed herself slowly up from the table and made her way out of the kitchen and into the hallway. 'There's a framed picture of him in the living room. I'll give you that.'

Back at the kitchen table, without Becca there to see him, Tom Parkinson pushed out his lips and puffed out his frustrations. To his mind, there were only two likely outcomes in the question of Philip McKeith's whereabouts. On the one hand, he might have fallen victim to the same unknown assailant who had murdered Lucy Lancefield. On the other, he might be alive and well, and looking like the prime suspect in a murder case. Either way, Parkinson wasn't looking forward to breaking the news to Becca Smith.

*

It was quiet in the library at Salvation Hall. Richard, his gaunt face hollowed further by the shock of the morning's events, settled back into his favourite shabby armchair to the right of the fireplace and regarded DCI Price through shattered eyes. 'I've known Philip McKeith since he was a boy, Chief Inspector. His father worked on my estate and Philip came to us as an apprentice for the garden at the age of sixteen. He has a flair for nature and a fine understanding of plants in particular. We paid for his training, of course, during his apprenticeship. But his real skill is born of instinct. He took over as head gardener on the estate when his predecessor retired, at the age of just twenty-two. He is now thirty-one. And an asset to our estate.'

Ennor Price, perched on the edge of a large wing-backed chair to the left of the fireplace, nodded thoughtfully and tried not to be distracted from the conversation by his surroundings. His investigations rarely brought him into such elegant territory. The crimes he dealt with usually led him to council estates and run down back-to-backs, to grime and smoke and dirt, and the stench of lives on the edge. To find himself in a private library, surrounded by privilege and heritage, was a novelty. 'I understand that Philip McKeith was close to your granddaughter?' It was a loaded question, and he was treading carefully.

'They more or less grew up together. Lucy was only a couple of years younger than Philip. On different sides of the fence, of course.' It was Richard's tactful way of referencing the class divide. 'Their friendship was never discouraged. Young people can learn so much from each other in the right circumstances.' He turned to smile at Nancy, who was sitting primly on the small damask-covered sofa in the centre of the room.

The policeman followed his gaze and smiled at the girl himself. He'd intended the smile to be reassuring but Nancy looked so self-possessed that it hardly seemed necessary. He drew his eyes away from her brunette waves and warm, bronzed skin, but it was a wrench that required some effort. Her beauty was striking but there was no conceit in her manner, none of the aloof superiority that so often lurked unpleasant and unwelcome behind a lovely face. Looking back at Richard, he said, 'I understand that Becca Smith has claimed they were having an affair?'

To his surprise, Richard met the question with a knowing smile. 'Two attractive young people, often in each other's company, a shared love of the outdoors and nature – Hardly surprising, would you think?'

'It didn't trouble you?'

'Is there any reason why it should?'

'Philip was already living with a partner and child, and Lucy was soon to be married. The trouble with affairs is that people are likely to get hurt.' And, he thought, when people get hurt they are apt to lash out.

The older man's eyes narrowed. 'Lucy and Philip were already friends when Philip met Becca. There was never any expectation that their friendship would be a lasting one.' If he meant that there was never any expectation that Lucy and Philip would marry, he stopped short of saying it. 'Philip met Becca when Lucy was travelling in Europe. She is a decent girl and we welcomed her into the Salvation family. She works for us as a housekeeper of sorts, lives with Philip on the estate, and never gives us any trouble. Their child Francesca is a delightful little thing, and we already have her name down for St Augustine's.'

'You're planning to fund a private education for your gardener's daughter?' St Augustine's was the finest private girls' school in the area.

Richard met the question with a weary smile. 'Francesca is my god-daughter, Chief Inspector. Were it not for the social and financial gulf between Lucy and Philip, she may have been my great-grandchild.' He sighed. 'I am fond of Philip McKeith. He is a fine gardener, a hard-working man, and an essentially decent human being. If he suffers from a flaw, from a tendency to give in to human passions, I will not judge him for that. We all have a weakness.'

The broad-mindedness of the old man's response caught Ennor Price momentarily unawares. He considered it briefly and then said, 'We need to find Philip as soon as possible. Would you have any idea where he might be found?'

'I hope you are not taking the easy option, Chief Inspector, and assuming that he is responsible for Lucy's death simply because no one knows where he is.'

'I've never been one for easy options, Mr Lancefield.'

Ennor Price smiled. 'Until we find Philip McKeith, we can't eliminate him from our enquiries. Later today we should be able to confirm the cause of Lucy's death. Until then, or until McKeith is found, whichever comes first, we will consider it accidental drowning.'

The old man's face grew solemn. 'Lucy's death can only have been accidental, Chief Inspector. My granddaughter had her faults, but no one would wish her that kind of harm.' He leaned an elbow on the chair's arm and rested his chin on his upturned hand, his eyes cast down now towards the carpet, his attention lost to a private and difficult thought. Eventually he turned back to face the policeman and said quietly, 'I'm sure you will do everything you can to discover what happened to Lucy. And everything you can to find Philip, and bring him home safely. Is there anything we can do now to help you move your investigations forward?'

'Thank you, yes, there is.' The question appeared to invite a truce, of sorts, and an opportunity that DCI Price wasn't in a position to ignore. He turned again to Nancy. 'I'd like to know more about Lucy while I'm here. Would you be good enough to take me to see her room?'

Nancy's face remained impassive, but she glanced across at Richard for approval. 'Would that be alright?'

'I don't see why not. I'm sure the chief inspector has a very good reason for asking. And as we are relying on him to get to the truth of what happened to Lucy, and to Philip, I wouldn't want it said that we didn't give him every possible assistance in his quest.'

7

Ian walked slowly into the hotel bar and steadied himself against a high-backed chair. He wasn't sure why the news had hit him so hard. He didn't really know Lucy Lancefield, except as the girl that Marcus was planning to marry. He drifted behind the bar, picked up a brandy glass, and rammed it against an optic. It wasn't his custom to drink during the day but he needed something now to steady his nerves.

It had been a long time since he'd heard a man cry. The young police officer dispatched to break the news of Lucy's death had been gentle in his approach to Marcus, but a sudden death was a shocking thing and Marcus had taken the news of Lucy's demise very badly.

Ian knocked back the contents of the brandy glass in one go and winced as the alcohol burned down the back of his throat. He contemplated another but thought better of it. Marcus was in no fit state to drive and he needed to go back to Salvation Hall. It would be incumbent on Ian to drive him, and he daren't risk a drink-driving charge on a day like this, however harrowing the circumstance. And in any case, he reasoned, he needed to keep a clear head. He may no longer practise as a solicitor, but that didn't mean he'd stopped thinking like one.

He'd been present when the news was broken to Marcus and quick to note that a detective, rather than a uniformed officer, had been assigned to the task. After breaking the news and giving Marcus time to absorb his loss the policeman, a tall and laconic young man with sandy hair and a determined gaze, had casually enquired when Marcus had last seen his fiancée.

The subtlety of the question was lost on the shocked and grieving Marcus and he had been almost too quick to answer. He hadn't seen her since breakfast yesterday morning, he'd said, a spell of nearly twenty-four hours. Within a few minutes, he had gone on to confirm that he hadn't seen Lucy the previous evening. He thought she had mentioned an invitation to dine with a friend in St Ives, but he may have been mistaken. Taken one by one, the detective's questions had seemed innocent enough. Taken together, the answers suggested that Marcus and Lucy almost led separate lives.

Unless, of course, Marcus was lying.

It was a possibility, and one which made Ian feel decidedly uncomfortable. The young detective had been remarkably vague on the subject of how Lucy had died, saying her body had been found in the lake but nothing could be confirmed until the pathologist had seen the body. Accustomed to police lines of enquiry, Ian had pessimistically translated this for himself as "it looks like a suspicious death".

There was no question that Marcus would be under scrutiny now until the cause of Lucy's death was established. If it proved to be accidental, Ian would be there to give him every support. If it proved to be otherwise...

He turned and eyed the brandy optic a second time. It had been three years since he'd practised law in any meaningful shape or form. If Lucy had been murdered, the police would look first at the immediate members of her family to find the killer. And Marcus would be right there in the middle of the frame.

He was still holding his empty glass and he looked down at it for a moment. There was no need to risk his licence. They could take a taxi out to Salvation Hall. Perhaps by the time they arrived, the pathologist would have made an initial report and the landscape would be clearer. But whatever the cause of Lucy's death, Marcus hadn't just lost his fiancée. He'd lost his future, his new opportunities, probably even the roof over his head.

Ian rammed his glass against the optic again and then downed the brandy in one gulp. Someone was going to have to go into the lion's den and stand up for Marcus and his loss. And as far as he could see, there was no other candidate available to take on the job.

*

Ennor Price heard the door close softly behind him and he glanced over his shoulder to check whether Nancy Woodlands was still in the room with him.

She was leaning against the door, hands clasped loosely in front of her, her head slightly lowered, her dark eyes watching him with a cool, almost feline curiosity. 'As you can see, Chief Inspector, Lucy had a suite of rooms to herself. She preferred to use this room as a sitting room for relaxing. Richard doesn't like modern technologies, so there is no television in the drawing room downstairs.' She paused and smiled. 'Please ask me if there is anything you want to know.'

He returned the smile silently and turned back to the room, taking in the luxury of the large Liberty sofa and polished glass console tables, the oversized television screen, and the marble fireplace against the innermost wall. The mantel above the fire bore a large collection of what he took to be family photographs, most of them in elegant silver frames, and he stepped forward to take a closer look. 'Could you tell me who these are? The people in the pictures?'

Nancy moved forward to stand beside him, bringing with her a fragrance that smelled like jasmine, and lifted a slender hand to point a slim finger at each picture in turn. 'The one in the centre is of Lucy and Marcus, the rest are of the family. Most are of Richard and Alice – that's Richard's late wife, Lucy's grandmother – and David and

Susanna, her father and her late mother.'

'They're all black and white.'

'Lucy preferred that. Many of the photographs were chosen because they were old black and white originals. The later ones were produced in monochrome to suit her taste.'

'Did you know Lucy's mother?'

'Yes, but only from her occasional visits to St Felix. She died in a car accident before I came to Salvation Hall.'

Ennor nodded to himself and picked up the large ornate frame that dominated the mantel. He studied the picture for a moment, his first sight of Marcus Drake, and noted thick fair hair, clear features and broad shoulders. He and Lucy made a handsome couple, smiling into the camera, their arms around each other's waists. 'So this is Marcus?'

'Yes. The picture was taken last year, at Lucy's birthday party.' She frowned. 'Are you going to ask me now if they were happy together?'

'Am I that transparent?'

Her smile became forbearing. 'Chief Inspector, I understand that you have to learn as much about Lucy as you can. And although you asked if I could show you Lucy's room, I do realise that you weren't planning to form a picture of her by examining the soft furnishings.' She held out the slender hand, took the photograph from him, and looked down at it thoughtfully. 'Marcus is a sweetheart, really. He's a handsome boy, as you can see from the picture. And Lucy subscribed to the old adage that everything in life should be either useful or beautiful. Marcus ticked both those boxes. I think that for Lucy, marriage was a business contract, and Marcus passed the interview with flying colours.'

'How did he come to apply for the job?'

'Nicely put.' She handed the picture back to him. 'Lucy and Marcus met when Lucy's father David announced that he was planning to marry Stella Drake. Marcus is Stella's son. He was engaged to someone else at the time, a girl he'd met at university. But Lucy wouldn't let a small detail like that get in the way. And I don't think he took a lot of persuading to break off the engagement. In fact, I think that was possibly what sealed the deal. He was everything that Lucy was looking for in a husband – handsome, educated, business-minded, and above all malleable.' She paused, and then added, 'Raw material, to be moulded and managed.'

Ennor held up a hand. 'I'm sorry, have I misunderstood, or are you telling me that Lucy and Marcus were stepbrother and sister?'

'Technically, yes. But it really isn't of any relevance. They weren't blood relations, Chief Inspector.'

It might not have been relevant in Nancy's view, but it was relevant enough for him. He looked thoughtfully at the photograph a second time and then put it back in its place on the mantel. The relationship between Marcus and Lucy may not have been incestuous in any literal sense, but the family dynamic was still an unusual one. He kept the thought to himself and ran an appraising eye across the collection of pictures as a whole to make sure he hadn't missed something. There was no picture of McKeith, but then of course there wouldn't be. Philip was Lucy's guilty secret. Except that their affair didn't appear to be a secret at all. Becca Smith was shouting about it, and Richard Lancefield seemed tolerant of it. It would be highly unlikely that Marcus would be in the dark about it if the rest of the household knew. He turned to look at Nancy again. 'Was Philip a guest at Lucy's birthday party?'

'Good heavens, no. Why would he be?'

Ennor Price shrugged. 'Just a thought.' He stretched out a hand and lifted another picture, this time from the left of the mantel, a striking shot of a young man in military uniform. 'Is this Richard Lancefield?'

Nancy softened visibly. 'Yes. During his national service.'

'Does he like Marcus?'

'Like him?' She looked bemused. 'I've never really thought about it.'

'He likes Philip McKeith.'

'I think "like" would be putting it a little strongly, Chief Inspector. He and Philip have the garden in common. It's not unusual for people who have a common interest to think well of each other.'

'He didn't seem perturbed by Lucy's relationship with Philip.'

'Richard has an unusual outlook on life. He's a lot more easy-going than people might think.' She smiled. 'I think it has something to do with the years he spent on St Felix. We have a very relaxed way of life on the island.'

The policeman replaced the picture and kept his eyes on the mantel. 'And when did you leave St Felix, Nancy? To come here and work as Richard's secretary?'

'About ten years ago. Although I think "secretary" is a rather fancy word for it. I'm more of a companion, really. I deal with his correspondence, but I also read to him. I drive him when he wants to go out, I prepare most of his meals and snacks, and I make his coffee. I run his errands. I even walk the dog when Richard feels too tired to go out.'

'Did Lucy mind?'

'Mind? Good heavens, no. She was relieved. It left her free to lead her own life. She wasn't the sort of person to run someone else's errands.'

'Were you friends, you and Lucy?'

'I hope so. We were rather thrown together, both living here in the main house.' Nancy looked suddenly downcast, as if the enormity of the morning's events had just registered. 'I will miss her if that's what you're wondering.'

Ennor Price turned to look at Lancefield's secretary. 'Do you think that Lucy was down at the lake with Philip McKeith yesterday evening?'

For the first time Nancy hesitated to answer him, and

he saw that the dark eyes had lost their coolness and had taken on a tinge of regret. 'I was hoping you wouldn't ask me that.' She looked uncomfortable now. 'It would break Richard's heart to discover that Philip was responsible for Lucy's death.' She lifted the eyes to meet Ennor's. 'And mine too, if I can bring myself to be honest about it.'

*

'Nancy has taken Chief Inspector Price up to see Lucy's room.' Richard rested his elbows on the arms of his chair and steepled his fingers. 'I realise that this morning's events are not the welcome you would have expected from Salvation Hall, Kathryn, but I do hope that you will stay and see things through.'

'I feel it would be an intrusion.'

'It would be abandonment. I didn't have you down as the sort of young woman who would walk away from an old man in his hour of need.'

They were sitting in the library, Richard still in his favourite shabby armchair, Kathryn seated again on the sofa. 'Surely I would be in the way of the family's grief?'

He coughed out a sour laugh. 'There's no grief here, Kathryn. Isn't that obvious? I loved my granddaughter, but I didn't like her. Very few people did. I cannot deny that she carried my blood, but she inherited the family's less creditable traits. She was not an engaging child, nor an endearing granddaughter. She was often arrogant, frequently overconfident and unquestionably self-serving. But she was a Lancefield. And although I do not grieve, I am shocked by her death, and angry that her life has been taken away so unnecessarily and at such a young age.' He took in a deep sustaining breath and blew it out through his thin lips. 'Have the police spoken with you yet?'

'Yes. They wanted to know why I was visiting Salvation Hall, whether I had met Lucy, and what I remembered of her body being found. It was a pretty short conversation.

But they're happy for me to leave now. I've given them a contact number, and they know I'm staying in Penzance until Sunday if they need to speak to me again.'

'If you are planning to stay on in Penzance, then I see no reason for your work not to continue. The family's documents still need curating and its heritage still needs recording. And I don't see Lucy's death as a reason for your work to stop. I fully expect the police to confirm that Lucy's death was an accident. My son David will be arriving tomorrow to take care of the funeral arrangements and Nancy will assist him. I cannot deny that there will be sadness in the house. But your work will give me something to think about, something to focus on. I will speak with Nancy about bringing the first tranche of documents down from the attic after lunch, as we discussed, and you may take up residence here in the library as a "centre of operations" if you will. The police should not need access to the room – Lucy was not in the habit of using it.' Richard leaned over the side of his chair and lowered his eyes. 'And Samson promises that he will keep you company, even if the rest of us must absent ourselves. Eh, boy?' The dog, huddled close to the side of the old man's chair, turned his eyes devotedly up towards his master and gave a hesitant wag of the tail.

It sounded like a heartfelt request, at least as heartfelt as Richard Lancefield could make it. Kathryn was in no doubt of that. But she couldn't be certain that his feelings for the late and seemingly unlamented Lucy were really that cold. Something, certainly, had touched him. She had seen that in his face as he'd stared down at Lucy's recumbent body in the lake. But her commission, after all, was purely a business one. She had no personal connection with the Lancefield family. She smiled and gave a nod of acquiescence. 'If you think it would help then, of course, I will stay.'

He turned the full force of his gaze upon her and studied her face. 'Thank you, Kathryn. I knew you would understand. When Nancy returns, I will ask her to prepare some lunch and serve it to us here in the library. After that I will give you a tour of the house and garden, as I promised, and then I will leave you here to begin work on the documents. The first boxes contain papers relating to Salvation Hall. They include family letters, details of births, marriages, deaths.' He thought for a moment. 'There will be some overlap between these documents and those relating to Woodlands Park, our plantation estate on St Felix, particularly for the eighteenth and early nineteenth century. For some years the Woodlands Park plantation was run on an absentee basis.'

'The family resided in England, and used an overseer for the day-to-day running of the plantation?'

'Yes. There will be correspondence between Salvation Hall and Woodlands Park for that period.'

'Then I would propose that I divide the documents into two, to begin with – those relating to the family, and those relating to the estates. Would you be happy with that?'

'If you feel it is the best approach.'

'And what about documents relating only to Woodlands Park? Are they still on St Felix?'

He gave a knowing smile. 'They are all here, Kathryn. Up in the attic.' He pointed heavenward with a crooked finger. 'I had them air-freighted over when you agreed to undertake the commission. Again, there are personal papers and estate documents. I'm sure the estate documents, in particular, will interest you.' His smile broadened at the thought. 'Account books, day books, land deeds.' He leaned forward a little and peered at her over the top of his spectacles, lowering his voice. 'Records pertaining to the purchase, ownership and sale of the plantation's slaves.'

It hadn't been an empty promise then. His letter of engagement had referred to "exclusive access to unseen documents of historical significance". That had been the promise, the carrot that Richard had dangled in front of Kathryn to tempt her to make the journey from Cambridge down to Cornwall. He had known she didn't work for money alone. Hugh Ferguson would have told him of her academic interest in the subject.

From their first ventures into the Caribbean in the early eighteenth century, their monopoly of the small Leeward Island of St Felix, the creation of vast wealth from the dubious practice of sugar production, and the investing of that wealth on English soil up to the present day, the Lancefield family of Salvation Hall had been meticulous record keepers. Everything was documented, every document retained, and everything kept private to the family.

Until now.

8

Detective Chief Inspector Price took the photograph from Becca's outstretched hand and moved closer to the window in the hope of better light. 'When was this taken?'

Becca, seated at the kitchen table, hugged herself and rocked slowly back and forth. 'Last year, on a day trip to Newquay. We took Frankie so that she could ride on the donkeys.' She didn't look at him. 'I don't know why you need it. I already gave your sergeant a picture.'

'DS Parkinson has sent that picture to have copies made.' He studied the grainy image in his hand. It wasn't the sharpest, but it would do for the time being. Philip McKeith was good-looking in an earthy, outdoor sort of way. Square jawed, his thick hair slickly combed in a left-hand parting, he wasn't smiling at the camera. His hands were thrust into the pockets of his beige chinos, and his blue denim shirt hung loosely over his broad frame. There was no sign of Frankie in the picture, and Philip himself looked disengaged, as if the last thing he wanted to do was spend the day in a local seaside resort playing happy families.

Price glanced at Becca with an awkward smile, and tried to visualise the two of them together. Becca was a homely creature, her badly-bleached hair almost tamed into an untidy bob, her short body clothed in a practical outfit of long-sleeved shirt and track suit bottoms. He couldn't imagine them a couple, but there must have been love at some time. Or perhaps just lust. Perhaps, he thought, it was the child that had made the difference. A woman could change after childbirth. Perhaps the girl had let herself go, capitulated to the ravages of sleepless nights and constant feeding, surrendered herself to the washing of endless nappies instead of caring for her appearance. He could see how that might be.

It wouldn't be like that for every woman, of course. He couldn't imagine that Lucy Lancefield would have let a small thing like a baby make that kind of difference. Lucy had been slender, blonde, groomed, and her eyes had shone out from the photographs he'd seen with a steely, determined gaze. If Lucy had been Frankie's mother, there would have been a nanny to take the strain while Lucy worked out at the gym and made time to have her hair tinted and her nails manicured. He offered Becca a more compassionate smile. 'I'd like to keep this photograph, Becca. Just until DS Parkinson can let me have a copy of the other picture.' He studied her face. 'I take it you still haven't heard anything from Philip?'

Becca flinched and looked away. 'I told Sergeant Parkinson. I haven't heard anything since yesterday afternoon. I thought he was with *her*.'

The policeman felt a sudden sympathy for the girl. He knew how it felt to have your trust betrayed, and although he'd seen no evidence to prove that she was telling the truth, he knew that she had little to gain by making up such a provocative lie. He pulled a chair away from the kitchen table and sat down. 'How long have you known about their affair?' His voice was gentle, almost avuncular.

'Since always.' She pursed her lips together in a forlorn attempt to stem the flow of new tears. 'I told Sergeant Parkinson already. It started after Frankie was born, but I never knew…' She sniffed and wiped her nose on the sleeve of her shirt. 'I knew they had been friends when they were kids, ever since Philip's dad came to work here. But I didn't know there had been an affair before I met Philip.'

'But you stayed with him, even though he was unfaithful?'

'He's Frankie's father.' She turned back to Price with a

withering look. 'I want my child to have a father in her life. If that meant putting up with him screwing Lucy on the side, then so be it.'

She was still in love with Philip McKeith, then, he thought. Although not really putting up with him screwing Lucy Lancefield at all, if her performance at Salvation Hall this morning had been anything to go by. But even a deceived woman might come to her lover's aid if the passion was strong enough, and Price didn't want Becca to make that particular mistake. 'I realise that if you did hear from him, you might be tempted to keep it to yourself. To protect him, if you thought he needed protecting.' Price slipped the photograph into the inside pocket of his jacket as he spoke. 'But it wouldn't be the right thing to do. It wouldn't be the right thing for Philip. The sooner we can speak to him, the sooner we can eliminate him from our enquires.'

'Enquiries?'

'The cause of death hasn't been confirmed yet. Lucy's death may not have been an accident.'

The colour began to drain from Becca's face. 'He didn't kill her.'

'Have you heard from him?'

'I didn't say that. I said he didn't kill her.' Becca blew out her exasperation. 'What reason could he have to kill her? The little tart was laying it out on a plate for him. There were no strings, she asked nothing of him.'

'How do you know?'

'Because I know Philip. He's a free spirit. If Lucy had made demands, he wouldn't want to be with her.' It sounded as if she spoke from experience, as if she'd tested the water, made demands of her own and learned the hard way that it wouldn't be a good idea. At least, not if she wanted Philip to stay in her life.

'Well, perhaps that was the problem. Perhaps she did make demands, and Philip couldn't think of any other way than killing her to get himself free.'

Becca shook her head. 'And lose his job and his home into the bargain? He works on the Salvation Hall estate. This cottage comes with the job.' She closed her eyes for a moment, thinking, then opened them and turned a ferocious gaze on Ennor Price. 'Has it occurred to you for one minute that there were plenty of other people who might have wanted Lucy dead?'

'No. But I'm always open to suggestions.'

'Well, you could start with Marcus Drake. How do you think he felt, knowing that Lucy was spending so much time rolling around in the grass with Philip?' Becca sucked in her cheeks. 'And then there's the old man. I know for a fact that Richard was sick and tired of her boasting that she was going to turn Salvation Hall into a hotel when he kicked the bucket.' She was growing belligerent. 'There's two suggestions for you to be going on with.'

Price leaned a little closer to the girl, folding his arms on the table. 'Thanks for the tip-offs, Becca. For what it's worth, I have a third suggestion to go with them. Someone who had every reason to be jealous, someone whose life was being turned upside down by the very fact that Lucy existed. Someone who resented the fact that Lucy had such overwhelming power and influence over the father of her child.'

Becca sucked in a breath and drew back from him, her pale blue eyes growing uneasy. 'But you can't think I would…'

He replied with a tilt of the head and a gentle, enigmatic curl of the lips. 'Oh, I can, Becca.' And what's more, he thought, I do.

*

'Now that the police have finished their search of the house and withdrawn to the gardens, I thought we might begin our little tour.' Richard paused at the bottom of the stone staircase in the hallway and put out a hand to the banister to steady himself. 'There is so much more here to explain our family's history than documents and papers.' He turned back and smiled at Kathryn. 'As I explained to you over lunch, Salvation Hall has been in the family since the early 1770s. The central part of the house was built much earlier than that, of course, around 1640. The Lancefields purchased both the house and its lands, and then added to the estate over a number of years.'

'So who originally owned the house?'

'Landed gentry by the name of Lister. The house was built for the second son and came with a parcel of land. In those days it was known as Penwithen Manor. It was my illustrious ancestor Thomas Moses Lancefield who renamed it Salvation Hall.' Richard looked a little abashed. 'I think, on reflection, that he hoped such a pious choice of name might bring a little personal salvation to his own world.' The old man looked up towards the galleried landing and pointed with his free hand to a large, dark portrait hanging above the staircase. Within the frame, a humourless-looking individual was seated at a grand mahogany desk, his stern, forbidding eyes peering out over a pair of pince-nez to study what appeared to be a sheet of accounts. 'Now, that is the only portrait we have of Thomas Moses in England, the rest are in St Felix. There is a matching one of his wife, Lysbeth Quintard, in the dining room. She used to hang in here but I had her moved out of the way.' He arched a meaningful eyebrow. 'Not the sort of face you want staring down at you every time you walk across the hall.'

Kathryn suppressed a smile. 'Was Thomas Moses responsible for extending the house to its present size?'

'Not entirely. He built the new east and west wings, but there was a later extension to the rear in the 1850s, and the conservatory was added in the 1920s by my father. But Thomas was responsible for a significant increase in the amount of farmland attached to the Salvation estate and for the building of Penwithen village to house the farm labourers. And he laid out the beginnings of the formal gardens close to the house.' Richard looked back at her again. 'He's interred in the village church, St Felicity's. Perhaps later in the week we might take a stroll down there. There are some well-preserved memorial inscriptions both inside and out which might be useful in your work.'

'I'd like that, Mr Lancefield.'

Mr Lancefield snorted a laugh. 'Come now, Kathryn, no unnecessary formalities. My name is Richard. We are all on first-name terms here. One big happy family.'

Kathryn followed in his wake as he slowly climbed the stairs and wondered, not for the first time, whether Richard Lancefield's determination to carry on as if nothing had happened could be attributed to the shock of the morning's events. His one big happy family was beginning to implode around him, his granddaughter's lifeless body had been removed from the estate in a body bag, his gardener and friend was missing and presumed suspect, and his housekeeper was confined to her cottage and assisting the police with their enquiries. At some point, he would have to face Lucy's bereaved fiancé, and tomorrow his estranged son and daughter-in-law would arrive at Salvation Hall to discuss funeral arrangements. Only his secretary appeared to be holding it all together, although during lunch even Nancy had appeared to be subdued.

'Now, here is something I must be sure to show you.' Ahead of her, Richard had paused on the landing. 'This is a fine oil study of Quintard Bay on St Felix. It shows our private beach, and if you look closely you can just make out the roofline of the Woodlands plantation house. Of course, it doesn't quite look like that now. The painting dates from the beginning of the nineteenth century.' He chuckled to himself and then set off upwards, ascending the next flight of stairs up to a further landing. 'Come along then, Kathryn. Let's go and take a look at the attic rooms. You can see where we've stored the documents, and we can make our way down through the house from there.'

'As you think.' Kathryn stopped behind him on the landing and cast her eye over the study of Quintard Bay. The picture was hanging between two small, stained-glass windows, and she was just about to ask its owner about the significance of the designs within the glass when the sound of tyres crunching on the gravel drive outside caught her attention.

She stepped a little closer to the left-hand window and bent her head to peer out through the palest pane of glass. A taxi had drawn up to the side of the house, and she was surprised to see a familiar figure emerge from it. Ian Mitchell slammed the front passenger door shut, and as he did so a slim, well-dressed young man with a head of thick, fair hair alighted from the back. As the taxi pulled away the two men stood for a moment, conversing in quiet tones, and then Marcus Drake – Kathryn couldn't assume it to be anyone else – stepped forward across the drive to make his way to the front of the house, Ian following close behind. As both men disappeared from view beneath the window she heard Nancy's voice call out to them from the path that swept around the side of the house towards the garden. For a few moments she heard a trio of voices in distant conversation, followed by the crunching of feet on the gravel path as Nancy led the newcomers back to retrace their steps and beyond, to the kitchen door at the rear of the house.

It appeared for all the world as if Nancy was leading them round to the tradesmen's entrance, and it occurred to Kathryn now that Marcus Drake no longer belonged here. If what she'd heard from Ian was true, then Marcus lived here at the hall only because he was engaged to marry Lucy. But now there was no Lucy to be engaged to.

'Kathryn? Are you with me?' Richard was hesitating at the head of the stairs above her. He didn't appear to have heard the taxi.

'I'm sorry, Richard, of course I am.' She began to climb towards him. 'I was just taking a moment to look at the view from this window.' It wasn't a complete lie. But she could hardly have admitted that, just for that particular moment, she had been watching more grief roll up to Salvation Hall in a taxi. Or that she was wondering just how Marcus now fitted in to what Richard insisted on calling his one big happy family.

*

Ennor Price leaned back in the passenger seat of Tom Parkinson's Audi and folded his arms across his chest. September sun was beating through the windscreen, and he closed his eyes for a moment and enjoyed its warming rays. The car was parked on the shore to the west of Marazion, facing out to sea, the vehicle itself lost in the usual ocean of family cars and camper vans that frequented the popular spot. It was a handy place for a detective chief inspector and his sergeant to take time out and they often used it to share notes and plan whatever moves a case required next. Parkinson's car was unmarked and the two men, dressed in smart civilian clothing, gave a fair impression of a couple of middle managers swerving the office on a sunny day. The surrounding mass of holidaying humanity gave them a degree of anonymity that couldn't be achieved anywhere close to a crime scene. And, of course, it didn't hurt that the mobile catering van that usually parked there served a decent range of coffees.

Fetching those coffees was Tom Parkinson's job. As he pulled the door of the Audi open and bent himself carefully into the driving seat, an unreliable cardboard tray holding two large Americanos balanced dangerously in his free hand, Price opened an eye and turned it in the sergeant's direction. 'Did you bring me a Mars bar?'

'Even though you didn't ask for one.' Parkinson placed

the tray gingerly on top of the car's dashboard, pulled the Mars bar from his trouser pocket, and tossed it to his boss. 'I thought you were cutting down?'

'It's brain food.' Price frowned and set about unwrapping the chocolate. 'The tougher the case, the more sugar I need.' He lifted a coffee from the tray and took a sip; they both took their coffee white with two sugars, so no need to ask which was his.

Theirs was an easy partnership, and they'd worked together for the best part of three years. Ennor Price, close to early retirement age and seriously considering the option, was an old-school detective whose world divided simply into two kinds of people – the good and the bad. Parkinson, fifteen years younger, had a far more pragmatic view that the world was full of all sorts, and that a person's experience of life usually determined their behaviours. Price believed in nature, that people were born a certain way, and that their true disposition would always emerge whatever the circumstance. Parkinson was firmly on the side of nurture, the belief that even a good person would change for the worse if subjected to enough pressure. More by good luck than good management, they usually managed to meet somewhere in the middle.

Parkinson took a sip of his coffee and peered through the windscreen at the causeway snaking across the water from the mainland to St Michael's Mount, the imposing rocky outcrop that rose from the sea in Mount's Bay. The tide was rising fast. In another thirty minutes, the road would be gone. He loved to watch those last few minutes as the water began to wash across the granite sets, and dithering tourists suddenly realised that they had only minutes to make it to one end or the other before the water would be up to their ankles. He sipped again and turned to look at Price. 'I can't see anything so tough about this case. You heard what the pathologist had to say. Lucy Lancefield was strangled before she went into the water. Philip McKeith is missing. All we have to do is find

McKeith.'

'Motive?'

'Jealousy. He wanted her to call off her engagement to Drake and she refused. Or maybe she wanted to call off the affair and he couldn't handle the rejection. Either way, they quarrelled, he strangled her with the scarf, dragged her body into the water, and he's gone to ground.'

'It's not like you to go for the easy option, Tom.'

It was a gentle gibe and Parkinson took it with his customary good humour. 'Just because it looks like the easy option doesn't mean it didn't happen.'

'I won't disagree with that. But I'd feel better knowing that we'd eliminated all the other possibilities.'

'Which are?'

'Come on, Tom. Apply a bit of brain power. Don't leave me to do all the work.'

The sergeant grinned. 'You want me to say that Marcus Drake is the obvious suspect because he was cuckolded by the affair. But McKeith had the opportunity as well as a motive. He knew the grounds, he regularly met Lucy there, and she had probably arranged to meet with him yesterday evening before Drake got back from work.'

'And?'

'And?' Tom beetled his brows. 'You think there's another?'

'I think there are two more.'

'Two?'

'Becca Smith had a motive and no firm alibi. We need to keep a close eye on that girl. She's besotted with McKeith, for all his infidelity, and it's possible that she knows where he is and is covering for him.'

'Unless she's the killer and she's done for him as well.' Parkinson turned a cynical eye to Price. 'That was a joke, by the way.'

The inspector raised an eyebrow. 'Many a true word spoken in jest, Tom.' He took a generous bite from his Mars bar and savoured the chocolate as he pondered the possibilities. He could imagine Becca strangling Lucy with her long green scarf. Becca was short but she was strongly built and feisty with it, and he didn't think that the slim and dainty Lucy would have been anything of a match for her. But somehow he couldn't see Becca murdering Philip, even if she had the strength. He washed the chocolate down with a mouthful of coffee and turned back to Parkinson. 'She certainly had a motive for murdering Lucy. And she led me to a motive for Richard Lancefield, too.'

'But Lucy was his granddaughter.'

'When I spoke to him, he showed very little grief at her passing. If anything, he seemed more concerned about the fact that Philip McKeith is missing. And according to Becca, the Lancefields were at odds about the future of Salvation Hall.' Ennor Price regarded the Mars bar's empty wrapper with a sigh, and then screwed it up in his hand and tossed it into the cardboard tray. 'We have to keep searching for Philip McKeith, and I want Becca Smith and Richard Lancefield questioned again. But we need to keep it gentle, I don't want to set hares running.'

'Are we going back to Salvation Hall now?'

'No. We're going back to Penzance.'

'But the family hasn't been advised yet of the cause of death.'

'If we tell them that this evening, Marcus and Richard and Becca will have a clear twelve hours to concoct their various statements before we question them again. I'd rather keep my powder dry on this one. Let's call it a day and go back to Salvation Hall in the morning. I want to see what falls out of the tree overnight.'

9

The library clock was beginning to strike four as Richard backed out of the room, taking Nancy and Samson with him, and leaving Kathryn alone to examine the contents of three stout cardboard boxes.

She was sitting at the large mahogany desk to the rear of the room, and she leaned down into the kneehole and pulled out the soft leather briefcase that held all the tools of her work. She had brought an old silk headscarf as a protective layer for the documents, and she shook it out and let it settle onto the desk's leather top. She pulled on a pair of white cotton gloves and looked down at the boxes, then lifted the first onto the edge of the desk and carefully levered off its lid.

The familiar musty smell of ageing paper wafted out into the room and met her nostrils, and she smiled and nodded to herself. The documents were certainly genuine. She reached into the box and pulled out a leather-bound ledger with the words "Woodlands Park" embossed in gold leaf on the cover and then gently prised the book open to reveal the first page.

The paper within was yellowed and showed signs of heavy foxing, but there was no surprise in that. A scrawling hand had written the words "Account Ledger" in large letters across the upper half of the page and the year 1736 beneath. The ledger was a little over two hundred and eighty years old. Hardly surprising that the paper had deteriorated, and oxidisation or humidity or some other misunderstood process had resulted in the pages being speckled with the telltale signs of old age.

She turned slowly to the next page and cast her eye

down the rows of neatly scripted words and numbers. The book began with details of the Lancefield family's acquisition of Woodlands Park in 1736, a brief summary of how one Thomas Proctor Lancefield inherited the whole from his mother's family, details of the attorneys who executed the transfer, and an inventory of everything he inherited. It was unlikely that anyone other than Richard had looked at this book in the last hundred years, possibly even longer.

She closed the book and shifted it carefully to the back of the desk, then dipped for a second time into the box and brought out a bundle of letters, their envelopes yellowed, the ink faded. The bundle was tied with a broad, blue ribbon and she suspected that they were personal, perhaps letters back and forth between members of the family separated by the Atlantic Ocean. She pulled gently at the ribbon, teasing it away from the uppermost envelope, and squinted through her reading glasses at the address on the front. The letter was intended for Mr Thomas Lancefield Esquire, resident of Salvation Hall. Tomorrow she would untie the ribbon, open up the envelopes, and read the contents.

She knew the opportunity was a privilege. Richard had promised her exclusive access to authentic historical documents and he'd been good to his word. He was paying her to curate the family's history, rewarding her in the traditional way for a job of work to be done. But she sensed that he also knew that for Kathryn, the documents themselves were the real reward. The contents of these boxes were a rich, untapped vein of history. They deserved to be seen by other eyes than hers and it crossed her mind that she might persuade Richard to donate the items to a museum, or at least to a university library. But not yet. Not until she'd had a chance to examine them herself, allowed herself the luxury of time alone with them.

She placed the bundle of letters down on the desk and was about to retrieve what looked like a roll of receipts from the box when a gentle tapping on the door of the library took her attention. She looked up to see the door swing partially open and watched as Ian Mitchell's head and neck craned tentatively around the door. 'Nancy said I would find you in here. Am I disturbing you?'

'Of course not.'

He stepped into the room and closed the door behind him. 'I was with Marcus at the hotel when the police came to break the news to him. About Lucy. He wasn't in any fit state to drive, so I brought him back in a taxi. He can pick up his car tomorrow.' Ian hesitated and then pointed vaguely in the direction of the desk. 'I was surprised when Nancy said you were still here. I suppose you'll be leaving us now, and going back to Cambridge.'

Kathryn leaned back in her seat and took off her reading glasses. She placed them down on the desk and smiled at him. 'On the contrary. My work is to go ahead as arranged. Richard says it will take his mind off things.'

'And you're happy to comply?'

'Of course not. But it feels like the path of least resistance at the moment. He's an old man and I don't want to upset him any further.'

'He is upset about Lucy's death then?'

It was a leading question, and Kathryn thought carefully before answering. 'I don't think it's registered with him yet. It's probably the shock. I'm just taking a look at some of the papers this afternoon and I'll come back tomorrow and see how the land lies.' She frowned. 'How's Marcus?'

'In bits. He usually puts on a good front when things upset him, but something of this magnitude' – Ian shook his head – 'I'm worried about how he'll cope but until we know just what happened to Lucy, all I can do is stand by him and make the right noises.' Ian looked momentarily sheepish. 'I don't suppose you've heard anything this afternoon? About the cause of death?' He was still probing.

'I'm afraid not. I was with Richard Lancefield this morning when Lucy's body was found. When the police arrived they said it was likely to be accidental drowning. I'm not aware that anything has changed. But in any case, they wouldn't include me in the discussion. I'm not a member of the family.'

'Do they have any idea how she came to be in the water?'

His persistence was beginning to make Kathryn feel uncomfortable. She wanted to help. And yet she didn't want to speak out of turn. 'I really haven't heard anything. Only that her father and stepmother are travelling down to Cornwall overnight. They should be here some time tomorrow.'

Mitchell let out a low growl. 'That's all we need. It's all Stella's fault that Marcus got involved with Lucy in the first place.' He moved over to an armchair and sat down, uninvited. 'Marcus was engaged when Stella married Lucy's father, and Judy was a really lovely girl. She was right for Marcus. And if it hadn't been for Stella and her ambitions, Marcus would have married her. And probably been a damn sight happier.' Ian's mood was beginning to darken. 'Stella pressured him into breaking off his engagement and making a play for Lucy. I think she thought it would cement the family's fortunes. She knew that she and David would never have children together.'

'You don't think that Marcus and Lucy were in love?'

'They certainly weren't in lust. The way I heard it, she was satisfying those appetites with the gardener on the estate.' Ian looked at Kathryn with an expectant expression that invited her to comment further.

But Kathryn looked away. She had overheard more than one conversation that day regarding the nature of Lucy Lancefield's relationship with Philip McKeith. She had witnessed Becca's anger in the morning, heard Richard's refusal to believe that Philip would do any harm to his granddaughter, and been unable to avoid the occasional fragment of chatter between police officers searching the house and grounds. But it was nothing to do with her. She made a tactful attempt to change the subject.

'What will Marcus do now? Will he stay on at Salvation Hall?'

'I wouldn't think so. He's going to stay here tonight but I've offered to put him up at the hotel in the short term if he would prefer. After that, he can look for a flat in the town.' Ian looked awkwardly down at his hands. 'Are you planning to come back to the hotel this evening, Kathryn?' He sounded coy. 'We have sea bass on the menu tonight, or rack of lamb if you would prefer.' He gave a self-conscious laugh. 'I quite enjoyed our dinner for two at separate tables yesterday evening. And God knows, after a day like today I really could do with some company.'

'I wish I could say yes, but Richard has asked me to come back to Salvation Hall this evening, for a working supper.' It was a convenient truth. Kathryn had enjoyed Ian's company too, the evening before, and without the day's events, she would have readily accepted the offer. But she was employed by Lucy's family, and Ian was an ex-solicitor setting out his stall to support the dead girl's bereaved fiancé.

If Moira had been there, she would have told Kathryn that her imagination was getting the better of her again. That she was seeing duplicity where no such deception existed. But it wouldn't have been the first time Moira had thrown that particular accusation at her sister-in-law.

And Kathryn knew to her cost just how much it could hurt when you listened to the words of others instead of trusting your intuition.

*

Richard Lancefield hung the crook of his stick over his left arm and lifted his right hand to rap at the cottage door. He looked down at Samson, sitting obediently at his heel, and muttered to him. 'Are we doing the right thing here, dog?'

Samson blinked and gave a quizzical tilt of the head.

'You think?' Richard grasped the door knocker. 'I wish I shared your confidence.' He rapped sharply on the door and rocked back on his heels as he waited for Becca Smith to answer. Inside he heard a toddler yell, and then the door latch was pulled back and the door swung open.

Becca was carrying Frankie in her arms and the swelling and dark rims around her eyes spoke of long bouts of prolonged crying. She looked surprised to see him, caught off guard in her misery. 'You didn't expect me at work?' Her voice was raw.

'Good heavens, no.' Richard shuffled from one foot to the other. 'We wanted to see how you are, Becca. You're one of the family. We don't want you to think we've forgotten you.'

She stared at him, suspicious now. 'Philip isn't here. I don't know where he is.'

'We didn't think he would be.' The old man put out a gnarled finger and rubbed it against Frankie's cheek. 'Hello there, Frankie. We haven't seen you for a while, have we?'

The child stared at him, bemused, and then her face broke into a smile. 'Unca Richie.'

'That's right, old girl. I'm Uncle Richie, and this is Samson.' He pointed down at the dog and then turned a frown towards Becca. 'What about it, then, girl? Are you going to let us in?' He watched Becca's face as she considered the request, then followed her into the cottage as she turned and led the way through into the small, untidy living room, Samson trotting obediently at his heels.

Becca lowered herself onto the sofa, the child still in her arms, and tilted her head towards an armchair, an invitation for Richard to sit. 'I'll try to be back at work tomorrow. My mum's going to have Frankie for the day.'

Richard sank into the armchair and balanced his stick between his knees. 'Nancy can cope. She's arranged for Mrs Peel to come in from the village tomorrow and do the cooking. The cleaning can wait.' His tone was kindly.

'They think Philip killed Lucy.'

'Well' – he drew out the word – 'we both know that's not true. Our boy Philip wouldn't do a thing like that.' Richard shook his head. 'But I am worried about him, Becca. And I'm worried about you. You're collateral damage in all of this, you deserve better.' He waited for a moment, but she didn't respond. 'You know, if you have heard from him, it might be best if you told me. Or the police. We all just want what's best for him.'

'Lucy deserved to die.' Becca's words came out quietly. 'And I'm glad that she's dead.'

Richard tutted under his breath. 'Now, I don't believe that for a minute. That's the pain talking.' He forced another smile. 'There was never going to be anything lasting between Philip and Lucy. There never could be. And once she'd married Marcus in the spring, likely as not all this nonsense would have stopped, and the three of you would have been a proper family again.' He fished in his pocket, pulled out a crisp, white, cotton handkerchief, and leaned forward to offer it to her.

For a moment it looked as though she would refuse, and then she stretched out her free hand and took it from him, and pressed it to her nose. 'Thank you.' She sniffed knowingly into the handkerchief. 'Richard?'

'Yes?'

'What do you think happened?'

'Truthfully? I don't know. I think the most likely explanation is that there was some sort of accident and that Philip is afraid to come forward and tell us about it. I honestly thought they would have found him by now, hiding out somewhere in the grounds.'

'You don't think he killed her?'

'Of course not.' He looked closely at Becca's face, at the dark rings beneath her eyes and the swollen, puffy cheeks, and took in a deep, deciding breath. 'Why don't I give you a bit of peace now? I just wanted to see that you were alright.' He put his hands on the arms of the chair and hoisted himself up. 'If you do hear from Philip, tell him that I'm there for him. Whatever happened, we can sort it all out.' He watched as she lifted her head, and an angry scowl began to cloud her face. 'Oh, I know, Becca. You haven't heard from him, and you don't know where he is. And you think I don't believe you. And maybe I don't. But I'm not judging you.' He picked up his stick. 'We'll be eating at around eight this evening. I'll ask Nancy to bring you both some supper over on a tray. If you want to speak to me at any time, I'll be at the hall.' He nodded to her and gently tapped his cane against Samson's rump to tease him to his feet. 'C'mon, dog. We're for home.' He gave the grieving girl one last smile. 'No need to see us to the door, we can find our own way.'

Out on the path outside the cottage, the door closed gently behind him, Richard straightened his cap and then thrust his cane forward to begin the steady walk back to the hall. He clicked his teeth at Samson, and the dog trotted obediently at his side.

It's a damn shame, he thought as he walked, what that girl is going through today. But she knows where Philip is alright. I'd stake my life on it. And if I can't get it out of her, then perhaps Detective Chief Inspector Price is the man to do it.

*

Ian pushed on The Zoological Hotel's front door and held it open for Kathryn to follow him. 'Thanks for the lift back to Penzance.'

'It was no problem.' She sounded almost convincing. In reality, the journey had been almost forty minutes of awkward silences, punctuated by lame attempts at polite if meaningless conversation. She crossed the hotel's hallway, hesitating at the bottom of the stairs. 'I hope you'll excuse me dashing off, but I don't have much time to shower and change. Richard's expecting me back at Salvation Hall by seven thirty.'

'Of course.' His smile was strangely guarded now. 'Perhaps we might have a drink when you get back later this evening?'

'I'd like that.' It occurred to her that perhaps she would, if only he would resist questioning her about Lucy Lancefield's death. 'I'll check in at the bar when I arrive, and see if you're there.' She turned to walk away, but he called her back.

'Kathryn? Before you go, I wanted to ask you about this.' He was standing behind the reception desk now, holding a slim cream envelope between the fingers of his right hand. 'It was Marcus who sorted the mail this morning, but he didn't know what to do with this. I meant to mention it to you earlier, but what with one thing and another it slipped my mind.' He watched her face closely as he spoke. 'It's addressed to a Mrs Kathryn Campbell, guest at the hotel. And as we don't have a Mrs Kathryn Campbell staying here, I wondered if it could be for you.' He paused, and added, 'It's postmarked Edinburgh.'

Kathryn took in a sharp breath and held out a hand. She took the envelope from him and gave it a cursory glance. 'Yes, it's for me.' She studied the hand-writing. 'It's from my sister-in-law. Thank you for making sure it reached me.' She began to turn away again.

'I'm sorry to ask, Kathryn, but you do understand I have an obligation to ensure that everyone who stays in my hotel is who they say they are?'

Stung, she spun back on her heel to face him. 'Once a solicitor, always a solicitor?' She caught the sudden flash of uncertainty in his eyes. 'There's no great mystery, Ian. My name is Kathryn Clifton. Clifton is my maiden name. I'm separated from my husband, whose name is Campbell. I'm not aware that I need anyone's permission to use the name I was born with.' He had touched a nerve and she couldn't keep the irritation from her voice.

He looked discomfited now. 'I'm sorry, I didn't mean – hell, Kathryn, I'm just worried about Marcus. You told me yesterday evening that you used to be a journalist. I thought…'

'Thought what? That I was here under an assumed name? That I was deceiving the Lancefields about my reasons for taking Richard's commission?' She licked her lips and gave an exasperated shake of the head. 'I've taken this commission to help me to put the past behind me. Not that it's any of your business. But for what it's worth, I couldn't have more sympathy for Marcus if I tried. Marcus isn't the only one around here who knows what it means to have your trust betrayed. In fact, Marcus and I have a great deal in common.' She narrowed her eyes, and when she spoke again her voice was low and steady. 'Not that that is any of your business either.'

10

Ennor Price had lived in Penzance for over three years, but he never tired of the view from his study window.

The study was on the top floor of the house, and its large and impressive arched window looked out over rooftops and chimneys and the tops of tropical trees that marked a straight line down to the harbour. It was his habit, after a tough day's work, to pour a chilled glass of Cornish ale and sink into his favourite armchair, carefully placed to enjoy the best of the view, and watch the twinkling lights of boats in the harbour until the stresses of the day had begun to subside.

And yes, he thought as he sipped on that evening's ale, this had been a tough day. It had been nearly eighteen months since he'd dealt with a murder case, and the circumstances of that one couldn't have been more different from today's unfolding events. Then, he had been hunting the lowlife who'd butchered two prostitutes in a bedsit. It had turned out to be the drug-addled son of one of the women murdered. There wasn't much in common with today's task in hand – working out who had murdered a wealthy, privileged heiress in the grounds of her own luxurious home – and Price was feeling uncomfortably out of his depth.

He'd heard of the Lancefield family, of course. There weren't many living around Penzance who hadn't. But he didn't know much about the detail. He understood that for several centuries they had lived in privacy behind their wrought iron gates, occasionally making an appearance to bestow their largess on a local hospital or school or cultural centre of some sort. No one seemed to know with any certainty where their wealth had come from. There were rumours that they owned property abroad, some thought in the Caribbean, and now he knew the rumours to be true. The assumption was that they had inherited money and land and that they lived on the rents of their tenants and the produce of their agricultural holdings. They were known for being aloof, suspected of being arrogant, and criticised for being detached from real life. But none of that was a good enough reason for murder.

And there was no doubt in his mind that Lucy Lancefield had been murdered.

The pathology report that had landed on his desk a couple of hours earlier had confirmed the pathologist's original view of the situation – that Lucy had been strangled with the long, green scarf that was still wound around her neck when her body went into the lake. The fabric had cut into the soft flesh of her neck, and there was bruising to her back consistent with the killer's knee being forced against her body as the scarf was tightened from behind. Fibres from the scarf had been found under her fingernails, suggesting that she had clawed at it in an attempt to pull it away. The dress she had been wearing, a long green shift, was made of a different fabric, and there was little hope of gathering more than the most basic forensic evidence from it due to its time in the water.

Price blew out a breath and tried to recall his first sight of the victim. She had been lying on her back in the lake, her face discoloured and bloated from the water, her yellow hair billowing out around her face, the green folds of her wet dress clinging to her boyish torso. One gold-coloured flip flop had still been attached to her left foot, the other was missing, presumably still somewhere in the water. She hadn't been wearing a bra. But she had been wearing an impressive collection of gold jewellery – a heavy belcher chain was still looped around her neck, hooped earrings floated from her ears, and a wide cuff bangle was tight around her wrist. The motive hadn't been theft, or the gold would be gone.

It would be easy, he thought, to subscribe to Tom Parkinson's obvious view that the motive here was jealousy of some sort, that Lucy and Philip McKeith had argued. There had been some damage to the grass around the area where Lucy had been pulled from the lake, signs of a struggle, and mud in the fibres of her dress where her knees would have hit the ground as she fell or was pushed forward. He closed his eyes and tried to imagine Philip murdering Lucy and, for some inexplicable reason, he just couldn't see it.

Nor could he imagine Richard Lancefield murdering his only grandchild. The old man may have been cold and matter-of-fact about the unexpected death, but it was evident to Price that Lancefield suffered badly from arthritis. Even if he could have lifted a creaking knee high enough to push into Lucy's back and cause the bruising, those gnarled fingers would have struggled to grasp the long, green scarf tightly enough to force the life out of her body.

But there were other possibilities for the role of killer in that unsettling, incomprehensible household – Marcus Drake for one, and Becca Smith for another. Both must have been angry with the duplicitous lovers, and Becca was hiding none of her resentment towards Lucy. Was she strong enough to have committed that particular crime? He was inclined to think that she was. She wasn't a tall girl, but she was stocky, and jealous anger was a great energiser. Many a violent crime had been committed by an unlikely-looking suspect when driven beyond their normal levels of strength by a raging passion.

It occurred to him that just about everyone he'd met at Salvation Hall today had a motive for murdering Lucy. Except, perhaps, the comely Nancy. Nancy was still an enigma to him. Petite and slim, her dark eyes were shrewd and knowing above exquisite cheekbones. And she carried herself with a confidence that far outweighed her claim to be only Richard's secretary and paid companion.

Of course, there was a player in this story that he hadn't taken account of yet. Tom Parkinson had interviewed the Lancefields' visitor, Kathryn Clifton, and believed she'd been invited by Richard Lancefield to work with him on some family papers. Something about documents and a family tree. Up until now, he hadn't thought it necessary to speak to Kathryn. But perhaps he was wrong about that. She would know about the family's past and any Caribbean connections, and she was in a good position to give him an outsider's view of what was going on inside the house. And he couldn't help thinking that an outsider's view was going to be invaluable.

Tom had already made up his mind that McKeith was the killer, that this was nothing more than a crime of passion, a simple case of lust gone wrong. But tomorrow morning, Ennor thought with a smile, they would be going back to Salvation Hall to begin the investigation in earnest. And then he could begin the thankless but otherwise necessary task of proving Tom Parkinson wrong.

*

Kathryn arrived back at Salvation Hall to find Richard sitting alone on the terrace, gazing out over the garden just as he had that morning after Lucy's body had been found.

'Nancy said that I would find you out here.' Kathryn pulled her shawl closer around her shoulders against the freshening evening breeze. 'I hope I'm not too early.'

'Not at all.' He turned his head and spoke over his shoulder without quite looking at her. 'Come and sit here with me a moment, Kathryn.' He patted the bench beside him. 'Samson and I often sit here in the evening to enjoy the garden in the twilight.' The dog was curled up at Richard's feet, gently dozing. 'Nancy has cooked supper for us, and she'll serve us in the Dower House when we're ready.'

Kathryn stepped forward and sat down beside him on the bench. 'It's been a difficult day.'

'Without question.' He gave a gentle cough to clear the emotion from his throat. 'I was thinking about Philip. So much of what you see before you is down to him. You know, we've always kept a good garden at Salvation Hall, but Philip is gifted. Gifted with plants, with nature. He's in tune with the landscape.' Richard heaved a heartfelt sigh. 'He wouldn't have killed her, Kathryn. Not my boy.'

Kathryn shivered, but not against the cooling evening air. It unnerved her that Richard's granddaughter was dead, and yet all his thoughts appeared to be with the man who may have been responsible for her death. 'Were you so very close to Philip?'

'I *am* very close to him.' The old man blinked slowly. 'Please don't speak about him in the past tense. He will show himself soon.' Richard seemed to be convinced. 'I can't imagine how he is feeling at the moment. But he will come forward when he's ready, and he'll tell us what happened to Lucy.'

'Have you heard any more from the police?'

'Only that they will have more information for me in the morning. I believe there are complications with the post mortem due to Lucy's body being so long in the water.' He flinched. 'Lucy had her faults, but she deserved a better end.' He leaned a little closer to Kathryn. 'She was an independent little thing as a child, and she grew into a headstrong teenager. Of course, we spoiled her. What grandparent doesn't spoil their grandchild? But there was no emotional connection.' He pursed his lips. 'The Lancefields don't "do" emotional connection.' He gave a quiet, hollow laugh. 'We must seem a very queer set of cold fish to you, Kathryn. But that's how we are. There is precious little bond between myself and my son David, over and above what is required by duty. And I doubt Lucy would have lived with me if I hadn't provided her with free board and lodgings in surroundings which befitted her natural sense of entitlement.' He turned to look at Kathryn. 'I can't help thinking that it ought to hurt, but it doesn't. I feel angry for her, but I cannot grieve.'

'That may just be the shock.' Kathryn placed her hand gently on Richard's arm. 'I've heard that Marcus will be moving back to Penzance.'

'The boy is in a difficult position. He's staying here this evening to pack his belongings. He has no desire to stay.' Richard lowered his eyes to his fingers. 'I'm afraid that his relationship with Lucy was not everything it might have been. Lucy was the kind of woman who saw marriage as a business arrangement. Marcus worked hard to give the impression that he felt the same, but I suspect he cared for her rather more than he would have us believe. And I think perhaps I might have been kinder to him at times. But he's not without friends. He has the reliable Ian, and his mother will be arriving tomorrow. That will be a comfort to him.'

Kathryn bit gently on her lip. It wasn't her place to suggest that the arrival of Stella Drake would be anything but a comfort to the newly grieving Marcus. In any case, she had only Ian's opinion of Stella, and she had long since learned not to judge another human being simply on the opinions of others. 'I suppose David and Stella will be staying here with you at Salvation Hall?'

'Indeed.' The thought didn't appear to please her host. 'And you will meet them both. I could have wished for a happier set of circumstances for such a meeting. But it cannot be helped.' Richard lifted his hands and rubbed them together against the cold. 'We really should be going in. Nancy will be ready to serve us. But before we do, there is something I would like you to see.' He pushed himself to his feet. 'Well, more to the point, there is something I would like you to have. A small gift that I think you will appreciate. A thank you, for not packing your bags and leaving us to our fate.' He pointed a crooked finger away from the house, and then turned and smiled down at her.

'It's in the old storeroom at the end of the path. I should have asked Nancy to bring it to the house, but there has been so much distraction.'

Kathryn rose to her feet. 'It's very kind of you, Richard, but there really is no need for a gift. I'm happy to stay.'

He was already making his way slowly down the York stone path. 'Nonsense. You're too well-mannered to refuse.' He clicked his fingers behind him, but the command was unnecessary. Samson was already picking his way carefully along the path in his wake. 'Come along now, girl. Don't dally. It will be too dark after supper.'

Kathryn turned and looked back in the direction of the house. Lights reflected from every window, and she knew that Nancy was waiting in the kitchen, and Marcus would be in his room, packing up his belongings. There was no reason to feel nervous, no explanation for the sudden apprehension she was feeling. And yet it was there. Perhaps it was the knowledge that Philip McKeith was still missing. Or still on the run.

She turned back to Richard and called after him. 'Is this something we could do in the morning, Richard?'

She heard him tut to himself. 'Never put off until tomorrow that which you can do today.' He was almost at the end of the path now. 'And never look a gift horse in the mouth. I promise that you won't be disappointed, Kathryn. I think I can safely say that what I have to give you is not only quite unique but that you will be the only woman in England to possess such a fascinating object.'

*

Becca tried to hold the mobile phone steady in her hand, but she was fighting a losing battle. Her palm was greasy with perspiration, her fingers shaking with the aftermath of shock, and the phone itself was slipping and sliding around in her grasp. She placed it down on the kitchen table and looked at it, squinting through teary lashes at the screen.

Forgive me.

It was such a short, simple phrase. Powerful. Humble. Unexpected. And so very, very unnerving to have arrived in a text from Philip.

Forgive him? Forgive him for what?

God knows there were enough reasons for him to need her forgiveness. Until this morning, she could have listed at least three to be going on with – lying, cheating, and screwing Lucy Lancefield. Now she could add disappearing without a word, rendering her sick with worry, and not thinking about the effect this nightmare was going to have on Frankie.

But Becca was too afraid to jump to any obvious conclusions. And she was too angry to make it easy for him. She pinned the mobile phone to the table with one clammy hand and jabbed at the keypad with the unsteady index finger of the other.

Why should I?

She counted the seconds it took for a reply to come through, one hundred and sixty-seven pounding heartbeats.

Because you love me.

It wasn't something she could contradict. She fought back a sob and pushed the mobile phone away to the other side of the table. The tears were coming thick and fast now, and she smeared them away with the sleeve of her blouse. For minute after minute, she stared at the silent, lifeless phone, unable to bring herself to reply, and then it juddered with the arrival of another incoming text. She snatched it up and held the screen close to her face.

I'm sorry I've hurt you. But you mustn't worry about me. I can't tell you where I am. But I'll text you again soon.

She knew there were questions that she ought to be asking. Are you warm, are you hungry, do you need money, what can I do to help you? The most obvious question she pushed to the back of her mind. Now wasn't the time to ask if he had murdered Lucy Lancefield. She tapped at the phone and sent one more simple, heartfelt plea.

Please come home.

The reply took barely twenty seconds to arrive.

Kiss Frankie goodnight for me.

Kiss Frankie goodnight? Becca dropped the phone back onto the table and stared horror-stricken at the display with unseeing, disbelieving eyes.

*

In the rising moonlight, Kathryn could see that Richard was standing in front of an old brick building which resembled some sort of stable block. He had paused by the first of two wooden doors set into the front-facing wall, and now was pulling gently at the handle. The door wasn't locked. He turned to smile at her. 'This room used to be the bothy for the estate gardeners, a rest room for them to take their meals. But it fell into disuse. The room next door is Philip's potting shed.' The door creaked as it swung inwards, and he reached inside to flick on a light switch. A single bulb hanging from the ceiling lit up what appeared to be some kind of storeroom. 'Philip was beginning to clean the place up a bit so that you would find it easier to work with the contents. I'm afraid it's still a bit dusty.'

Kathryn followed him into the room. It was cold and damp and smelled of neglect and decay and something foetid that she couldn't quite place. She gazed slowly around. The floor was covered with packing trunks and tea chests, and against one wall a thick tarpaulin covered a row of rusting iron tools - a legacy, she supposed, of the estate's agricultural past. 'Do you expect me to curate the contents of this room at some point?'

'I would hope so.' He was rummaging in one of the packing cases. 'These items have been shipped back from Woodlands Park over several years. I didn't want them to be lost.' He lifted his head and looked up at her through hopeful eyes. 'I did mention when I engaged you that there would be artefacts to curate as well as documents. I hope that what is here is of as much interest to you as it is to me.' He put his hand deep into the packing case, pulled out something wrapped in crumpled tissue paper, and tentatively peeled the end of the paper away to better examine what was inside. 'Ah, here it is. I knew it would be here.' He looked pleased with himself. 'A bit of a risk, offering it to you as a gift before I'd tracked it down. But no harm done.' He pulled at the tissue paper, dropping it to the floor, and then held out to Kathryn what looked like a slim, silver stick. 'My mother used to tickle me with this when I was a child. It was passed down by her mother, and by her mother before her. I don't know the actual date it was made, but I believe it to be eighteenth century, and I know it's solid silver. There must be a hallmark.' He pulled it back for a moment and squinted up and down its length. 'My eyesight's just not good enough. We can take it back to the house and give it a polish. Perhaps when we've removed the tarnish we might learn a bit more.' He offered it to her again. 'With my very best compliments, Kathryn. I know you will appreciate its value and its heritage.'

Kathryn stretched out a hand and took the item from him. At first, she thought it was some kind of toy, a silver rattle perhaps, or a stick for a small child to play with a hoop. Such extravagances would have been common in a wealthy colonial family. Whatever it was, and despite the heavy tarnishing, she could see that it was indeed made of solid silver, and old enough to be of significant historical value. 'Richard, it's too generous. I couldn't possibly accept this.'

'Oh, please, my dear. You are probably the one person I know who *could* accept it.' He was watching her closely. 'You do know what it is?'

There was evidently something that Kathryn was

missing. She held the stick up to her eyes, and looked more closely at the delicate engraving. It gave no clues. She held it away again and considered it as a whole. It was pointed at one end, and at the other the silver was fashioned into a small, empty loop. She looked up at Richard, bemused.

He looked momentarily disappointed. And then he smiled and held up a finger. 'It's lost its end. Of course, you can't tell what it is yet.' He gestured for her to give the silver stick back to him, and then bent down into the packing case a second time. 'Now,' he said, straightening his back and handing the object back to her. 'That's better. Now you know what it is?' He had attached something to the loop at the end of the stick, a hank of leather strands, each almost as long as the stick itself.

As realisation dawned, a shiver of horrified fascination rippled across Kathryn's skin. 'It's a whip.' Her mouth had turned dry, and the words came out as a hoarse whisper. Then louder. 'A lady's whip?'

He nodded with a tired smile. 'That's right. At one time every lady on St Felix possessed one. They were essential, you know. How else was one supposed to keep order and discipline in the household?'

Kathryn felt suddenly light-headed. How could she answer such a question? There was no answer. She stepped forward, closer to the packing case, and peered inside. 'What else is in there?'

'Mostly clothing, I think. Nothing much of interest.' He had moved away to examine another packing chest. 'This one is more interesting.' He leaned in and pulled out something black and heavy. It came out with a clanking noise, like a heavy chain. 'These were generally used on the wrists, to keep a gang together. There are several sets of these.' He seemed distracted. 'Now where on earth…?' He turned again, towards the items leaning against the wall. 'Perhaps under here.' He pulled the tarpaulin covering them away with a flourish, like a magician revealing a trick.

Kathryn watched as the oiled cloth slid away, feeling her pulse quicken and her forehead become clammy. She opened her mouth, but no sound would come out, and she lifted the silver whip, still in her hand, to point at the artefacts lined up against the wall.

She had seen something like them in a museum on more than one occasion, but nothing could have prepared her for the feeling of repulsion that was sweeping through her body. Leaning against the wall was an iron neck collar, its protruding irons sharp and pointed, and next to it were the recognisable lines of a human yoke. A pile of iron chains lay heaped on the floor beneath them – the unmistakeable trappings of human bondage.

The undeniable accoutrements of slavery.

'Richard, these things should be in a museum.' Her voice was low, her tone as calm and steady as she could make it.

At the other side of the room, Richard didn't appear to be listening. He was rummaging behind the packing crates and muttering to himself, and then he looked up at her. 'When I stopped by yesterday afternoon, I could have sworn that there was a fine set of leg irons in here. I can't imagine what Philip must have done with them.'

'Leg irons? You mean manacles?'

'Yes, if you like.' He frowned. 'I don't suppose you've spotted them?' He spoke casually, as if losing a set of manacles was as usual as misplacing the gardening shears, or forgetting where he'd left his spectacles.

'Spotted them?' The absurdity of the situation was indisputable, yet there was nothing Kathryn could do but cast her eyes absently around the room. 'I really don't know. There are some chains beside the wall there.' She pointed beneath the neck collar and tried hard not to look too closely at it.

'Ye-es.' He drew out the word, but looked uncertain. 'Those are manacles, but those were made for women. You can tell by the size of the ankle cuffs. No' – he shook his head – 'I'm talking about a big chunky set. The sort they used for a chain gang.' He stopped and considered for a moment. 'I'm absolutely certain they were here yesterday.' He looked up at her perplexed. 'Now why on earth would anyone want to help themselves to a rusty old set of iron manacles?'

11

DS Parkinson placed a paper cup in front of DCI Price, then perched gingerly on the edge of the desk and began to sip on his first Americano of the day. Price muttered his thanks without looking up. His eyes were still glued to the detailed report on his desk, an early morning gift from the pathology department.

'It doesn't give us much more than we knew yesterday.' Price tapped impatiently on the document. 'We have an approximate time of death now – somewhere between seven thirty and eight thirty in the evening. And she was dragged into the water immediately after death occurred. Also' – he licked his index finger and used it to turn the page – 'it doesn't appear that there was any sexual activity immediately prior to death. So if she *was* meeting Philip McKeith, intercourse hadn't taken place.' The policeman leaned back in his seat and folded his arms. 'We're not going to get much more in the way of forensic evidence from the body or the clothing. She'd been in the water too long.'

At the other side of the desk, DS Parkinson was listening intently. 'She wasn't carrying keys or a mobile phone?'

'No, she wasn't. But then she was in the garden of her own home.'

'Have we had any information back yet on Philip McKeith's phone?'

'No. We're still waiting for the service provider to get back to us. But it should be today. If it's been used since Lucy died, we might get a trace on him.'

'So how do you want to proceed this morning?'

'Well, more than one member of the household has a motive, but as McKeith has gone to ground, let's start with a working assumption that he strangled her. We've given the family overnight to come to terms with Lucy's death. It's time that we told them she was murdered. And I want to take a closer look at their alibis. Just because we're starting with the gardener doesn't mean I'm taking my eyes off the others.' Price again tapped thoughtfully on the desk. 'We'll start with Richard Lancefield. I don't think he was physically capable of the murder himself, let alone of dragging the body into the water, but let's break the news to him and see how he takes it. If I talk to Lancefield, could you walk over to Becca Smith's cottage and break the news to her? See how she reacts. And see if you can get her to cough up whether she has heard from McKeith yet.'

'And Marcus Drake?'

'If he's at the hall, I'll speak to him. Otherwise, we'll have to come back to Penzance and break the news.' Price frowned. 'I'd like to know why he didn't report Lucy missing. She was expected to go out on Tuesday evening, yet no one seemed to notice that she hadn't come back. Not even her fiancé. Wouldn't you think he would notice if she wasn't safely tucked up in bed? I mean,' he looked perplexed, 'even if he was used to her staying out late, wouldn't you think he would have popped into her room the following morning to speak to her before he went to work?'

'It's certainly what I would have done.' Parkinson thought for a moment, and then said, 'There aren't many of them, are there? In the family, I mean.'

'No, there aren't. Lucy's father and his wife should be arriving today, but they were the best part of six hundred miles away when she was murdered. There's the enigmatic Nancy – I still can't work out where she fits in. She's supposed to be employed as Lancefield's secretary, and yet she claims Lucy was a friend.'

'So?'

'I don't know. I'm just not sure I believe her.' Price was looking thoughtful. 'You spoke to their visitor yesterday, Kathryn Clifton. What's she like?'

'She came across as cool, but I think she was shaken by what had happened. She's been engaged by Lancefield to do some sort of historical work, something to do with the family papers. She said it was her first visit to Salvation Hall, and she'd never met either Lucy or McKeith.'

'How long is she going to be in Penzance?'

'Until Sunday. I think the intention was for her to assess the documents over the next few days, and then return home to work on the assignment.'

'And where's home?'

'Cambridge.'

Price raised an eyebrow. 'Academic?'

'I'm not sure. A writer, I think. But she specialises in genealogy, particularly where there are links to the Caribbean.'

'Does she now?' That Caribbean connection just wouldn't leave Price alone. 'I think it might be worth another chat with Kathryn Clifton. She might not know the family well, but it's possible she might be able to provide some background for us on the kind of family they are.'

'Is that relevant if our primary suspect is Philip McKeith?'

Price swivelled gently in his chair and regarded the sergeant with a tolerant smile. 'Everything is relevant, Tom, until we know beyond all doubt who murdered Lucy Lancefield, and why.'

*

'I can see why the contents of that room would shock you.' Nancy regarded Kathryn with a look of mild concern. 'Richard sometimes forgets that what he takes for granted is abhorrent to people in the outside world.'

'The outside world?' It was a curious turn of phrase. 'You mean the world outside the family?'

'I suppose so.' Nancy shrugged and dropped the letter she was holding onto the left-hand side of the library desk. 'The left-hand pile is "personal papers", that's right isn't it?'

Kathryn nodded. They had been sifting through documents since her arrival at nine thirty, and the desk was so heavily covered with documents now that little of the blue silk scarf covering its surface could be seen. 'When we've finished emptying the first box, it might be an idea to drop all the personal papers into it. Then when we start on the second box, the estate documents can go onto the desk, and the personal ones into the first box.' She lifted a discoloured envelope from the desk and glanced at it. 'Do you know exactly what's in that room, Nancy. I mean, have you seen it for yourself?'

Nancy laughed, a light chuckle of amusement. 'Of course I have. I brought some of the items over from St Felix myself.' She had just lifted another roll of papers out of the box and she paused, resting it on the edge of the desk. 'Kathryn, we are a family from St Felix. I thought you understood. What is in that room is a part of our shared history.'

If Kathryn had had a suspicion, Nancy had just confirmed it. Nancy had been introduced to her as Richard's secretary, but no one had mentioned her origins. 'You're from the Woodlands Park estate, aren't you?' She asked the question with a gentle smile, already confident of the answer.

A coy expression spread across Nancy's face. 'Of course. I was born and raised there and offered the chance to come to England and train as Richard's secretary when I was eighteen. There was never any question, it was the opportunity of a lifetime.' She frowned. 'You do understand, Kathryn? You understand that Woodlands

Park is one big family, regardless of any blood ties. That we are related by the history that we share? And that the past – for us – is dead and buried?'

'I understand, I think, that Woodlands Park is a working plantation. And that the island of St Felix is a small one, so it is likely that those who live and work on the estate are members of families who have been there for generations.'

Nancy stretched out a hand and placed it on Kathryn's arm. 'You don't need to be so careful with me, Kathryn. I was born at Woodlands Park and yes, I am a distant descendant of the first slaves who were carried to the island. I'm not ashamed of that. In fact, I'm proud of it. I'm proud that my ancestors fought against the adversity that took them to St Felix, and I'm proud that they survived.'

Her candour was complete, and for a moment Kathryn could only stare at her. 'Is it really that simple for you?'

'Of course. Richard is my employer. In a different life, I might have been born here, in Cornwall. I might have been descended from the original serfs who toiled in the fields planting wheat and barley for the benefit of their masters. Would you look at me with those careful eyes and ask me if I was descended from a serf?' She laughed again. 'What am I supposed to do with the hand that life has dealt me? I could be angry, or I could be content. And trust me when I tell you that I am very, very content. Richard is a lovely man. He is kindness itself to the people on the estate in St Felix. Here in England he is seen as a curmudgeon, a misery, a secretive old man who closets himself in this grand house and doesn't mix with the local community. But I see only sadness in his eyes most of the time. For much of his early life, he divided his time between Woodlands Park and Salvation Hall, but there was never any question about where he wanted to be. He maintained a presence here in England out of duty, but his heart is in St Felix.'

'Still, those things that are in the storeroom…'

'They are barbaric. And they serve to remind us of what must never happen again.' Nancy was regarding Kathryn with a concerned eye. 'We can choose to be horrified by them, or we can choose simply to observe. I believe that if we choose to be horrified, then we give them power over us.' She was still holding the roll of papers pulled from the box, but she placed it on the desk now and pushed herself up from her chair. She rested her hand on Kathryn's shoulder with a gentle touch. 'I'll make us some coffee. Then when I come back, we can begin the work again.' She moved towards the door and then paused, turning to look at Kathryn over her shoulder. 'I am so pleased that you're here, Kathryn. I think you'll be good for us. I think you have the capacity to understand, where others would only judge.'

Kathryn watched Nancy leave the library, then sank back into her seat and raised her eyes to the ceiling. Whatever Nancy thought of her, Kathryn herself wasn't all that sure that she would be able to understand the Lancefield family at all. She had arrived at Salvation Hall that morning to see Richard at a distance, setting off for his morning walk with the ever-faithful Samson trotting at his heels. He was striding out with purpose and couldn't have looked less like a man who'd just lost his granddaughter if he'd tried. Now Nancy was cheerfully assisting her with her work as if she hadn't just lost a close friend. Even Marcus, the bereaved fiancé, appeared to have left for work in Penzance as if nothing untoward had happened.

She glanced down absently at the second box of documents, so far unopened, and wondered whether Richard had said anything to Nancy about the missing set of manacles. It might be nothing, just the fancy of an absent-minded, forgetful old man. But she couldn't help thinking that someone should mention it to the police. And she couldn't help wondering whether she was the only person in the Salvation Hall household who thought it was important.

*

'And there is absolutely no doubt, Chief Inspector Price?' Richard Lancefield looked away, out of the drawing room window, as he asked the question.

'None whatsoever, sir. I'm very sorry.' Price stood awkwardly beside the fireplace and waited for the old man to absorb the news. He hadn't been sure what to expect but now, seeing Richard's demeanour, he realised that Lucy Lancefield's grandfather was more affected by her death than he had given him credit for. And he couldn't help feeling slightly ashamed for judging the man so harshly. He'd been in the job long enough to know that there was no predictable reaction to unexpected death. He'd seen it all in his time. Sorrow, grief, guilt, denial, indifference, feigned indifference, and the reaction itself, born of the shock of hearing the news, was no reliable indicator of the true feelings of the recipient. Men in particular, especially elderly men like Richard Lancefield, were conditioned to keep their feelings hidden and apt to feign indifference to hide any hint of weakness. It was possible, he thought, that Richard Lancefield's behaviour yesterday was down to denial, the refusal to admit that his granddaughter was, in fact, dead. He took a step forward. 'Would you like me to call for someone? For Nancy?'

'No, thank you.' Richard put up a hand but kept his gaze focused on the view through the window, across the terrace and the garden. For several minutes he didn't speak, and they stood in awkward silence, then he turned to Price and asked, 'What is to be done now?'

'I know that you are concerned for Philip McKeith. If we are to eliminate him from our enquiries, then it is imperative that we find him as quickly as possible.' The words were carefully chosen to keep Richard Lancefield on side. 'I would like your permission to search the house and grounds more closely. I could apply for a warrant, and there is no doubt that the warrant would be granted, but we could move more quickly if you gave your consent. I don't want this to drag on any longer than it needs to. And I think you would appreciate a swift resolution.'

Richard backed away from the window and lowered himself into an armchair. 'Very prettily put, Chief Inspector. I appreciate your efforts to spare my feelings.' He put a hand up to his face, his thumb pressed into his cheekbone, his fingers spread across his forehead. 'Forgive me.' It was impossible to tell what was most on his mind, the fact that Lucy had been murdered, or that Philip McKeith may be the prime suspect for the crime. He turned a rheumy eye towards the policeman. 'I will give you my permission, Chief Inspector, on one condition. That you treat my household with respect. No one is to be bullied, and no one is to be manhandled. If Philip is found on the estate, and even if he admits to being involved in Lucy's death, I do not want him judged. I want him treated with compassion.' His voice was firm. 'And I want your word.'

Ennor Price smiled, a business-like curve of the lips. 'I would be compromising my principles, Mr Lancefield, if I did anything less. It isn't my job to judge. And' – he cleared his throat – 'I might add that I will be extending the same compassion to any other member of your household who comes under investigation.'

The old man's eyes narrowed shrewdly. 'You consider someone other than Philip under investigation?'

'As I advised you yesterday, Philip McKeith is the obvious subject, but it has never been my way to take the easy option.' He paused and then ventured a dangerous question. 'Can I ask what you really thought about your granddaughter's affair with McKeith?'

'As I explained to *you* yesterday, Chief Inspector, I did not judge them. I take on board your point that Marcus and Becca may have been hurt by their behaviour. But Philip and Lucy have known each other for many years and were naturally very close. There had been an attraction between them since Lucy was too young for any liaison to be legal.' He gave a throaty laugh. 'I have shocked your sensibilities, but I can assure you that I would not have condoned any underage liaison. But once Lucy was of age, it was her decision. Young people today are quite liberal in their habits and, at the beginning, they were not hurting anyone. And to be perfectly frank, if Lucy was going to be liberal with her favours, I considered it better it be someone close, someone I knew and trusted.'

Trusted? Price couldn't help but wonder if it occurred to the old man at all that his trust might have been misplaced. But now wasn't the time to raise the point. Instead, he asked, 'Was Marcus Drake aware of their relationship?'

'I cannot comment on that with any certainty. Marcus does not hold me in his confidence. We have a polite but distant relationship.'

'He lives in your house.'

'It pleased Lucy to have him here. He is a polite, respectful, hard-working young man. In my opinion, he wasn't husband material for her. Lucy was a headstrong girl, and Marcus couldn't control her. There would have been tears in the end.'

'Did you ever witness any confrontation between Marcus and Philip?'

'No.'

'Between Marcus and Lucy?'

'I never heard a cross word between them.'

Price was momentarily thankful that he wasn't playing Richard Lancefield at poker. 'Will Marcus stay here now?'

'No. He returned to Penzance this morning. But I hope he will stay in touch with us. We are a small family and will need each other's support more than we think.' The old man turned his head away, lost in thought, and when he turned back his voice was strangely resolute. 'I'm relying on you, Chief Inspector. Lucy's murder was an affront to her, and an affront to the family, and suspicion has fallen on a young man in whom I place the utmost trust. I will give you every support in your investigation. And in return, I will be looking to you to find Philip McKeith and bring the person responsible for my granddaughter's death to speedy justice.'

DCI Price bowed his head. There was no question that he and Richard Lancefield wanted the same thing. He only wished that he shared Lancefield's confidence in his ability to deliver.

12

DS Parkinson watched Becca's face with genuine concern. The confirmation that Lucy Lancefield had been murdered had stunned her into a silent daze. 'Why don't you sit down. I'll put the kettle on and make you a brew.' His voice was kind.

She lowered herself onto a chair at the kitchen table without a word. He could only guess at the thought processes working away somewhere behind her eyes. He thought tears were close at hand, but they were unlikely to be tears for Lucy. For as long as it took him to locate mugs, coffee, milk and sugar, Becca sat in silence, her gaze fixed on some distant unseen point. Only when he sat down next to her at the table did she make any kind of movement, turning her head a little towards him, then looking down at the mug of coffee he'd placed before her on the table. She wrapped her hands around the mug and stared into it.

Parkinson cleared his throat. 'I have to ask, Becca. Have you heard from Philip since we spoke yesterday?'

He saw her wince, a tiny backwards jerking movement of the head, an unmistakable flinch of the eyelids. 'No.' Her voice was hollow and unconvincing.

'The sooner we can find him, the sooner we can eliminate him from our enquiries.'

'You don't want to eliminate him. You want to truss him up like a scapegoat and hang him out to dry.'

Her words surprised him. 'Is that what you think, Becca? Or is that what Philip thinks?'

'I haven't heard from him.'

'Where's Frankie today?'

'She's with my mum. I'm supposed to be working today.'

'Did you stay here last night?'

'Of course I did. I wanted to be here if Philip came home.'

He couldn't tell if she was bluffing. 'He doesn't deserve your loyalty.'

She turned and looked at him with unforgiving eyes. 'How would you know?'

'He's not thinking about you, or Frankie.' He stared hard into his mug of coffee. 'I have a wife. And a daughter. My little girl is four years old. And they are at the front of everything I do from the minute I wake up in the morning until the minute I go to bed.'

A sarcastic smile twitched around Becca's lips. 'Even when you're leaning on a potential witness?'

He didn't miss a beat. 'Even now. Because I'm looking at you and I'm thinking of them. I'm looking at you and I'm thinking that I would never place them in the position that Philip has placed you and Frankie in.' And, he thought with a guilty twinge, I would never be so mean as to lean on Claire the way I'm leaning on you, or use Ella as a pawn to lever information, but sometimes I have to cross my own line. He pushed his mug of coffee away from him and rested his forearms on the table. 'There's such a thing as assisting an offender, Becca. When we find Philip – and we will find him – if it turns out that you've been covering for him – do you really want Frankie to be on her own?'

'Frankie?'

'If he goes down and you've been covering for him, he could take you with him. Is that what you want? To be separated from your little girl?' The sergeant was trying to sound solicitous and not sure if it was working. 'They'd take her into care.'

'She'd go to my mum.'

'So you've already thought about it?' She was almost in the trap.

But she knew it. 'Richard Lancefield came to see me yesterday. He doesn't think that Philip was responsible for Lucy's death. And he said he's going to look after us.'

'That was before he knew that Lucy had been strangled. She was strangled with the scarf she was wearing. It was a violent death, Becca. Whoever murdered her throttled the life out of her body and dragged her into the lake after she was dead.'

'He wouldn't. Philip wouldn't have done that.'

'We're tracing his phone. If he's made or taken any calls since Lucy's death, if he's exchanged any texts, we'll know by this afternoon.'

Her eyes flicked towards him, and for the first time he saw fear, and then just as quickly she turned her head away. He followed her gaze. She was looking across the kitchen to a tall pine bookcase. The shelves were packed with books and magazines, but the top was empty save for a sorry-looking potted geranium in need of water and a slim, silver mobile phone. It was one of those moments, more familiar to him than he would have wished, when he realised that he was right and would have preferred to be wrong.

'I wanted him to come home, to turn himself in. But he still denies it.' Her face began to crumple, tears beginning to flow.

The tension finally broken, Tom relaxed. He wouldn't have to push her any further. He slipped a hand into the inside pocket of his jacket and pulled out a small leather-bound notebook and a ballpoint pen. 'I'll do everything I can to help you, Becca. But you're going to have to tell me everything. From the beginning.'

*

The quiet tap on the library door was unexpected. The door was already slightly ajar and Nancy and Richard came and went through the doors of their own home without a second thought. Kathryn looked up from the handwritten journal she was examining and peered over her reading glasses towards the door, watching as it swung quietly open.

'Miss Clifton? I'm Detective Chief Inspector Ennor Price. I'm leading the investigation into Lucy Lancefield's death. I wonder if I could speak with you about your work here?'

'Of course.' She took off her glasses and placed them down on the desk. 'You'll have to excuse the mess, I'm afraid I'm not exactly a tidy worker.'

'My sergeant tells me you're working on the family's history.' He pointed at the pile of papers on the desk as he walked towards her.

'Yes, amongst other things. The Lancefield family seem to have been voracious document keepers.' She smiled at him. 'Richard Lancefield has asked me to curate all the papers, and also some historical artefacts that belonged to Woodlands Park, his estate on St Felix.'

Price frowned. 'In the Caribbean?'

'Yes. The Leeward Islands. It's a small island close to Barbados. The family were amongst the first settlers there.'

He leaned against the desk and glanced down at the growing piles of documents. 'And by "curate" you mean what?'

'The documents relate to the family and their estates here in Cornwall and on St Felix. Richard has asked me to study the documents and to write a history of the family. I think he sees it as a legacy, to document the family's heritage, their way of life, before his own life comes to an end.'

The inspector looked mildly amused. 'This may sound a little harsh, but would anyone other than the family be interested?'

'What, apart from me?' Kathryn laughed. 'You would be surprised. According to Richard, even his family think it's just the vanity of an eccentric and elderly patriarch.

But, the subject matter is sensitive, and many families with similar histories have been reluctant to share details of their affairs. I've only sifted through the material so far but, from an academic perspective, it's priceless. It provides evidence of social, political and economic practices across a period of around three hundred years. Opportunities to access material like this come along once in a lifetime. And that's if you're lucky.'

Price looked interested now. 'You said the subject matter was sensitive.'

'Woodlands Park is a sugar plantation, Chief Inspector Price. Without mincing words, the Lancefields were a slave-owning family. The estate was initially built using white indentured labour but over time, and in line with the practices of the time, it came to rely increasingly on slave labour. By the time ownership transferred to the Lancefields, the practice would be well-established.' Her frown deepened. 'Forgive me. What does this have to do with Lucy Lancefield's death?'

He shook his head with a smile. 'Nothing directly. I'm just interested to know what you're working on because it helps me to form a picture of the family.' He thought for a moment and then asked, 'You didn't actually meet Lucy Lancefield, did you?'

'No. Yesterday was my first visit to Salvation Hall. And it was my first meeting with Richard. Previously we have only communicated by letter and telephone.'

'And he's happy for your work to continue? In the light of Lucy's death, I mean.'

'I'm not sure he's happy, Chief Inspector. But he's keen. I think perhaps it's helping to take his mind off things.' She frowned. 'Do you think my work should stop?'

'No. In fact, I would be pleased for it to continue. Sometimes these things have a way of opening doors for us when we least expect it.' Price folded his arms. 'You mentioned that the estate on St Felix was called Woodlands Park. I believe that Mr Lancefield's secretary is also called Woodlands. Nancy Woodlands. Is that a coincidence?'

Kathryn gave a knowing smile. 'Hardly. Nancy is called Woodlands because her family hail from the Woodlands Park plantation. That's generally how it is for families of slave descent on St Felix. Their ancestors were usually named after the plantation owner or the plantation itself. The name carries on through.' She watched with amusement as his face contorted through a series of emotions, and finally settled on incredulity. 'Don't be shocked, Chief Inspector. It's a fact of history. There are many things in the past which are abhorrent to us today, but we can't change history. We can only learn from it.'

'But slavery? The Lancefield family really made their money from slavery?' He'd lowered his voice as if the subject could only be discussed in a whisper.

'As far as I am aware, they made their money from sugar production. At least Richard's branch of the family did. The use of slave labour was fundamental to sugar production in the West Indies until the first part of the nineteenth century.'

'That must be quite a legacy to live down.'

'And more of our country is trying to live it down than you would imagine.' Kathryn gave an enigmatic smile. 'Sugar production, and the wealth it generated, has left a legacy in this country that seeps into just about every aspect of our daily lives. Banks founded on it are still operating today. Charities were funded by it. Plantation owners who poured wealth into their home cities in England were honoured by having streets named after them. Sugar money was used to fund successful political careers. It bought advantageous marriages for daughters and first-rate university degrees for sons. There is no escape from it. It's one of the great foundations of privilege in this country.'

She had caught his interest, and he straightened his back and moved a fraction away from the desk. 'So why don't I know about it?'

Kathryn shrugged. 'Because we bury the unbearable. Because it's easier to hide the truth than face up to it. Or perhaps sometimes the moral maze we've created would be so convoluted to unravel and would take so many innocent victims with it, that we can't even bring ourselves to contemplate the task. It's much easier to just pretend it never happened.'

'A form of self-denial.' Price gave a smile of resignation. 'I have a complex task of my own to deal with, Miss Clifton… Kathryn. And I can't pretend that it never happened. I've just had to inform Richard Lancefield that his granddaughter's death was murder.'

For a moment Kathryn was silent, contemplating. Then she quietly asked, 'Do you suspect the gardener?'

'Let's say we are keeping a very open mind, but that is one line of enquiry we are considering.'

'Then I'm glad you came to speak to me, Chief Inspector. Something happened yesterday evening that frankly has been troubling me and, well, I'm sure it's nothing to do with Lucy's death, but I wanted to make you aware of it in any case.' She looked uncertain. 'As well as the documents you see here, Richard Lancefield has asked me to curate some artefacts that were shipped over to Salvation Hall from Woodlands Park. And last night, when he was showing me where those artefacts are stored, he discovered that one of them was missing.'

Price looked at her expectantly. 'And you think it may be relevant to our enquiries?'

'I can't say that, Chief Inspector. But the missing item is a set of iron manacles, and it was taken from a storeroom next to the potting shed that was used by Philip McKeith. And, under the circumstances, it does seem rather worrying that they should go missing at the same time as your primary suspect.'

13

The mobile phone skittered across the table with the vibration of another incoming text. Marcus didn't need to look at it to know that it was yet another message from his mother.

She had been sending him texts at approximately hourly intervals since the news of Lucy's death had been broken to her yesterday afternoon. He had responded to the first few with his customary filial obedience, and his mother had sounded surprisingly sympathetic, a turn of events which later he could only subscribe to the shock. But as the day wore on, each new text had taken on a firmer, more judgemental tone. "Marcus, darling, I'm so very, very sorry" had soon become "She has no one to blame but herself." In the late afternoon he received "It's not your fault", and soon afterwards "Have they caught the adulterer?", and the evening closed with "Don't move out of the house, you have every right to be there."

He had stopped responding at "Don't move out of the house". Stella Drake Lancefield might be his mother, but he was under no illusion about the shallow motivations by which she lived her life. Marrying David Lancefield and living at his expense would never be enough for her. She wanted control of the Lancefield estates, and Marcus was the tool by which she hoped to secure it. If nothing else, he mused with a slight tinge of shame, Lucy's death removed any possibility of the two women in his life declaring open warfare with him caught helpless in a no-man's-land between them.

His decision to stop answering his mother's texts had done little to stem the flow. If anything, the frequency had increased, and her tone had become correspondingly more demanding. Worse still, her arrival in Cornwall was imminent. There would be no avoiding her then. He had accepted Ian's offer to bed down at the hotel, but The Zoological was public territory. One way or another, he knew that she was going to track him down.

He got up from the table and moved over to the window. He was in the small administrative office that Ian had set up in the hotel's attic, and he looked down through the dusty glass at the gardens laid out below. School term in England had already begun, but the late summer's day had drawn young women out of doors with babies and toddlers, and the lawns and benches of Morrab Gardens were littered with pushchairs and picnic blankets. It was an experience of childhood that he didn't recognise.

He leaned against the window frame and thought with a sinking feeling that his experience of adulthood wasn't turning out to be much better. Persuaded by his mother to abandon the girl he loved so that he could nail his colours to the Lancefield mast, he'd found himself with even less control over his destiny than he had felt as a boy. At least during his early years, there had been friends at school, and a grandfather to watch over him, and his mother had mostly forgotten about him while she played the role of wild child and muse to a succession of self-absorbed and mostly drug-addled musicians and artists.

But as her beauty had begun to fade, as her striking green eyes had begun to narrow and grow hooded, and the flesh around her sharp chiselled cheekbones had wrinkled and sagged, her power had begun to diminish. Blonde hair from a bottle was yellow and harsh and her once full lips had thinned to a supercilious smirk, rather than the alluring and sensual pout of her youth. And then one day her sights had landed on the unfortunate and unsuspecting David Lancefield. An artist, yes, but only in name. Even Marcus could see that his stepfather's work lacked any real expression of talent. But he knew that as far as his mother was concerned it hardly mattered if David stood one day to inherit the Lancefield millions.

Marcus turned away from the window and looked back at the mobile phone on the table. He knew what Stella wanted of him now. He had been so close to marrying Lucy, so close to cementing their access to the Lancefield fortune, and Lucy's death had swiped that from their grasp. He closed his eyes and for a moment his young face screwed up against the risk of tears. It had been so long since he had lived his life for himself that he could barely remember how to do it. His future had been so bound up in his mother's plans for him to marry, and Lucy's plans for him to be an off-the-shelf husband, that beyond his job and a temporary bed in the hotel he no longer had any idea just what the future held for him.

He was about to sink deeper into the well of self-pity when the mobile phone shuddered with another incoming text, and he opened one eye to look at it. He couldn't avoid his mother for ever. He may as well talk to her now and get it over with.

*

'Thank you for showing me Lucy's rooms again.' DCI Price smiled amiably at Nancy Woodlands.

She met the smile with an inscrutable expression and what might have been a hint of wariness in the dark, expressive eyes. 'Richard has asked me to help you in any way that I can.'

'Has he told you that Lucy was murdered?'

'Yes.' She looked uneasy. 'I can't believe it of Philip. Neither of us can.'

'Well, we're keeping an open mind on that. No man is guilty until proven so. At this stage, we'd just be glad of the opportunity to speak with him.' Price let his gaze linger on her face for a moment, and then turned his attention back to the task in hand, beginning to walk slowly around the small, exquisitely furnished room. 'Did Lucy use this sitting room much? I mean, rather than the drawing room downstairs.'

'Yes. We both did.' Nancy was still standing beside the door, her hands clasped modestly in front of her like an obedient servant. 'The drawing room is Richard's domain. Sometimes in the evenings I will sit in there and keep him company. But if Lucy and I wanted to watch a film, we would sit in here.'

'Did you do that often? Watch films together?'

She hesitated before answering. 'Yes, pretty frequently. We both enjoy – I mean, enjoyed – a good adventure movie. Especially historical ones, the ones we grew up with.' She gave a gentle laugh. 'We used to argue over who was the best, Indiana Jones or Jack Colton. Lucy was a big fan of Michael Douglas.'

'Do you also have a sitting room, Nancy? You or Marcus?' Price half turned his head towards her as he asked the question, and saw a momentary loss of composure.

'No, of course not.' She made the question sound absurd. 'If it's a matter of the household's living arrangements, they are quite simple. I have a large bedroom, dressing room and bathroom to myself in the attic. It was originally the servant's quarters, but you really shouldn't read too much into that. Richard had it modernised and furnished for me, and I enjoy a great deal of privacy up there. It's almost like a self-contained apartment, and my room is so large that it accommodates a sofa, coffee table and television stand without encroaching on the sleeping area.' She sounded proud of the arrangement. 'Like all the family, I take my meals in the kitchen.' Her laugh was self-deprecating now. 'Well, I would, wouldn't I, considering that I cook most of the meals for us?'

'Doesn't Becca do that?'

'She's meant to, and she usually attends to breakfast

and lunch. She brings Frankie with her, or else leaves her with her mother in the village. But Richard isn't so keen on Frankie being in the house in the evenings now that she's growing up and becoming noisy, so I tend to arrange the evening meals.'

Price turned and began to examine the books on a nearby bookshelf. 'Did you cook Lucy an evening meal on Tuesday?'

The question seemed to catch Nancy off guard. Then she said, 'No. Lucy had told me she was going out to dine with friends in St Ives. I saw her at around six thirty, when we had a coffee together in the kitchen. And then she went up to her room to freshen up and change.'

'Did you hear her leave the house?'

'I'm afraid not, Chief Inspector.'

'So that was the last time you saw her?'

'Yes. Until the following day, when her body was found in the lake.'

Price gave a nod of satisfaction. 'So you ate alone on Tuesday evening?'

'I cooked a St Felix jambalaya. It's a favourite dish of Richard's, a bit like a paella with a Caribbean twist. Richard ate his in the Dower House. He often likes to be alone in the evenings. I took his supper over to him on a tray. I ate mine alone in the kitchen, and I left a portion in a casserole dish for Marcus to reheat when he was ready.'

'And what time was that? When you ate alone in the kitchen?'

'I served Richard just after eight o'clock and then ate mine directly afterwards.'

'And what time did Marcus come in?'

Nancy was beginning to look a little flustered. 'I honestly can't remember exactly.' She furrowed her brow. 'We don't live in each other's pockets, Chief Inspector. I believe he came back around seven thirty.'

'While you were cooking?'

'Yes.' She sounded more positive.

'But he didn't eat with you?'

'No. When I went over to the Dower House to serve Richard, Marcus went up to his room to shower and change.'

'And after you'd eaten?'

'I made myself a coffee and read the paper.'

'And later?'

'I think I prepared a mug of cocoa for Richard. I took it over to him at about nine fifteen. Marcus was in the kitchen by then, eating his supper. When I came back to the house we sat and chatted for a while.'

'What about?' Price tried to make the question sound casual.

'I can't remember.'

'And in the morning, did no one miss Lucy? Wasn't she expected for breakfast?'

'We all breakfast separately. Marcus tends to grab a bowl of cereal before leaving for work. Becca usually cooks for the rest of us. I take Richard's down to the Dower House on a tray, then eat mine in the kitchen. Sometimes Lucy joins me. Sometimes she stays in bed, especially if she has been out late the evening before.'

Price turned slowly towards her and smiled squarely into her face. 'Thank you for being so helpful, Nancy. I know this can't be easy. I have just one more question if you don't mind.' He tilted his head to the right and swivelled his eyes up and around towards a framed print hanging to the left of the fireplace. It was a fine art print, a colourful period portrait of two young women in exquisite silk gowns, and it looked incongruous hanging amongst a collage of muted modernist works. 'I couldn't help noticing this yesterday. I've never seen anything quite like it. Do you know how it came to be here? Where it came from?' He flicked his attention back towards her face and was rewarded with a momentary narrowing of the eyes.

'Why would I?' She stepped forward and appeared to examine the picture in more detail. 'The house is full of art, Chief Inspector. This picture is only a print, but there are also many originals on display. I'm afraid I have nothing to do with the choice of furnishings in the house. It may have been in the family for many years, or it may just be something that Lucy acquired on her travels.' There was no emotion in her voice, but there was a guarded, almost suspicious look in the expressive, dark eyes.

And for the first time since he had begun his investigation, Ennor Price couldn't help thinking that he was getting a little closer to the truth.

*

Despite the unnerving presence of DCI Price and a posse of uniformed officers, Kathryn had made unexpectedly good progress with her work that morning. The first boxes of documents were now neatly sorted, and she had taken the opportunity to catch some fresh air before spending another afternoon indoors inhaling the unavoidable aroma of musty, mouldering paper.

It had been Nancy's suggestion that she take a stroll down to the nearby village church. The weather was set fair for the rest of the day, but due to turn fickle the day after. And so, Kathryn had picked up her camera, donned her sunglasses, and embraced the opportunity for an hour's fresh air and freedom.

The church was barely a ten-minute walk from the house, a pleasant stroll along the winding country lane that linked Salvation Hall with the small manorial village of Penwithen. It stood proudly in the centre of the village, flanked by a pair of impressive chestnut trees, and directly across the village green from an inn. The inn itself looked ancient enough, white painted and gabled at both ends, and Kathryn could only smile at the name board hanging above the hostelry's door. It wasn't really any great surprise that it should be called The Lancefield Arms.

There was no denying that the church was also a fine-looking building, constructed entirely from granite with a strong, square tower at one end, and a fine perpendicular window at the other. The churchyard around it was compact, at least to the front, with neatly mown grass and a selection of shrub roses planted at random between the surviving gravestones. The stones themselves, like most gravestones in an almost-coastal churchyard, were showing signs of wear, their letters scraped and smoothed by the blowing of salty winds off the nearby English Channel.

There was a board to the right of the lichgate, burgundy-painted, and the church's provenance was written in neat gold letters. The Church of Saint Felicity and All Saints had been founded in 1363. Beneath the details of Sunday services and the Reverend James MacArthur's telephone number, the words "familia super omnia" were discreetly painted in small, gold, Italianate script.

Familia super omnia. Family over everything, the Lancefield family motto.

Kathryn smiled to herself, then opened the gate and followed a curiously modern concrete path to the entrance to the church. She pushed gently on the weighty oak door and it swung open without resistance. Inside, a strong shaft of sunlight was shining through the window at the back of the church, throwing the blues and greens and reds of the stained glass within it down to dance on the stone floor of the aisle. She turned, and gently closed the door behind her, and as she did so a muted bark echoed from the altar end of the church.

Samson was sitting at the end of the aisle, his blue-grey head on one side, his curly tail wagging with its intermittent sweep. On the pew beside him, Richard Lancefield sat in silence. He put his hand down to Samson to quiet the bark and then turned to look over his shoulder. 'Kathryn, my dear. What a welcome surprise. Come and keep an old man company.' He slid along the pew to make room for her at the end. 'I was indulging in a moment of peace and reflection.'

She eased herself into the pew beside him. 'I didn't mean to disturb you.'

'You're not disturbing me. I'm pleased to see you. I needed something to brighten my day.' He looked weary. 'They have told me that Lucy was murdered. I am trying to prepare for the worst.'

Kathryn could only venture to guess what might be worse than hearing that his granddaughter had been murdered. 'Have they identified the murderer?'

'Not in so many words. But I think they are convinced that Philip was responsible.' Richard looked down at his hands. 'No man likes to think that his trust has been betrayed. I trusted him with her, you know.' He turned sorrowful eyes to Kathryn's face. 'I knew that she was wilful, that she'd have her own way when it came to earthly pleasures, and I trusted him to be the one because I believed that he would treat her kindly.'

'And perhaps he always did. Just because he hasn't been found doesn't automatically mean that he was responsible for her death.'

'Do you really think so?' The old man brightened for a moment, and then his shoulders sank deeper into the pew. 'It's a cowardly act, though. Not facing the music. She deserved better.' He looked suddenly vulnerable, older even than his eighty-eight years.

It occurred to Kathryn now that Richard Lancefield wasn't cold so much as unable to express himself. His hand was resting on the back of the pew in front, and she stretched out her own to wrap it over his. It was a spontaneous gesture that surprised them both, and for several minutes they sat together, virtual strangers, linked only by the gravity of the situation and a tenuous understanding of humanity.

It was Kathryn who eventually broke the silence. 'I've told Chief Inspector Price about the manacles. That they've gone missing.' She licked her lips. 'He's asked me to be present this afternoon when he examines the storeroom. I think he would like me to explain what some of the items are. But it will give me an opportunity to at least get everything photographed and catalogued.' She paused, and then added, 'If the police think that the contents of that room are relevant to their enquiries, they may remove some of them. And we must protect them. They... because of the nature of them, I'm worried that they may impound some of them.' She turned to look at him. 'Richard, I would like your permission to lie.'

He turned a quizzical eye in her direction. 'For what purpose?'

'I think it would be helpful if I made out to DCI Price that the items have already been promised to a museum. I have a contact in Cambridge who would be prepared to confirm that, if the police thought it necessary. I don't think we can prevent any of the items from being removed. But we're more likely to have them safely returned if they have already been promised to a third party, especially one in the public domain.'

'As you see fit.' Richard smiled to himself. They were co-conspirators now. 'I suppose you are making this suggestion because you believe that the items belong in a museum.'

'In the short term, I just want to buy some time so that I can photograph and catalogue them. But I know that any museum would be privileged to have them.'

'Including my gift to you?'

'My silver whip?' Kathryn squeezed the gnarled hand beneath her own. 'Most certainly not. I shall look upon that as my own private piece of the Lancefield family history.'

He looked pleased. 'Then we must speak of museums when this drama is done.' He coughed to clear the emotion from his throat. 'In return, Kathryn, I would like you to do something for me.' He slipped his left hand into his jacket pocket and pulled out a small, basic mobile phone. 'Lucy bought this for me last year. She was trying to bring me into the twenty-first century.' He smiled at the thought. 'I don't understand how it works, but I have a use for it now. I believe that Lucy stored some phone numbers in it for me, those people she thought I may want to contact at some time or other. I would like you to send a text message for me.'

Kathryn took the phone from him and pressed the keyboard with her thumb. 'Of course. What would you like me to send, and who would you like me to send it to?'

'I would like you to send it to Philip. And I would like you to ask him to come home.'

14

DS Parkinson looked down at his hands, and then lifted his gaze to Drake's face. 'I'm sorry to have to tell you that we have confirmed the cause of Lucy's death. And it was not due to an accident.'

Marcus blinked and turned to look at Ian. 'She was murdered then?'

They were standing in the bar of The Zoological Hotel and Ian, seeing distress beginning to loom, moved swiftly behind the counter, picked up a glass, and pumped the brandy optic several times before handing the glass to Marcus.

Marcus took it from him and swigged back the brandy, flinching as its heat hit the back of his throat. He placed the glass gently down on the counter and turned back to Tom Parkinson. 'How?'

'She was strangled with the scarf she was wearing. Before she went into the water.'

'Have you found him yet? Philip. Have you found him?'

'No. But I must stress to you, Mr Drake, that at this stage Philip McKeith is only a person of interest. The fact that he is missing doesn't necessarily make him guilty of Lucy's murder.'

'Doesn't make him guilty?' Marcus muttered the words under his breath. 'Philip McKeith has murdered my Lucy, and you don't think he's guilty?'

Ian stepped forward towards the policeman. 'It's all come as a shock, sergeant. Perhaps if you could give Marcus time to come to terms with the news?'

DS Parkinson responded to the suggestion with a smile

that suggested Marcus would be lucky. 'I'm afraid I have several questions for Mr Drake.' He pointed towards a small table in the corner of the empty bar. 'I will try to keep it as brief as possible.'

'I'd like Ian to be present while you put those questions to me.' Marcus moved towards the table. 'That's alright, isn't it?'

'Of course.' Parkinson nodded as he took his seat. 'If Mr Mitchell agrees.'

'I'm happy to sit in.' Ian settled in a chair beside Marcus. 'But I need to advise you, Sergeant Parkinson, that I used to practice as a solicitor. I'm not in a position to represent Marcus on a formal basis, but I do intend to support his interests.'

Parkinson gave Mitchell his best reassuring smile. 'The questions I have are informal. But I appreciate the heads-up.' He pulled a pen and small notebook from his pocket. 'Mr Drake, can you tell me, please, when you last saw Lucy Lancefield?'

'On Tuesday morning, before I went to work.'

'And at what time did you return home on Tuesday evening?'

Marcus paused. 'I think it was about seven thirty. Lucy had already gone out for the evening. I chatted to Nancy for a while, and then went up to my room to shower and change. Nancy had prepared some supper and left it in the kitchen for me to reheat.'

'I apologise for the next question. You were aware of Lucy's relationship with Philip McKeith?'

'It wasn't a relationship.' The reply was hissed through clenched teeth. 'It was a fling. Nothing more. It would have stopped after the wedding.'

Ian placed a cautioning hand on Marcus's arm. 'You only need to answer the sergeant's questions, Marcus. You don't have to add anything.' It was a warning shot, but Marcus understood.

The policeman appeared untroubled by Ian's

interference. 'Can I ask where you were until seven thirty that evening?'

'I met a client for a drink in Penzance just after six. I was with him for about an hour. And then I drove home. I think I stopped for petrol on the way.'

'And the client can confirm that?'

'Yes.'

'And after you'd eaten supper, what did you do then?'

'I sat in the kitchen and chatted with Nancy. She'd taken Richard some cocoa while I was eating, and she came back and made some for us.'

'What did you talk about?'

'I can't remember.'

Parkinson looked up at him and smiled. He guessed that Marcus had been crying on Nancy's shoulder. 'And you didn't see Lucy again that evening?'

'No. I chatted with Nancy until around ten thirty, and then I went to bed.'

'And the next morning, you went into Lucy's room to speak to her before going to work?'

Marcus look startled. 'Who told you that?'

'No one. I just assumed that as you hadn't seen her the previous evening, you would look into her room and say hello before going to work. I know I would if it were my fiancée.'

A crimson flush began to seep into the young man's cheeks and his eyes took on a wary look. 'I assumed she must have come in very late. I didn't think she would appreciate being woken so early.' It sounded lame.

DS Parkinson eyed him thoughtfully and then closed his notebook. 'Where will I find you if I need to speak with you again? Are you going back to Salvation Hall this evening?'

The flush in Drake's cheeks deepened. 'Yes, but not to stay. My mother is due to arrive today, and I'll be going over to the hall to see her, and to collect the rest of my belongings. I've decided to move out. I'm going to be staying here for a few days.'

The policeman nodded in quiet understanding. He wanted to probe deeper, to ask more questions about Lucy's relationship with Philip McKeith. But he hadn't reckoned on Ian Mitchell being a retired solicitor. He needed to get Marcus away from his guard dog.

And the best way to do that was to back off and wait until Marcus returned to Salvation Hall.

*

Stella Drake Lancefield turned a critical eye to her husband. 'Why are we always made to feel like intruders in this house? Nancy couldn't wait to get away from us.' They were alone in the drawing room at Salvation Hall, and Stella had draped herself over the generous Chesterfield sofa with her usual affectation. 'David, are you listening to me?'

David Lancefield stepped closer to the large bay window overlooking the garden, and tried very hard not to tell his wife that he had done nothing *but* listen to her all the way down from Edinburgh. He was still coming to terms with Lucy's death, the news broken to him by Richard the previous evening in one of their longer telephone conversations. Somewhere between replacing the receiver and climbing onto a train at Waverley Station, David had decided to pull down the shutters, but it hadn't stopped Stella from sharing her every waking thought. He answered his wife in a quiet voice without looking at her. 'We *are* intruders in the house. We don't want to be here, any more than my father and Nancy want us here.'

'Marcus wants us here.'

David held his tongue. He had a good deal of sympathy for the easily-manipulated Marcus and thought it highly unlikely that his step-son would welcome the appearance of his mother. But it wasn't an opinion he was prepared to share with his wife.

His silence did nothing to stem the tide of Stella's complaints. 'I can't imagine what my poor boy is going through. I hope Richard and Nancy have been kind to him. Bereaved before his wedding day. It doesn't bear thinking about.'

'And what about me, Stella?' David turned to her with a spat of unexpected venom. 'Can you imagine what I'm going through? Lucy was my daughter, after all.'

'Oh, darling… ' His wife threw up her arms towards him and pouted. 'You didn't care for her. You told me yourself.'

'I wasn't close to her. A poor relationship is not the same as "not caring". She was my flesh and blood.'

'She was a spoiled child. She was spoiled by her mother. And how many times have you told me that she *reminded* you of her mother? You didn't even love the woman. You told me you were relieved when Susanna died.'

'Stella, that's an unforgivable thing to say.'

'You were the one who said it. I just repeated it.' She wrapped an arm around her head. 'How long are we going to have to stay here?'

'Until the day after the funeral.'

'Well, you must include Marcus. In the arrangements. Lucy was his fiancée. He should choose the music. And the readings.'

'I know.' David tried, with only moderate success, to keep the exasperation out of his voice. He craned his neck around to look at her. 'I've just seen my father come in through the conservatory door. For pity's sake straighten your dress and sit up properly. He will expect some respect.'

'He doesn't deserve respect.' Stella sounded bitter. She swung herself around, her legs primly together in front of her, and rested her hands gently on her lap. 'Will this do?' Her tone was wheedling, just a fraction short of facetious.

David stepped away from the window and walked

towards the sofa, just as the door of the drawing room opened. There was a rattle of china as Nancy wheeled in a small tea trolley, pushing it into the middle of the room. She smiled at him warmly. 'I've made tea for you both – Assam for you, David, and Earl Grey for Stella. There is milk and lemon, if you want it. And I wasn't sure if you'd eaten, so I've brought you some smoked salmon sandwiches. And biscuits, of course.' She stiffened the smile and turned it towards Stella. 'I'll be in the kitchen if you need anything else.'

David visibly softened. 'Nancy, you are literally an angel. Before you leave us, can I ask if you have any idea when Marcus will be back?'

'He called me to say he'd be here about four.'

'He called *you*?' Stella's voice rose by an octave and she turned to glower over her shoulder at Nancy.

Nancy didn't answer but simply blinked at David before attempting an escape through the doorway behind her. Stella rose to her feet and turned towards the door, preparing to vent her frustrations on the innocent and retreating Nancy. But as she did so, Nancy almost collided with an unexpected figure in the doorway, and Stella found herself unexpectedly face to face with Richard Lancefield.

For a moment she froze and her gaze darted from Richard to David, then back to Richard. And then she skirted the sofa, her arms outstretched. 'Richard, my poor darling. This whole situation must have been hell for you.' She rested her hands on the old man's shoulders, enveloping him in a cloud of patchouli, and air-kissed his cheeks. 'But we're here to help you now.' She turned her head and widened her eyes at her husband, her hands still clamped to Richard's shoulders. 'David, for heaven's sake, don't be so distant. Come and say hello to your poor father.'

15

DCI Price paused in the doorway of the small, brick-built storeroom and took in the packing crates, the jumble of clothing and toys on the floor, and the row of iron instruments neatly lined up against the wall. Stacked together casually, they were unmistakably relics of a bygone age, and at first glance might have been any other set of rusting, agricultural paraphernalia.

Kathryn watched the policeman's face as he took in the scene and smiled at him as he turned to her with an enquiring look. 'Most of these things have been shipped over from the estate on St Felix.'

'And Richard Lancefield thinks that something has been taken from this room?'

'A set of iron manacles. He thinks it was a double set. They would have been heavy, it would have taken a strong person to lift them.'

'Manacles? Like the sort of thing that was used to restrain convicts?'

'If you like. Although these will have been used to restrain workers on the plantation. They were most commonly used to shackle runaways after capture. A double set would have had four individual leg cuffs. Two runaways would have been chained together, to make a further escape more difficult.'

Price narrowed his eyes. 'How could anyone be so cruel?'

Kathryn shrugged. 'They were different times. How could anyone send a six-year-old child up a smouldering chimney to clean it?' She walked across the room and bent down to pick something up off the floor. She turned to

Price and offered him what looked like an iron chain with a cuff or ring at each end. 'This is the sort of thing you're looking for. This is a single leg iron made to restrain a woman. The one that's gone missing will be much bigger and will have four of these leg cuffs on it, with two lengths of chain. The intention was to apply restricted movement using the cuffs and the chain binding them together, and the chain was intentionally heavy to weigh down whoever was wearing them.'

He took the small set of irons from her with a wince of disgust. 'And these were used on women?'

'And probably adolescents.'

'We found nothing like this anywhere near Lucy Lancefield's body. And the pathology report made no mention of bruising around the ankles or wrists that might indicate the use of metal cuffs. In any case' – he looked away with a frown, thinking – 'wouldn't the killer have taken this smaller set if the intention was to use them on Lucy?' He shuddered at the thought and dropped the irons gently to the floor. 'I'm not sure I can see any relevance to our case, Kathryn. Although you were right to bring it to our attention.' He rubbed his hands together to remove a dusty residue. 'As a policeman, I have to say that this room is unlikely to be relevant to our case. As a human being' – he looked solemn now – 'I have to say that I am truly disgusted.' He turned to look at her. 'How on earth can you bear to work with this stuff?'

'How on earth can you bear to work with criminals? Thieves, drug dealers, murderers? People traffickers?'

'That's different. I'm working on the side of justice.'

'How do you know that I'm not on the same side?' She leaned over to a packing case and pulled out what looked like a poker. 'See this?' She held it out towards him. 'It's a branding iron. If you look closely, you'll see a motif carefully worked into the disc at the end. That motif is a seahorse, drawn within an orchid flower. It's effectively the trademark of the Woodlands Park estate. Every beast on the estate would have been branded with an iron like this to show that it belonged to the Lancefields. And every human they owned would have carried the same mark.'

'You can't own a human being.' Price had begun to put out his hand to take the iron from her, and he suddenly recoiled. 'They branded human beings?'

She answered with a knowing look. 'This iron would have been searingly hot and pushed into the flesh of men, women and children, so that everyone would know that they belonged to the Woodlands Park plantation. That they were Lancefield property. Have you ever smelt burning flesh, Chief Inspector Price? Can you imagine the screams of those men, women and children as they were branded?' She tossed the iron back into the packing case. 'I have no issue in helping Richard Lancefield to document his family history. In fact, I welcome the opportunity because writing it down is the first step on the road to acknowledging what happened. Families like the Lancefields have been hiding the shame of their legacy from public view for too long. We can't obliterate the past. We can't heal those wounds. But we can make sure that the story is known, and that it never happens again.'

'Does Richard Lancefield know that's how you feel?'

'Not yet. But he will, when I discuss it with him. I've already begun to persuade him that this stuff should be in a museum, where it will be preserved for everyone to learn from. But now isn't the time to broach the subject with him. He needs to come to terms with Lucy's death and Philip's disappearance.' Kathryn paused, and then added, 'Which brings us nicely back to the real reason we're here.'

DCI Price smiled. 'It does. And I'd like to know more, but I don't have the time to talk about it right now.' He hesitated, and put up a hand to pull awkwardly on his ear. 'I don't suppose you could spare me some time this evening?' He coughed, embarrassed at the inference. 'A working dinner, perhaps? Call it a favour. Or an opportunity to educate an ignorant policeman. It would help me to know just what makes the Lancefield family tick.'

Kathryn bit her lip to stifle a smile. 'A lesson in Caribbean history in return for a glass of wine and a pizza?'

'Well, I hope I can do better than that. There's an excellent seafood restaurant near the shore in Marazion. I could pick you up from your hotel, say seven thirty?'

'And you really think that I can help your investigation?' She thought for a moment. 'Before I accept, can I ask what you're planning to do with this room, now that you don't think the contents are relevant to your case?'

'We'll seal it off while the investigation is ongoing, in case anything leads us back here.'

'In that case, it's my turn to beg a favour. I'm negotiating the transfer of the contents of this room to a museum, in the hope that Richard Lancefield agrees to my proposals. Can you give me half an hour to photograph the contents before you seal it up?'

'Of course I can. As long as you promise me not to remove anything after you've finished.'

'You have my word.' Kathryn gave an enigmatic smile. If DCI Price was only concerned that she didn't remove anything after she'd photographed the contents, there would be no need to confess that the silver lady's whip, a rather fine example of a slave family Bible, and a reel of film intriguingly labelled "St Felix, 1937" were already packed away safely in the boot of her Volvo.

*

Marcus dropped the empty holdall onto the bed and unzipped it, then set about transferring the contents of a chest of drawers into its cavernous interior. He could feel his mother's eyes burning into the flesh at the back of his neck. But this time, it wasn't about her. He'd had enough of being pushed and prodded into shape to please the women in his life. If the last couple of days had taught him anything, it had taught him that it was time to live life on his own terms.

Somewhere behind him, Stella was huddled into a small wicker chair in the corner of his bedroom, watching him with a mixture of dismay and contempt. 'I'm only thinking of you, darling.'

Her voice crackled with a mother's disappointment, but it didn't touch him now. He knew that she could turn on more or less any emotion at will if she put her mind to it. 'If you're only thinking of me, then you'll understand why I want to move out.'

'But, darling, where will you go? This is your home. You're part of the family.'

He pulled angrily on the bag's zip to close it, then lifted it off the bed and dropped it noisily to the floor. 'You don't give a damn about Lucy, do you?' He turned to eye his mother with undisguised hostility. 'You don't give a damn that she's been murdered.'

'Of course not. Good heavens, Marcus, I didn't think that you loved her. How could you love her when she was carrying on with that Neanderthal that worked in the garden?'

'It was a fling. Nothing more. It would have been over when we married. You know how strong Lucy was. Do you honestly think she would have married me if she'd really wanted McKeith? She would have dumped me and taken him from Becca without a second thought.' Marcus blew out a snort of contempt. 'They would never have made a couple. It was just a game to them, to both of them. Half the fun was in the deception.'

'Darling, it seems so wrong to me that you should lose out just because the silly little tart wanted to play Lady Chatterley with her own private Mellors. And everyone seems to be forgetting that it turned out to be a very dangerous game. I don't remember any point in DH

Lawrence's novel where the lover strangles his mistress and drowns her in the ornamental lake.'

'You really can be vile.' Marcus turned away and set about divesting the wardrobe of its contents, pulling out armfuls of hanging clothes and dumping them onto the bed. 'If Lucy made a mistake, then she paid with her life. And I have no intention of profiting from that.'

'Well, I think you're being very selfish. There is no heir to the Lancefield estate now. David will never have another child. Have you forgotten that you were meant to provide the family with an heir?'

'What makes you think David will never have another child? Maybe he'll throw you over now and find a younger wife. Maybe he'll have to. Maybe Richard will insist on it, as part of his inheritance.' Marcus turned to his mother with a self-satisfied smirk. 'This may come as a shock to you, but I'm not going to hang around here and fawn all over Richard Lancefield just to please you.'

Stella pursed her lips and wrinkled her nose. 'David will never leave me. David loves me. But you may be right about Richard. Making David's inheritance conditional is just the sort of controlling, malicious thing he would consider. No' – she shook her head – 'you have to stay here. It's best for everyone.'

'It isn't best for me.' Marcus was tiring of the argument now. He walked around to the far corner of the bed and sat down on its edge, 'Look, I didn't love Lucy when I met her. I was flattered by the attention and blinded by the possibilities of marriage to her. But I did grow to care for her. And I'm sick to the stomach that McKeith has murdered her. And not just because he's ruined my future, but because he's taken Lucy's life.'

Stella's eyes searched his face. 'You believe he's guilty then? Poor David is quite distraught to know it was murder and not an accident.'

'There is no other possibility. It's down to the police to find him, and bring him to justice. But until they do, I have to get out of here. I'm going to stay at The Zoological with Ian and concentrate on my job. And once the police investigation is complete and the whole sordid bloody mess is over, I'm going to take a very long holiday somewhere to get the taste out of my mouth, then start my life again.'

For one unexpected and fleetingly sweet moment, his mother appeared to soften. She leaned forward in her chair and put out a hand to stroke his face. 'My poor boy.' She ran her fingers down his cheek and under his chin and lifted his face so that she could look directly into it. And when she did so, her expression had once again grown cold and calculating. 'If you move out of this house, you may never get back in again. This isn't just about you any more, it's about both of us. While David has been bleating about denying his family heritage, Lucy has been playing fast and loose with the gardener, and you have been dithering about on the sidelines, Richard Lancefield has turned his attention to the family's history. You know what that means don't you?'

Marcus stared blankly into her face. 'He wants the family history documented so that it won't be forgotten when he's gone?'

Stella threw her gaze heavenward. 'Oh for pity's sake, Marcus. Am I the only one around here with any brains? Do I really have to spell it out for you?'

*

Kathryn gently closed the library door behind her, skirted the oak table in the centre of the hall, and paused outside the door of the drawing room. It was barely four o'clock, but she was beginning to tire and the atmosphere at Salvation Hall was growing increasingly uncomfortable. The police presence on the estate had been bordering on low key the day before, as if they were sensitive to the family's distress. Officers had gone about their business quietly and with minimum disruption to the household. But the news that Lucy's death had been far from accidental had brought a distinct change to their approach. There was nothing low key about a murder investigation.

Intent on taking her leave of Richard for the day, Kathryn lifted her hand to knock on the drawing room door, but a sudden awareness that he was not in the room alone gave her reason to pause for a moment. She could just make out the muffled sound of what might have been an argument, two men evidently at odds, and by the tone of their voices both entrenched in opposition. She drew in a breath and then tapped loudly on the door to attract their attention.

'Come.' An angry bark from Richard summoned her into the room, and she turned the door's handle and pushed it slowly inwards. He was sitting in the armchair beside the fireplace, and at the sight of her his tone softened and he lowered his head. 'Kathryn, my dear, forgive me. I didn't know it was you.' He lifted his eyes and forced a smile. 'Come in, come in. Tell me what I can do for you.'

She closed the door behind her and returned his smile as she dropped her bag to the floor. The other man in the room was standing beside the fireplace and his face bore an impatient scowl and a distinct determination not to look at her. She looked back at Richard. 'I just wanted to let you know that I've finished here for the day. I'm going back to the hotel to spend some time consolidating the catalogue I've been putting together. But I'll be back in the morning.'

Richard tutted quietly to himself. 'Why don't you come back and join us for dinner?' He seemed to have forgotten that there was someone else in the room with them. 'I would enjoy your company.'

'That's kind of you, Richard. But I've already made plans for this evening.' As those plans included Detective Chief Inspector Price, she thought better of sharing them.

She waited for a moment, hoping that Richard would introduce her to the man she assumed was his son, but he just went on staring at her. There was no choice then. She stepped towards David Lancefield and held out her hand. 'I'm Kathryn Clifton.'

David Lancefield glowered at his father and then turned a sullen face towards her. There was no doubt that he was unhappy, and yet he didn't look unkind. He took her hand and pressed it unconvincingly. 'So I had assumed.' He took in a breath and blew it out again. 'I think I should warn you, Miss Clifton, that I don't agree with my father when it comes to the family heritage. If you are looking for support for your work, then you won't find it here.'

Kathryn gave a demure smile. 'Your father's support is quite enough for me. But I would welcome the opportunity to discuss your views some time.' She smiled at him again, an open and disarming smile that she hoped would reassure him that she hadn't come to start a fight.

For a moment he hesitated, unsure how to respond. Then he said, 'I think at the very least your work should be postponed out of respect for Lucy.' He flashed angry eyes at his father. 'I might have said, out of respect for me. I am still trying to come to terms with the news that my daughter was murdered. But I am not accustomed to being respected in this household, so I won't waste my breath.'

If Richard Lancefield felt the sting of his son's words, his face did not betray it. 'Kathryn, did you meet with the chief inspector this afternoon?' It was a deliberate change of subject.

'I did, yes. He doesn't think the contents of the storeroom have any bearing on Lucy's death. But he's going to seal the room temporarily while the investigation continues. And he allowed me to photograph everything in there before the room was sealed.'

'Well, he seems to be a good man. And at least he's local. I may not have warmed to him yet, but I think he's up to the job. The sooner he finds out who murdered Lucy, the better.' The old man thought for a moment, and then asked, 'Where is he now?'

'I believe he's with Sergeant Parkinson. They were going to search the potting shed.'

Richard finally turned to look at his son. 'I think you should go over there, David, and introduce yourself. See what they're up to.'

David scowled his irritation. 'Can't Nancy go?'

'Nancy isn't here to run around after you. She's gone over to the cottage to see if Becca needs anything.'

For a moment it looked as though David Lancefield had no intention of following his father's suggestion. And then he straightened his back and began to walk slowly towards the drawing room door. Halfway across the room, he turned to look again at Kathryn. 'Can I take it, then, that you will postpone your work, at least until after Lucy's funeral?'

'You most certainly may not.' It was not Kathryn who answered the question. Richard's voice was raised. 'I will decide how Kathryn's work will proceed. And I might add that in the light of Lucy's death I consider it to be more important than ever.' He groaned and sank back into the armchair. 'It doesn't seem to occur to anyone around here other than myself that Lucy's untimely death has left us with a most undesirable predicament.' He put an unsteady hand up to his face. 'It had never occurred to me until now that it is one thing to consider disinheriting one's heirs. It is another thing altogether to have that decision taken out of your hands by a malicious twist of fate.' His lips contorted into a snarl of despair. 'No man should have to live to see the death of a child or a grandchild. Especially when there is no one left to continue the family line.'

16

The potting shed at Salvation Hall was one of those quaint, brick-built affairs so beloved of Victorian gardeners, and had once been the middle room of a block of three built on to the western wall of the old walled garden. The room to the left was now used as a storeroom, as DCI Price had found earlier that afternoon. The room to the right had been used to store fruit from the orchard, but during the Great War, when all the young men on the estate had gone away to fight for their country, there was no one left to pick and store the fruits, and the room had fallen into disuse and crumbled away.

It had taken around twenty minutes for Price and Parkinson to convince themselves that there was nothing of use to be found in the potting shed. There was no evidence to support a theory that Philip McKeith was hiding out on the estate. McKeith was obviously a tidy workman. The room was pristine and orderly, the tools of his gardening trade neatly placed along the length of a sturdy timber potting bench, and stacks of upturned terracotta plant pots standing regimented along an eye-level shelf that ran the length of the bench.

A search behind the pots had yielded some evidence of the gardener's nocturnal habits in the shape of half a bottle of Irish whiskey, two mismatched wine glasses, and an unopened bottle of burgundy. These might not have meant much on their own, but coupled with the large lightweight duvet and the inflatable mattress that Parkinson had found behind a makeshift screen at the back of the shed, they had spoken of the evening trysts that McKeith had been sharing with Lucy Lancefield.

'Still no trace of his mobile phone.' Price was beginning to sound discouraged. He wasn't sure what he'd expected to find here – perhaps some evidence that McKeith was using the potting shed as a hiding place, if not for himself then at least for food and drink. 'Have we made any progress on his mobile phone records?'

'I've been promised the data by the end of the day. I'll chase them when we've finished here. If Becca Smith is telling the truth, and there have been texts from him, we should be able to evidence them.' Parkinson leaned back against the potting bench. 'I should have just asked her to show me her phone. But it's not easy keeping her on side. I didn't want to frighten her off.'

'She wouldn't have shown you anyway.' Price turned his attention to the wall opposite the bench. The upper portion was used as a sort of display area, and he moved closer to take a look. The display was a mixture of photographs and awards: a small, framed picture of Frankie as a toddler-in-arms, various certificates awarded for horticultural merit, and a larger, more heavily framed photograph of Philip with Richard Lancefield at a local flower show. They were smiling cheerily into the camera, each holding a handle of a large, pewter jug presumably awarded for some exhibit they had prepared together. Ennor put his face up to the picture and peered at it. If pushed, he could see a resemblance between Richard Lancefield and his gardener. Or maybe he was imagining it, just trying to find a reason beyond noblesse oblige for Lancefield's concern for Philp McKeith's wellbeing.

He turned back to Parkinson. 'I don't think there's anything else for us here. Let's pay another visit to Becca Smith. She's definitely hiding something.' He turned towards the door, pulled it open, and was about to step outside when he caught sight of an unfamiliar male figure striding out down the path from the terrace. 'Then again,' he said quietly over his shoulder to his colleague, 'I think I might let you do that on your own. I'm just going to hang on here for a few minutes. I've got a feeling that things are about to get interesting.'

*

The hallway at The Zoological Hotel was deserted when Kathryn returned and she had just reached the foot of the staircase when Ian emerged from the bar. 'Ah, Kathryn. I missed you at breakfast. I'm glad I've caught you now.' He crossed the hall to the reception desk as he spoke. 'I wanted to apologise to you. For what I said yesterday evening.' He had the grace to look repentant. 'I was out of order. No excuses.'

Kathryn responded with what she hoped was an equally gracious shake of the head. 'And I'm sorry if I was rude to you. But my personal life… well, it's been pretty difficult lately. I've come here to forget who I was. Not to be reminded of it.'

'And I suppose that's just what your sister-in-law was trying to do by addressing the letter to you in your married name. Remind you of who you were.'

Kathryn took in a deep breath and blew it out slowly through her lips with an almost-defeated smile. 'And I suppose it must be the solicitor in you that leads you to ask so many intrusive, personal questions.'

He blinked at the rebuke, and then looked away, contrite. 'Kathryn, I'm sorry. You won't hear it mentioned again. At least, not by me.' He turned back to her. 'I heard the news about Lucy. That it was murder, not an accidental death. I was here when the police came to break the news to Marcus.' He had turned away from one subject that she didn't want to discuss and stumbled straight into another.

'I heard that too. But it's police business. I'm just trying to focus on my assignment.' She dropped her soft leather bag onto the floor and leaned against the wall. 'Marcus must have taken the news pretty badly.'

'That's putting it mildly.' Ian looked worried. 'Haven't

you met Marcus yet? He's been at Salvation Hall all afternoon, picking up the rest of his things.'

'No. There was no reason for our paths to cross. I've been trying to keep to myself in the library for most of the day.' She frowned. 'I did meet David Lancefield this afternoon.'

'Did you meet Stella?'

'No, I think she was upstairs helping Marcus.'

'Well, that would be a first.' Ian laughed now, an unconvincing snort. 'She was probably leaning on him to continue living at Salvation Hall so that she could keep her nose firmly in the family trough. I just hope he doesn't cave in to her demands. He's got more than enough on his plate now that they're looking for Lucy's killer.'

'You really are concerned for him, aren't you?'

'Someone has to be. Marcus is one of those unlucky creatures who go through life like a universal orphan. His mother only thinks about herself and his father didn't hang around long enough to even register on the birth certificate. There was a grandfather on his mother's side, he looked out for Marcus when he was a boy. But he died years ago.'

'There was the girl he was engaged to, before he met Lucy.'

Ian looked thoughtful. 'Yes, there was Judy. I can't help thinking how much he must regret what happened there.'

'And your son. Didn't you tell me they were friends at university?'

He gave a melancholy smile. 'They were good friends at one time. But Laurence is ambitious. He's moving with a different crowd now. It takes him enough time to remember that he has a father, never mind a friend in Marcus.'

So that was it then. Marcus needed a father figure, and Ian was missing a son who had well and truly flown the nest. 'Is Marcus coming back to have dinner with you this evening?'

'I believe so. I was hoping to persuade you to join us.' He seemed to sense her hesitation. 'As my guest, of course. It's the least I can do to make up for yesterday evening.' His gaze was expectant.

'There's nothing to make up for.' Kathryn smiled. 'It's a very kind offer, but I'm afraid I've already made plans for this evening.'

Ian raised an inquisitive eyebrow. 'Back to Salvation Hall to enjoy dinner with the extended Lancefield family?'

'No.' She didn't want to explain. But his disappointed expression left her in no doubt that some explanation was going to be necessary. 'I'm meeting an acquaintance of the family. Someone interested in the work I'm doing for Richard Lancefield.' She tried to make it sound inconsequential. 'Not exactly the most exciting way to spend an evening, especially as I've spent most of the day indoors and buried under a mound of historical documents. But it's what I do for a living, so…' She forced a sigh, and hoped it didn't sound too artificial.

Ian gave a nod of the head and the disappointment in his eyes was joined by a hint of mistrust. 'Perhaps tomorrow evening, then.' He made the suggestion without any real expression of conviction.

Kathryn felt a sudden stab of remorse. She was beginning to realise now that Ian's concern for Marcus ran well beyond that of an employer for his right-hand man, and crossed over the line into the personal. It was too late now to back-pedal, to completely re-arrange her evening. But not too late to send a discreet text to DCI Price suggesting they meet somewhere other than the hotel before dining out this evening. She couldn't do anything about how Ian was feeling. But perhaps she could make sure that she didn't make things any worse.

*

'Why didn't you call me?' DS Parkinson, usually placid,

was finding it difficult to conceal his irritation. 'I thought we'd agreed that you would contact me if you received another text?'

Becca's face folded into an angry scowl. 'What would you do, if it was your wife who was hiding out?' The scowl turned into a sneer. 'No, don't answer that. You would have shopped her to your mates. Once a copper…' She was sitting at the kitchen table with a large glass of wine, a sullen light in her eyes.

Parkinson pulled a chair away from the table and sat down opposite her. He was losing – had probably already lost – her trust. But there was something else going on here, something he couldn't quite fathom. He would have to take a firmer line. 'I've been trying to play fair by you, Becca. I got it in the neck from DCI Price because I didn't lean on you to show me the texts you got from Philip last night. Now I want to see them. I want to see all of them.' He pulled his notebook from his jacket pocket and flipped to an empty page. 'Well?'

'I'm not telling you. You need a warrant.'

'Not if you agree to help, I don't.'

She gave a sarcastic waggle of the head. 'I'm still not telling you.'

He leaned forward over the table. 'We've been searching the grounds for Philip today, and we've just searched the potting shed. That's a nice duvet and mattress Philip's keeping in there. Is that from the cottage?'

The words stung her, and a violent flush lit up her cheeks. 'You're lying.'

'Come and see. I'll show you.' He let her think about it for a moment and then said, 'You don't owe him anything, Becca. He's been playing fast and loose with Lucy Lancefield and you're still defending him? I thought you had more backbone.'

He'd pushed too hard. Tears began to stream down her cheeks and her face crumpled into a mask of anguish. 'I'm scared.' She looked up at him through the tears. 'I thought the texts were from Philip, but now I don't know.' She sniffed loudly and rubbed her sleeve across her nose. 'The first couple just said that he was okay. That he was sorry, and he wanted me to forgive him. I asked him to come back, but he didn't answer me. But he said to kiss Frankie goodnight for him.'

Parkinson put down his notebook and gently pulled the wine glass from her hand. 'You don't need this. Just tell me what happened.' He put the glass down on the table where she couldn't reach it, took her hand in his, and squeezed her fingers. 'What's happened, Becca?'

She looked at him through tear-laden eyelashes. 'He never kissed Frankie goodnight. I used to ask him to, and he said he couldn't. There was a special reason he couldn't. And I know it sounds stupid, but it didn't feel right. Him asking me to do something for him, that I know he would never do. I know he's in a mess, but…' She gave another sniff. 'I sent him a text that said his mum was worried about him.' She paused, and turned her gaze away from the policeman, staring across the room, her mouth working hard to suppress a sob. 'And I got a text back that said, "Tell her not to worry, I'll be okay."'

'Well, that's not so strange, is it?'

Becca turned the swollen, tear-stained face back towards him. 'Philip could never kiss Frankie goodnight because of what had happened to his mum. She kissed him goodbye one night, when he was a boy, then went out to work her evening shift at the pub and was knocked down by a car.' Becca began to cry. 'Now you tell me, Sergeant Parkinson, why would Philip tell his mum not to worry, when she's been dead this past twenty-three years?'

17

'Ennor.' Kathryn said the name slowly with a teasing smile. 'Is that a Cornish name?'

'Very.' The policeman looked different without a collar and tie. Casually smart in an open-necked shirt and black jeans, he appeared to have shed his professional confidence with his formal attire and now, despite his greying temples, he looked strangely boyish and decidedly self-conscious. 'I have my mother to thank for that. She's obsessed with the Cornish heritage. My brother is called Gryffyn. At least we get to shorten that to Gryff, which sounds pretty normal.' He stifled a smile and looked down at the table. 'And his name is only a boy's name. I have a half-cousin also called Ennor but, luckily for me, she lives in Wales now, so I don't have to put up with the gender jokes.'

Kathryn leaned over the table and lowered her voice to a conspiratorial whisper. 'I promise I won't tell anyone.' She leaned back again and eyed him with more than a little curiosity. 'So what is it that you think I can tell you? It must be important for you to bribe me with this.' She circled the air with her finger, indicating their surroundings. They were seated outside a small restaurant in Marazion, enjoying the unseasonal warmth of the evening, and if her tone of voice was teasing she certainly wasn't complaining.

'It's not a bribe.' He looked serious for a moment. 'I really would like to know more about the Lancefield family, and what makes them tick. I don't expect you to breach any confidences but I'm not as convinced as my sergeant that it's a straightforward case of jealousy.'

'Fair enough. But if I'm going to help, I'd like to know something about the person I'm going to be helping.' Kathryn took off her wristwatch and laid it down on the table, face up, and then looked up at Ennor through mischievous eyes. 'Give me your history in two and a half minutes.'

'What?'

'I'm serious. Tell me about yourself in two and a half minutes. Then I'll tell you about myself and, after that, we'll be able to talk more openly.' She looked down at the watch and ticked the seconds off with her forefinger. 'Four, three, two, one, go.' She flicked the finger at him with a smile.

Ennor looked away from the table, thinking, then looked back at her and gave a self-conscious laugh. 'You don't mean it?' He blew out his disbelief. 'You *do* mean it.'

'You're losing precious time here, Chief Inspector.'

'My name is Ennor.'

'I'm not calling you Ennor until I know something about you.' She looked down at the watch again. 'Two minutes eleven seconds left.'

He puffed out a deeper sigh. 'Well, I was born in Penzance.' He sounded awkward. 'Raised in Penzance. One brother who lives in London. Parents have retired from the country to live in the centre of Exeter. Don't ask. I started to read law at Warwick University, found it dull, dropped out after two years and joined the police. The West Midlands force. Married a girl from Coventry.' He paused, a hint of sadness in his eyes. 'No kids. Divorced. Wanted a fresh start. Came back to Penzance to start again. But decided to hang on to my career. I live in the old part of town. I'll be fifty-five in October. Could retire, might seriously consider it.' He blinked, and then grinned, relieved that the ordeal was over. 'Will that do?'

'You have thirty-two seconds left. I'd hate you to leave something out.'

He let out a groan. 'I read a lot. I spend as much time

as I can by the sea.' He pondered, solemn for a moment, and then added, 'And justice matters to me. It makes me tick. I might not have had much time for Lucy Lancefield when she was alive, but I'm damned if I'll let the bastard who murdered her get away with it.'

Kathryn arched an eyebrow and looked down at the watch. 'Two minutes and forty-seven seconds. But I'll allow you the seventeen-second overspill. That last bit was worth the wait.'

Ennor reached out across the table to pick up Kathryn's watch. He turned it round to face him, his expression relaxed now the ordeal was over, but there was a smile brewing around his lips that suggested he was about to enjoy turning the tables. 'Your go.'

Kathryn rested her elbows on the table and clasped her hands together. She rested her chin on her interlocked fingers and smiled at him. 'Born in Cambridge to an academic father and dissatisfied mother. Raised in Cambridge. No siblings. Parents retired but still in Cambridge. Read history at Edinburgh University, studied British West Indian history, never looked back. Tried all sorts of jobs in Edinburgh that I couldn't settle to, including journalism and publishing. Married' – she gave a wistful twist of the lips – 'also no kids, almost divorced, don't want to talk about it. Took a holiday in Barbados after my marriage fell apart, met a guy called Ferguson whose family had been out there for three hundred years. Agreed to curate his family's history in return for a fee. Moved back to Cambridge, and rented a cottage on the outskirts. I survive by freelancing, editing other people's books mostly, though I've written one or two of my own. I turned forty-one in March. I also read a lot.' Her face straightened. 'And justice matters to me too. I want people to know more about our shared history with the Caribbean. I don't believe that it's overtly suppressed, but it isn't openly talked about.' She looked thoughtful. 'And I think it should be.'

For a moment he held her gaze and she had the impression that if he didn't quite understand, at least he wanted to. He looked down at the watch and laughed. 'Two minutes and fifty-nine seconds. Coffee and liqueurs are on you.'

She laughed with him. 'I really shouldn't talk about myself so much. But I hope we've broken the ice now. I'd rather talk to you as a friend than as a police inspector.' And, she thought, there are so many more interesting things we could be talking about. 'So now we've got the ice-breaker out of the way, tell me why you think that Lucy Lancefield's murder isn't just a straightforward case of jealousy.'

Ennor relaxed back into his seat. 'There's something about the Lancefield family that makes the hairs stand up on the back of my neck. I've always known about them as philanthropists, but I've never stopped to think about where the wealth that funded their charitable work came from.' He scratched at his forehead. 'I can't help wondering what sort of people they are, to live down a legacy like that as if it never happened.'

'But they're not living it down, are they?' Kathryn bit her lip. 'And I don't think that's what you're wondering about at all. I think you're wondering to yourself whether the Lancefield fortune has caused some kind of fall-out.'

Ennor laughed. 'Am I really that transparent?' There was a bottle of Semillon chilling in a wine bucket beside the table and he pulled it out and topped up Kathryn's glass before refilling his own. 'Richard Lancefield has engaged you to document his family's history and heritage. But he tells me that his son would rather obliterate every shred of Lancefield history so that he can't be reminded of his family's sins. Lucy, meanwhile, thought she had come up with a plan to commercialise the Lancefield estates so that no one would remember where the money originally came from. And Nancy Woodlands?' He paused and took a drink from his glass. 'Well, I just don't know what to make of Nancy Woodlands. Is she staff, or is she family?'

'Does it matter? In terms of your investigation?'

'It might. If Nancy had an objection to Lucy's plans. Or David's plans. Or even to Richard's plans.'

'Where does Philip McKeith fit into this train of thought?'

'I don't believe he had a motive for Lucy's murder. I get the impression he was too fond of her.'

'So where is he now?'

Ennor scowled. 'Now you're trying to disrupt my theory.' He sipped again on his wine and changed the subject. 'I met David Lancefield for the first time this afternoon. He came to the potting shed to find me, specifically to tell me that he wanted your work to stop. In fact, he asked me to insist upon it. On the grounds that it was interfering with the police investigation.'

'He went that far?' Kathryn felt a genuine pang of disappointment.

'You already knew that he had objections?'

'Yes.' She cast her eyes down into her glass. 'Are you going to stop me?'

Ennor lifted his glass to his lips and smiled into it. 'To please David Lancefield? Do I look as though I might?'

*

The evening air at Salvation Hall was finally beginning to cool, but Becca didn't notice. She was beyond the normal recognitions of daily life now, immune to pangs of thirst and hunger, impervious to the normal human sensations of cold and discomfort. She had taken up her spot by the lake just as the moon had begun to rise, throwing an old tartan car rug down on the grass, and sinking heavily down onto it with a heavy heart. There was nothing left now, she knew, but to hold vigil.

Something had happened to Philip.

What other explanation could there be? The realisation

that she'd been exchanging texts with a stranger had been a blow to the gut. A stranger using Philip's phone, masquerading as the man she loved, some faceless being pretending to be him, sending her messages of reassurance, of love. Gaining her confidence, taking her in, making a fool of her. She choked back the rising bile. Some unspeakable bitch or bastard laughing at her.

She had been staring at the cool, level waters of the lake but now she looked up and to her left, across the lawns and the terrace, to the warmly glowing windows of the house. Was it one of them? She knew that the Lancefields didn't want her there. One by one they had come to the windows to stare at her. She had seen David Lancefield first, beside that bitch he was married to, Marcus Drake's mother, the two of them peering out at her from the small leaded window on the landing. And then Nancy, looking out first from her own attic window, and then a short while later from the French windows that opened out from the drawing room onto the terrace. On that second occasion, Richard Lancefield had been with her, the two of them staring out in silence, and then Nancy had opened the window and stepped out across the terrace and the lawn to the lake, and pleaded with Becca from a distance to go home to the cottage.

It would take more than Nancy Woodlands to make Becca walk away. Who cared if she was upsetting Richard Lancefield? Her own unbidden feelings of resentment startled her, and she looked away from the house. *She* cared. It wasn't Richard's fault that his granddaughter had been a selfish little slut. And he cared about Philip. She knew that much to be true. But she still wasn't going to give up her vigil.

She turned her gaze back to the lake and tried to focus on the surface of the gently rippling water. They had pulled Lucy Lancefield's body out onto the grass just a few feet away from the spot where Becca was sitting and police tape still fluttered between flimsy stakes driven into the ground, an ineffective barrier to protect the crime scene. Becca had watched in morbid fascination from a distance as the pathologist examined the body, and as a police diver searched the shallow waters around the spot where Lucy had been found. But he hadn't gone any further. Sergeant Parkinson had explained that they had searched for any evidence of who might have dragged Lucy into the water. But they hadn't searched for any sign of Philip.

A cold and nagging thought was beginning to form now in Becca's tiring mind. They had searched for Philip in the grounds, but they hadn't searched for him in the water. She lifted her eyes across the lake, across the vast expanse of water lilies that stretched for several hundred metres until it met the driveway that dissected the grounds. Philip had told her once that the lake was only shallow where the waters met the lawn, that when it was built a deeper shelf had been excavated to accommodate the fish. She felt her breathing quicken, a mild panic rising in her stomach, and she pushed herself to her feet and began to walk around the lake to the spot where it met the driveway.

Instinct was leading her now, or perhaps it was the triumph of hope over rational thought. She picked her way carefully around the water's edge, the ground before her illuminated by the moon, until she reached the point farthest away from the spot where Lucy Lancefield's body had been dragged into the lake. She paused and stared solemnly into the gently rippling waters, watching the shadows of night-feeding carp darting here and there beneath the surface. The water lilies were less vigorous at this spot, their rooting baskets challenged to find an anchoring point in the lake's greater depth, the lucky ones finding a safe haven above the heavy limestone boulders that had been used in the construction of the lake. Philip had tried to teach her the names of the resourceful lilies that had made this spot their own and she frowned now at the remembrance. She had only ever been able to remember the simple names. Mayla, with its showy, fuchsia-coloured blooms. Mrs Richmond, pale pink and lightly fragranced. And Masaniello, whose name she could only recall because it rhymed with Limoncello, her favourite Italian liqueur. There was a fine spread of Masaniello here and she peered out across the water in the moonlight, trying to pin it down. It was hard to tell one lily from another when their flowers were closed against the moonlight.

She found it just a couple of metres beyond her present spot, and closer to the edge of the lake than she remembered, a broad sweep of generous leaves, its luscious strawberry-coloured blooms furled up against the darkness. It took a moment for her to register that it looked different from how she last remembered it. The once extensive spread appeared to have suffered some sort of fracture, and where the glossy leaves had previously appeared as a pool within a pool, there floated an untidy horseshoe of bruised and broken foliage.

An insidious chill began to creep across her scalp and neck, and when it reached her shoulders she gave an involuntary shiver, and a suffocating blanket of dread descended across her being with such relentless strength she could barely catch her breath. Her chest began to heave as her lungs fought against the constricting muscles of her chest, and her mouth felt suddenly dry. She tried to open her lips, but her mouth was frozen, and she turned wide and panicked eyes back in the direction of the house.

There was no one at the windows now. No one to see her panic, her fear, her despair. She looked down into the murky water, her breath still heaving, and forced her lips open, whispering into the night air. 'Oh dear God, please, no.' Still battling back the tears, she pulled her mobile phone from the pocket of her jeans and with trembling fingers began to dial her one and only hope.

18

Kathryn pulled her shawl around her shoulders. It was still a balmy evening but a cool breeze was blowing inland off the bay. She turned back to look at the restaurant to see Ennor emerging from the front door, distracted for a moment as he tucked a receipt for the meal into his wallet. She hadn't expected him to be good company, nor to be quite so interested in her favourite subject, and so far the evening had been much more enjoyable than anticipated.

She smiled as he came closer. 'This isn't really going on your expense account, is it?'

'That depends on whether I decide to put you down as a copper's nark.' He looked relaxed. 'I appreciate what you've done this evening, Kathryn.'

'What, sting you for a three-course meal, a bottle of Semillon, and an Irish coffee?' She laughed. 'I wish all my assignments were so easy.'

'Tell me a bit more about the Lancefields and I'll throw in a free taxi.' His tone was light. 'If we walk up into the village there's a taxi rank. That doesn't mean there'll be a taxi, of course. But if there isn't, there's a decent pub where we can wait until one comes out from Penzance to pick us up.' He set off walking at a slow pace, waiting for her to fall into step, then asked, 'What did you make of David Lancefield?'

'He wasn't what I expected. I thought he would be grieving the loss of his daughter. But he just seems, I don't know. He seems angry, somehow. And not necessarily about Lucy's death. I think he's angry at his father, and I think it goes back a very long way. I almost felt that his determination to stop my work was more about his feelings regarding the family's history than about it being disrespectful in the light of Lucy's death.'

'You know that his wife is Marcus Drake's mother?'

'Yes.

'It doesn't seem right to me, step-brother and sister getting married.'

'There was no blood tie between Lucy and Marcus, Ennor. No legal or biological reason for them not to marry.'

'Still' – Ennor glanced down at her – 'there was Philip McKeith. Marcus must have been desperate to marry into the family money, to put up with that. Salvation Hall and all its estates, never mind the property on St Felix. He would have come into that, wouldn't he, when Lucy inherited?'

'*If* she'd inherited.'

'There was some doubt over that?'

Ennor's tone was casual, but the question still brought a smile to Kathryn's lips. 'You really do think I'm a copper's nark, don't you?'

'You haven't earned your taxi ride back to Penzance yet.'

'Haven't I? Well, you already know that David is uncomfortable with the legacy. His solution so far has been to move away to Edinburgh and re-invent himself as an artist, having as little to do with his father as possible. Except I think he collects some sort of allowance from the estate. Richard thinks that if David inherits, he will immediately dissolve the estate, sell off all the assets and pocket the cash.'

'And is this why Richard Lancefield wants you to document the family history? Because he thinks that David will just get rid of any trace?'

'It's one reason, I think. There had been some talk of the inheritance bypassing David and going straight to Lucy – certainly Lucy seems to have been working on her grandfather to persuade him to settle Salvation Hall and

Woodlands Park on her. But she wasn't planning to dispose of it. Her grand idea was to turn the house here into a hotel and health spa, and Woodlands Park into a Caribbean golf resort. The properties would remain in the family, but everything relating to their history would be lost in a commercial reinvention. That way, she figured that the property would stay in the family, but the stigma of sugar production and slave ownership would be lost.'

'Who told you all this?'

'Nancy.'

'And how does she know?'

'I suppose because she's Richard's secretary. And she did spend a lot of time with Lucy, so perhaps they talked about it.' Kathryn fell silent for a moment and then said, 'Nancy told me that she believes her own family tree can be traced back to the first African slaves who were purchased for the Woodlands Park plantation. That was before the Lancefields owned it. She thinks her family have been there even longer than theirs.' Kathryn turned to look at Ennor. 'Can you imagine that? I've promised that when I've finished my official work for Richard I'll spend some time with her to look into it in more detail.'

'Even more time with those dusty old documents?' Ennor's eyes creased, and he turned his head away so that she couldn't see him laugh. 'You certainly know how to enjoy yourself, don't you?' They were close to the centre of Marazion now, and within clear sight of an empty taxi rank. 'Still, it looks like you'll get an unexpected bonus glass of wine while we wait for a taxi. If you can answer my next question.' He turned back and grinned at her. 'What did Richard Lancefield think of David's and Lucy's plans for his estate?'

'He wasn't happy about them. But I don't think he'd made up his mind yet to disinherit them. I think he's conflicted.' The question made her uncomfortable. 'I think you need to speak to Richard about that. In any case, I'm not sure I agree with your theories about Lucy's murder. It seems far more likely to me that her affair with McKeith is at the bottom of it.'

'That's what my sergeant would like. He thinks it's a straightforward crime of passion, that Lucy and Philip argued and that Philip murdered her, and now he's gone on the run.'

'And what's wrong with that theory?'

'It's too easy an assumption to make. I don't like things too easy. I need to know there is definitely no other angle before I'll grab at the obvious.' Ennor pulled his phone from his pocket and flicked at it with his fingers. 'Do you know anything about art, Kathryn? There's a print on the wall of Lucy's suite that intrigues me. So much so that I took a photograph of it.' He held out his hand, the phone screen turned towards her. 'Have you any idea what it is?'

Kathryn took the phone from him and glanced at the screen with a smile of undisguised pleasure. 'Is this really on Lucy's wall? Don't you find it stunning?' She turned to him with a quizzical look. 'You really don't know what it is?' He evidently didn't. She handed the phone back to him, still smiling. 'It looks like you'd better get a move on then and buy me that glass of wine. I think I'm about to earn it.

*

'I shouldn't be doing this, Becs. You need to get the police involved.' Robin Smith hauled himself out of the lake and sat on the grass beside his big sister. She'd sounded so distraught on the phone that he hadn't the heart to turn her down, but it had never been his intention to actually go into the water and look for Philip. Rather, he was sure that if he drove over to see her, he could persuade her that the exercise would be futile.

His mistake, of course, had been not to remove his diving gear from the van before setting off for Salvation Hall. Once there, once subjected to her pleading and cajoling, he had no excuse not to make a cursory search. He'd donned his wetsuit and mask, taken a small, half-filled air cylinder from the van, and grudgingly made a cursory search of the area underneath the damaged water lilies. Now he pulled off the mask and tried some earnest pleading of his own. 'I just don't have the right equipment for this sort of dive. It's not like a dive at sea. And I shouldn't be doing it on my own. It's not safe. Once you get below the water you can't see a thing.'

'But you have a diving light.' Becca's tone was pitiful.

'I know I do. But there's so much weed down there, and every time I try to push it out of the way it just releases clouds of mud and sediment.' He shivered against the evening cold and hugged himself, rubbing his hands against his arms in an attempt to warm himself. 'There's no way I could find him, Becs, even if he was down there.'

'He *is* down there. I just know he is.' She pointed at the water lilies, floating bruised but innocent in the moonlight. 'Something has disturbed the lake. And I can't ask the police. They think he's the killer. They just can't see him as a victim.'

He gave a deprecating laugh. 'To be honest, neither can I. If Philip had fallen in, he would have made his way out. He's a stronger swimmer than I am.' He stopped short of adding that Philip was one of life's survivors, that if he fell in a ditch full of horse manure he'd come up smelling of roses.

'Please try again. Please try just one more time.' Becca grabbed his arm, her grip vice-like.

'It's too dangerous.'

'Please, Robin. I'll never ask you for anything again. If you won't do it for me, then do it for Frankie. Philip is her father. Do you want her to grow up not knowing what happened to him?' His sister was almost hysterical now, her voice rising with her sense of panic.

'For God's sake, Becca, keep your voice down.' He shook himself free of her grip. 'They'll hear you in the house. What if they call the police?'

His apprehension gave her something to latch on to, something to turn against him in her desperation. 'They'll hear me if I scream. And if you don't try for me again, I will. I'll scream until they hear me in Penzance. And then you'll be in trouble for going into the lake.'

'Alright.' His voice was sharp. 'I'll go down once more. But if I don't find anything this time, that's it.' He grabbed her wrist and shook her harshly. 'I'll do it once more, and I'll do it for Frankie. But I'm not risking my life.' He pulled his mask back over his face and reattached his air cylinder. 'Count slowly to one hundred. If I'm not back out by then, you'll need to go for help.' He slid noiselessly into the water and disappeared beneath the pool of glossy leaves.

Beneath the surface of the lake, everything was opaque. He forced his body down, counting silently in his mind, six, seven, eight, nine. Below the lilies, a large basket of mud anchored individual plants together, and hanks of matted roots trailed like tentacles towards the limestone boulders that had been used to construct the lake. Robin wrapped the fingers of his right hand around the corner of a boulder, and used it to force his body further down towards the bottom of the lake, still counting, twenty-two, twenty-three, twenty-four. Mud swirled around his mask, and dimmed the glow from his diving light, until he was all but blind. He used his other hand to reach out into the darkness, looking for the next boulder along, finding instead something unexpected, something soft, something yielding. He wrapped the fingers of his left hand around it… forty-one, forty-two, forty-three, forty-four… and let go of the boulder with his right, using his free hand to rub at the front of his mask so that he could take a better look.

For a moment he hung rigid in the water, and then the contents of his stomach began to heave and he was pushing himself up and up and up, towards the surface of the lake, no longer counting, no longer thinking of anything but making his escape from the water, of finding dry land, of getting away from the nightmare he'd just seen.

He thrust his head up into the night, clawed the mask away from his face, and tried to draw clean air into his lungs. But the contents of his stomach had other ideas, and he launched himself out of the lake and onto the grass in a choking, heaving, spluttering mass of watery vomit. He ripped off the mask, buried his face in the ground, and began to sob.

Somewhere behind him he heard Becca quietly whisper. 'Oh my God, I was right. I was *right*.' And he knew that any minute now she was going to fall noisily apart.

19

Nancy paused on her way down the stairs and turned to look out of the small, leaded window on the landing, across the lawn to the lake. She had worked so hard yesterday evening to keep the household on an even keel, comforting Richard, pandering to David, even ministering to Stella's complaints to keep her quiet. She might as well have saved herself the trouble.

DCI Price had arrived at Salvation Hall just after seven that morning, in the first of a succession of police vehicles – marked, unmarked, some laden with officers, others carrying what appeared to be diving equipment. From the window, Nancy could see events unfolding, and more blue and white police tape being unravelled around the ornamental lake. Beside the water, DS Parkinson appeared to be deep in conversation with the chief inspector, and behind them other officers were suiting up, preparing for the dive to search the cold, unwelcoming waters rippling underneath the trembling lilies.

And she could still see Becca Smith.

She could almost believe that Becca hadn't moved since the evening before, since she, Nancy, had tried to persuade the girl to go home. If she had gone home, Nancy thought, we wouldn't be watching this pantomime now.

'Do you think they've found the gardener?' A brittle voice behind Nancy broke the silence.

She didn't turn to answer. 'I have no idea, Stella. All I know is that Becca's brother claims that he dived the lake last night and found a body down there.'

Stella, on her way down to breakfast, had reached the

landing now, and she peered over Nancy's shoulder out towards the lake. 'God, what a terrible thing to do for a living. Diving for dead bodies.' She gave a shiver so fierce that Nancy could almost feel it. 'What on earth made Becca's brother dive into the lake at night in the first place?'

'I suppose Becca persuaded him to go in and look for Philip.'

'Would it have occurred to her that he might have committed suicide? In remorse for murdering Lucy?'

'I have no idea. The only thing I know is how distressed Richard is by all of this. If they confirm it is Philip, he'll be heartbroken. He's had a dreadful night. I don't think he's slept at all.'

Stella uttered a quiet groan. 'I suppose he's going to mope all over the place today.' Unseen by Nancy she rolled her eyes. 'He was very fond of Philip, wasn't he? Do you think there was a reason for that? There was a resemblance between them. I've often wondered whether he was Philip's father.'

A sudden blush of anger suffused Nancy's cheeks. 'I've never thought about it. But if he was, I suppose that would have made him your brother-in-law, wouldn't it?'

'It would have made him Lucy's uncle. That would have been incestuous, wouldn't it? Uncle and niece?'

'Just as well then that they weren't related.' Nancy smiled through gritted teeth, and made a conscious effort to steady her breathing. 'I hope, Stella, that you're going to be supportive to Richard today. He's an old man, and he's already grieving Lucy's death. You might show him a little compassion.'

'Compassion?' Stella gave a disparaging laugh. 'This family deserves everything that is visited on them. Their past is shameful. They should have every expectation of retribution. And their present is shameful too. You seem to have forgotten that Lucy and Philip were making a fool of my son. Marcus had to endure their disgraceful carryings-on. Her treatment of him was unforgivable.'

Nancy closed her eyes and steadied herself. 'Are you going to see Marcus today?'

'Yes.' Stella's voice softened. 'I'm going to have lunch with him in Penzance. But I'll have to phone him now, to tell him what's happening here. He deserves to know that the two people who were causing him so much pain are gone.'

'That should be a great comfort to him.' Nancy inclined her head and turned a little towards the woman standing behind her. 'What do you think he will do now, Stella? I mean, he doesn't really belong at Salvation Hall now, does he?'

The stinging words hit their mark. 'Of course he belongs here.' Stella's voice lowered to a hiss. 'He's staying in Penzance for the moment because he finds all this' – she thrust her hand towards the scene through the window – 'too distressing to cope with. He is grieving Lucy's death. But he will come back. He has to come back. After all, he is David's heir. He needs to take his proper place within the family.' She paused, and then added defiantly 'I'll be speaking to Richard about it later today.'

Now Nancy turned fully to face her. 'Richard needs to be left alone. He's very upset this morning. He's taking breakfast in the Dower House, and he's asked not to be disturbed unless it's either Chief Inspector Price or Kathryn.'

'Thank you, Nancy. I don't think that instruction applies to members of the family. And as David and I are family, we will decide what's best for Richard.' Stella's tone was beyond condescending. 'The poor darling really is beginning to decline, and all this upset is making him worse. We're going to reassure him today that we are here for him as long as he needs us.' She licked her lips. 'And as for Kathryn Clifton, all this ridiculous family history nonsense has to stop. We're going to insist that she is sent packing. The estate will go to David, and then David will leave it to Marcus. And that's an end of it.'

'Kathryn isn't here because of Richard's estate, Stella. She's here to curate the family's history. It's to preserve the family's heritage. It has nothing to do with any legacies.'

'Doesn't it?' Stella arched a scornful eyebrow. 'You do surprise me, Nancy. I didn't think even you could be quite that naïve.'

*

'There's definitely a body down there, Ennor.' Given the early hour, the cold water in the lake, and the nature of a police diver's job, Mitch Nicholson was inhumanly perky. 'Based on the picture you've shown us of Philip McKeith I'm ninety per cent certain it's him. It's a well-built male, maybe late thirties, and he's wearing jeans and a green polo shirt. He's been down there a while, judging by the state of the body. But we couldn't have gone down there last night. That young lad who found him needs a talking to, diving in that mess on his own in the dark. If he'd got into trouble we could have been fishing two bodies out of the water this morning.' Mitch shook his head. 'How long did you say the victim might have been down there?'

'We're guessing anywhere between twelve and thirty-six hours.' Ennor Price frowned. 'The pathologist should be here within the hour. How long after that will it take you to bring the body up?'

Mitch winced and looked uncomfortable. 'It depends how she wants us to tackle it. It's going to be tricky. Didn't it strike you as odd that he hadn't come up to the surface?'

'Is the body trapped under something?'

'Not exactly. He's been weighted down by something heavy, something made of iron.' Mitch looked troubled. 'I know this sounds daft, but it looks like a set of leg irons fastened around his ankles.' The diver gave a self-deprecating laugh. 'But it can't be that, can it?'

Price felt a cold prickle run across the back of his neck,

and he blew out his frustration through pursed lips. 'Yes, it could be that.' He saw disbelief register on his colleague's face, and he put up a hand. 'Don't even think of asking, Mitch.' His smile was withering. 'Will you be able to get them off him?'

'We've tried the catches to see if they'll open, but they're locked. In any case, it depends what Dr Frinton wants us to do with him. If she wants to see the body in situ, we're in trouble.' It wasn't the first time Dr Gina Frinton had been called to examine a body submerged in deep water. Nor the first time someone in the team had drily commented that there was a definite gap in the market for a curvier kind of wetsuit. 'We'll either need a key or else we'll need lifting gear to get him and the irons out of the water in one piece. But given the state of the body, I can't guarantee it won't be damaged further if we have to lift him out with the irons attached.' Mitch blew out his frustrations. 'I can't see we'll have much choice, really. I mean, there's not going to be any chance of a key, is there?'

Price turned away and glanced towards the house. He could see Nancy and Stella watching from the small window on the landing. 'There might be. I can ask Richard Lancefield.'

'A key?' Mitch let out a laugh of astonishment. 'Who the hell keeps a set of leg irons handy, with a key?'

'Believe me, you have no idea what this family is capable of.' Price turned back to the lake. 'You're going to need the lifting gear anyway. Even if you free up the body, the manacles will have to be brought up, and they're not going to float to the surface.' He flinched at the thought. 'Could he have put those things on himself?'

'What, weighting himself down so he couldn't get out again?' The diver considered the possibility. 'It could be suicide, I suppose, if he was determined enough. But it's a bit early to be making that sort of a guess, isn't it?' Mitch shrugged. 'Mind, that's your job. Coming up with the theories. I'd best get on. We'll go down again and take some photographs while you're asking about the key, but they won't show you much.' He set off walking back towards the lake, but turned his head to throw one last cheery comment at Ennor Price. 'If we have to bring him up with the irons on, we'll try to keep him in one piece, but I can't promise.'

Price shuddered. He supposed that being flippant was Mitch Nicholson's way of coping with the unexpected horrors of his day-to-day job, that behind the insensitive comment was probably a very real fear that the body would disintegrate as it was raised up and out of the water. And if it did, then whatever they gleaned from the pathology report would have to be taken as only partial evidence. There may be no way of knowing with any certainty whether McKeith's injuries – if it even was McKeith – were sustained before death or as a result of winching the body out of the water. Price didn't envy Mitch that responsibility.

What a bloody mess.

He turned his gaze towards the right of the lake, and the sloping lawn where Becca Smith was leaning into DS Parkinson, watching the proceedings from a distance. Parkinson had a protective arm around her shoulders but she was leaning forward, straining for a closer view, her face an anxious mask, pathetic in her longing for the body not to be Philip's.

And yet it had to be Philip.

Price glanced back the other way, towards the house again, and wished Kathryn was there. She might have been able to tell him more about the leg irons. He wished to hell that he'd listened to her yesterday, instead of dismissing her information as irrelevant to his enquiries. Now he would have to tackle Richard Lancefield directly, and he'd already seen the old man once this morning, seen the pain in his eyes at the news of another body. Now he would have to inflict more pain, by telling him to prepare for confirmation that the body was Philip McKeith's, and then add insult to injury by asking if there was a key to the leg irons. He glanced at his watch. He knew Kathryn was planning to be at Salvation Hall, but not until ten o'clock. And it was only eight fifteen.

Maybe it would be beneficial not to break the news to the old man until Kathryn had arrived. Having spent the previous evening in her company, Price was beginning to understand why Richard Lancefield seemed to set such store by her presence. She had an easy-going gravitas, a self-assurance that made you feel both at ease in her company and yet confident that if a crisis occurred, she would find a way to cope.

And in any case, he thought, Becca Smith was effectively Philip McKeith's widow now. If anyone deserved to hear the news first, it surely had to be her. He turned and began to walk across the lawn towards Becca, his eyes cast down, his face as non-committal in expression as he could make it. But he knew he would have to raise his gaze sooner or later to look her in the face. Why put off the agony any longer?

Even the blank look was enough to tell Becca the truth. She let out an agonised wail and then crumpled forward, Parkinson's strong hands grasping onto her waist as he struggled to stop her falling to the floor.

This could be a game-changer, Price thought, as he watched Parkinson wrestle to bring the girl back to her feet. And it's going to go one of two ways, depending on the cause of McKeith's death. Either McKeith murdered Lucy, then drowned himself in the lake in a fit of wretched remorse.

Or I'm dealing with a case of double murder.

*

'I know it's only nine o'clock but Nancy thought you wouldn't mind if I came over early this morning. In the light of what's been going on.' Kathryn's voice was gentle, her concern for Richard Lancefield genuine. 'She called to let me know about the body.'

The old man was sitting huddled in his shabby armchair in the library, the ever-present Samson curled up in his lap. He seemed to have aged overnight, the rheumy eyes now red-rimmed, his thin face sallow and drawn. 'Nancy was right. I'm very pleased to see you, girl.' He forced a fleeting smile that was no less genuine for being transient and flicked a finger in the direction of the window to the garden. 'You will have seen our current performance as you came down the drive. They are attempting to bring up a body which Becca believes is Philip's.'

'How did she know about it?'

'I understand that she asked her brother to dive into the lake yesterday evening. Into our lake, without our permission.' He snorted his disapproval. 'I don't know why she didn't just ask. I've tried my very best to consider her these past few days. But it would appear that she considers me an ogre.' The disapproval made way for disappointment. 'I would have tried to help, if she'd spoken to me. But' – he looked up at Kathryn – 'it would appear that she was right. And the police are now diving the lake to recover the body. I am prepared for it being Philip.' His eyes moistened. 'My poor boy. I fear the worst.'

Kathryn observed him with compassionate interest. The news of Philip's body being found seemed to have affected him far more than his granddaughter's death. Or perhaps she was just imagining it. 'I can see this is all very upsetting, Richard. Do you think that we should stop work on the history, at least for the time being? I know we agreed to press on despite Lucy's death, but…'

'Not at all. The prospect of your arrival today is the only thing that has kept me going. You know, for the whole of yesterday evening I had David and Stella to contend with. They carped at me and disagreed with me on just about every topic of conversation we tried. And do you know what kept me going despite all that unpleasantness? Nancy's smile, and the prospect of your company today. I am relying on my two girls – you and Nancy - to keep me sane in the midst of all this madness.' He forced a brighter smile. 'What are your plans for today? Have you brought something that might keep my mind occupied?'

'Well, if that's really what you want.' Kathryn wasn't persuaded, but she could see no point in arguing. 'I began work before breakfast on a simple family tree. It's only drawn by hand, and it needs more work, but it's a starting point. It would be a huge help if you could validate what I've found. I could lay it out on the desk in here, and perhaps Nancy could make us a coffee and we could go through it together.'

'I would like that very much. You know, we have always been a reclusive family. The various branches have never really mixed. But perhaps the time for reticence is over. Perhaps it is time I got to know my broader family a little better.'

'You mean their history?'

'To begin with.'

Kathryn suddenly felt a little uneasy. 'You plan to reach out to your broader family at some point?'

'I do.' Some of his spark was beginning to return.

'May I ask how David feels about that?'

'I don't know. I haven't discussed it with him. But in any case, it's not up to David. In a sense, I'll be doing it *for* David. He will have no family when I am gone. Just that unspeakable harpy that he was foolish enough to marry, and her hapless son.'

Kathryn thought for a moment before speaking again, then she said 'I'm only looking at the deceased family, Richard. It will be easy, to look for the links back, there is so much information available online these days to supplement the family's documents. But tracing the living is not so easy. You would have to engage a private investigator. That isn't my line of work.'

He smiled back at her. 'Don't worry, my dear, all I need from you is the tree you are building. My solicitor will do the rest.' He paused, and then said, 'It may come as a shock for someone to realise that they are related to the Lancefield family. We have never had much of a public persona.' He looked back towards the window. 'Were there people outside the gates this morning when you arrived? Have we become newsworthy yet? Have the vultures descended?'

'I can only say yes. There are a few people hanging around outside. I think I saw a photographer, so at least one of them is probably a journalist. A police officer is keeping them at bay.'

He nodded sadly. 'We've done well to keep the news about Lucy private, but there is so much police presence today that I fear the rumours will be spreading.'

'Richard, are you absolutely sure that I'm not going to disrupt the household too much today? I feel I'm intruding.' Feeling unsettled would be closer to the mark, but she kept the thought to herself.

'Your discretion does you credit, Kathryn, but you are not making things worse, you are making them better.' He turned back to look at her. 'Today's unfolding events are going to stretch Nancy's time and capabilities to their limit, especially with the effect this will all have on poor Becca. Today I need you to be a part of my team, to be our navigator and keep us on the straight and narrow. The work you are doing will anchor Nancy and me to our true world while the storm rages all around us.' His assertiveness was returning. 'Now you set out your stall here in the library and I will rally Nancy to bring us coffee and biscuits.' He pushed the reluctant Samson from his lap and levered himself up out of his seat. 'And let's see if we can't make some normality out of this damned day before some other disaster befalls our Godforsaken family.'

20

The washing-up bowl in Becca Smith's kitchen sink was full to the brim with greasy, stagnant water that had long since lost any hope of detergent properties. DS Parkinson pulled up the cuff of his shirt and tentatively dipped his fingers into the bowl, hoping to find a teaspoon. He couldn't blame Becca for her lack of domestic diligence. God knew she had more than enough on her mind. But perhaps, he thought, we ought to get a liaison officer round here to the cottage to help her get things under control. He rinsed the only teaspoon he could find under a running tap and dried it on a piece of kitchen paper torn from a rack on the wall. He'd seen a tea towel slung over the back of a kitchen chair but, given the oily sheen that ran across its grubby surface, he wasn't prepared to risk it.

Mugs had been easier to find than the teaspoon, and he quickly spooned instant coffee from a jar into two retrieved from a kitchen cupboard and added boiling water and a splash of milk. The coffees stirred, he carried them through to the sitting room; one for Becca and one for Robin Smith. Brother and sister were huddled together on the edge of the sofa, holding hands for comfort, and Parkinson put the drinks down on the coffee table in front of them without a word. Neither of them acknowledged the gesture.

DCI Price was leaning against a nearby armchair, silent, watching the siblings with a probing, inquisitive look that Parkinson had seen before. Price thinks they did it, he thought. Or at least, he suspects that one of them is involved. The atmosphere in the room was taut, the tension growing rapidly in the silence and, not for the first time since Tom Parkinson had found himself partnered with Ennor Price, he took it upon himself to defuse the tension. 'Will you be able to stay with Becca until we can get a liaison officer out here?' He directed the words at Robin. 'I really don't think she should be left on her own.'

The young man turned to look at him, his face still pale and drawn after the shock of the previous evening, his eyes vacant and unseeing. But he seemed to hear, and he mumbled in Parkinson's direction. 'I can stay for an hour. I'll call our mum, she can come out and take over.'

Becca turned to him sharply. 'I don't want Frankie here.'

'She won't bring Frankie. She'll take her to Auntie Jean's.' Robin sounded irked. 'We're not stupid, you know. We do know that Frankie needs to be kept out of the way.' He turned to his sister and pulled his hand sharply away from hers. 'She ought never to have been brought up in a place like this, with all these perverted goings-on. She deserves better.'

'Philip's her dad.'

'Philip *was* her dad,' he corrected. 'And he ought to have thought more about her than carrying on with that Lucy while his child was sleeping just a few yards away. And you' – he was becoming angry now – 'ought to have left him to it, and brought Frankie home to us.' He seemed to be finding his voice, waking from his shock, and he turned to DCI Price. 'Inspector Price, will Mr Lancefield make a complaint against me for diving into the lake? I was only doing what I thought right. I didn't mean to cause any trouble. I did it for Frankie. So that she might know about her dad. Will you tell him that I'm sorry if it made him angry?'

Price gave the boy a brief but reassuring smile. 'I'll pass your message on, Robin, but I don't think Mr Lancefield will hold it against you. If he does, I'll do my best to talk him out of it. You may have helped to move our investigation forward, and that can only be a good thing.

At least now we might know where Philip is.' The policeman turned his attention to Becca. 'I know this is hard for you, but I have to ask you to stay as calm as you can, and not do anything to make the situation more difficult. We still haven't had a formal identification of the body.'

'Those bastards killed him.' Becca was beginning to seethe, the anger she'd been suppressing all night gradually beginning to rise to the surface. 'They're to blame. They could have stopped it.'

'You don't know that, Becca. And I have to caution you against making any wrongful accusations. If you want us to find out exactly what happened to Philip, I need your word that you'll stay at home, answer our questions, and give us the space we need to do our jobs.'

'You'll let them get away with it.'

'And that's another unfounded allegation.' Despite her tone, Price took the accusation in his stride. 'As soon as we know for sure that it is Philip's body in the lake, and we have a confirmation of what happened to him, one of us – me or Tom – will come and tell you. Until then, we don't know whether Philip is still alive, whether he was murdered, or whether he committed suicide.'

'Or whether it was an accident?' It was Robin who asked the question, a slight inference in his voice that the police already knew enough to dismiss the possibility.

'Whatever happened to the body in the lake wasn't an accident. That much I can tell you.' Price looked uncomfortable. But he wasn't one to mince words.

'Well it's obvious, then, isn't it.' Becca's anger was growing. 'It was one of them. One of them killed him.' Her eyes grew suddenly wide. 'Oh my God, it was one of them, wasn't it, sending the texts on Philip's phone? It was one of them who put him in the water, and then started sending texts to make me think he was still alive?' She turned to DS Parkinson. 'You said you'd know by now. Where the texts were coming from.'

Parkinson felt his cheeks grow warm. He knew where they were coming from alright, the report had landed in his inbox the previous evening, and he'd had time to cast his eye over it quickly before setting off that morning. But he hadn't yet had time to share the information with DCI Price. He flashed a warning look at his superior officer, but Price shook his head with a wan smile. 'Just let it out, Tom. We're going to tell her sometime today anyway.'

The sergeant shrugged. 'As you say, sir.' He licked his lips, still uncomfortable. 'As far as they can pinpoint, the phone was operating in this area. It pinged off the mast over the other side of Penwithen village. So it looks pretty much like the texts were being sent from somewhere close.' Somewhere, he thought but didn't say, as close as Salvation Hall.

*

'I'm going to spend some time with Kathryn this morning, and then I'm going to go over and visit Becca.' Richard lowered himself onto a chair at the kitchen table. He was looking a little less frail now and resuming something of his patriarchal authority. 'Have you heard anything from her?'

'I haven't spoken to Becca since before the police arrived.' Nancy was standing at the kitchen counter and concentrating on the task at hand, placing chocolate-covered ginger biscuits neatly in a ring on a fine china tea plate, an accompaniment to the cafetiere of coffee that she'd already added to a tray. 'I know she spent a miserable night out on the lawn. She camped out beside the lake, waiting for the daylight to come. Her brother told me that she refused to leave Philip.'

'The dear girl loved him, that's for certain. She put up with a great deal.' Richard looked grave. 'We must look after her, Nancy. And little Frankie. We mustn't lose them from the family. I shall let her know that her job and the cottage are safe for her.' He seemed to be growing aware of the maudlin quality in his voice, and he straightened his posture. 'Now, we must be strong during this family crisis. Can you make sure that the household keeps running on a day-to-day basis? Kathryn and I will require lunch, and you will need to be on hand to assist the police if they need anything. Make sure that they are catered for as necessary. Mobilise Mrs Peel from the village if you can, let her know that Becca is still indisposed, I'm sure she'll rise to the occasion and give us a hand. But impress upon her the need to be discreet, won't you?' He paused and then added, 'Perhaps you could call the florist in Penzance and arrange for some flowers to be sent to Becca. When I go over, I'll check that she's eating and whether she needs anything.' He slapped his hands to his knees. 'Well, I think that's it for now.'

Nancy glanced over her shoulder and offered him an indulgent smile, as if he were a forgetful child. 'And what about David and Stella?'

'What about them?' He barked the question with a huff of exasperation. 'Nancy, you are a wicked girl, you know just how to take the wind out of my sails.' He clicked his teeth. 'I will speak with David later this morning about Lucy's funeral arrangements. I suppose we should make a start, even though we don't know yet when the body will be released. And we must be prepared for the news that it is Philip's body they have found in the lake. The impact of that on the family must also be considered. Becca will need our assistance for the funeral.' His face folded into a frown. 'Perhaps I should call a family conference. Yes, we'd better have a more formal family dinner this evening. Could you manage that on top of everything else?'

'Of course.'

'And I want Kathryn here. I'll extend the invitation to her this morning, but if she's reluctant I'll be looking to you to help me persuade her. And we'd better have Stella's boy. If nothing else it will stop Stella from spending the evening bleating that we haven't included him.' Richard braced himself against the kitchen table and slowly pushed himself up to his feet. 'And now I'm going to spend a little time with Kathryn in the library. If anyone wants me in the next half hour, then that is where they will find me.' He clicked his fingers and Samson emerged from underneath his chair. 'After that, I'll be outside walking the dog. The routines must be honoured. And Chief Inspector Price will be looking for me again before long. I want some fresh air in my lungs before I have to deal with the stench of more death.'

*

The air in the small office above The Zoological Hotel was stifling, the late summer sun outside beating directly against the large sash windows. The windows were open but there was no breeze, and the small electric fan that Marcus and Ian shared to keep the place cool was struggling to cope. Marcus put a clammy hand up to his forehead and rubbed at his temple, but it did nothing to improve his ability to concentrate.

Somewhere behind him, impervious to the debilitating heat, Ian was chatting away to a client on the phone, discussing the finer details of a corporate lunch booking. He could hear Ian's conversation, the day-to-day chatter of a man with nothing on his mind but the task in hand, nothing to drag him down. And he couldn't help wondering what that felt like. To be free to live in the moment, not haunted by the past, not living in fear of the future.

Marcus had barely slept since Lucy's body had been discovered in the lake, and it occurred to him now that he had never cared for her as much when she was alive as he had since her death. And not just because of the comfortable life they would have shared. Lucy died because of her affair with Philip, but she didn't deserve to die the way she had. Only now was Marcus beginning to realise how much he had grown to love her, despite her more obvious faults, and how much he was hurt by her infidelity. Yet despite those hurts, despite her betrayals, he would never have raised a hand against her. That was the real difference between him and Philip McKeith.

Such thoughts were beginning to haunt him during daylight hours now. He couldn't stop thinking about Lucy and Philip together, about how they must have looked, lying on the grass in the warmth of that September evening, and about how Lucy had paid for the privilege, and found herself soon afterwards lying in the cold, stagnant waters of the ornamental lake.

He had to get away from this place. It was the only way he could stop the thoughts from crowding in upon him. Everywhere he turned there was a memory of Lucy: at Salvation Hall, in Penzance, he couldn't even get into his car without imagining her sitting in the passenger seat. He glanced up at the clock. It was only ten thirty. In a minute, he thought, Ian will hang up his call and cheerily ask if I want a coffee. And if I do, he'll ask me if I want a biscuit or a slice of cake to go with it.

But it was hardly Ian's fault. And Marcus knew he wouldn't be coping now if Ian hadn't cheerfully given him a room in the hotel free of charge for as long as he needed it. That's what Ian was like. Nothing was a big deal. Ian was uncomplicated. And he had been more of a father to Marcus than Stella Drake Lancefield had ever been a mother.

He let out a sigh. His mother was coming into Penzance today to meet him for lunch. It wasn't a meeting he wanted but, with Stella, there was very little choice. You either accepted the invitation and tolerated the hour in her company, or spent the next few days navigating her sulks and feeling guilty because you didn't care enough about her to let her have her own way. Experience had long since taught him that the hour of earache was always the easier option.

And yet he knew that today's hour was going to be a tough one. He knew that her sole topic of conversation was going to be "Marcus moving back into Salvation Hall". He was just a pawn in her game to secure control of Richard Lancefield's fortune. And he didn't want to be involved. He was tired, so very tired of being controlled by other people's agendas.

It wasn't as if the family had ever warmed to him. David barely spoke to him, and although Richard was as polite as he would be to any guest under his roof, probably for Lucy's sake, he knew that Richard had little time for him. There was Nancy, of course. Practical, efficient, kind-hearted Nancy. Nancy hadn't just known about Lucy and Philip, she had known how Marcus felt about their deceptions, and she hadn't judged him when he'd needed her support. But Nancy wasn't really one of the family, and it would take more than a little understanding to sustain him against David's indifference, Richard's coldness, and his mother's misplaced sense of entitlement. No, he was better here with Ian for now, better where he was appreciated, where no one judged him or found him lacking.

'Ready for a coffee, Marcus?'

Marcus started, shocked out of his musings by Ian's voice, despite the predictability of the question. He swivelled a hundred and eighty degrees on his chair and regarded Ian with vague, unseeing eyes. 'Sorry?'

'You're done in, boy. Why don't I make us a coffee? I can bring you a biscuit, or there's chocolate cake this morning to go with?' He didn't wait for an answer but headed for the steep staircase down to the hotel kitchen without another word.

Left alone, Marcus could only go on thinking: about his mother, about Lucy, and about Salvation Hall. And the need to break free. *I have to do it.* And the starting point would be to call his mother, and cancel their lunch date.

To take the other route for once. To give up the hour together and risk the days and days of retribution. Because he wouldn't have to listen to the retribution any more. He didn't have to see Stella again.

He turned back to his desk, stretching out his hand towards his mobile phone, and as he did so, the phone began to vibrate with an incoming call. He picked it up and examined the display. Synchronicity. The incoming call was his mother. And for once, he took an incoming call from his mother to be a positive thing. She'd saved him the trouble of calling her to cancel. He prodded the phone's answer button and lifted the phone to his ear. 'I was just about to call you. About lunch.'

'Never mind about that now, darling. I have something I need to tell you. You simply won't believe it.' Her voice at the end of the line was breathless, but her tone was almost exultant.

'I was going to cancel lunch.'

'Cancel lunch? No, no, darling, we have to meet now. You haven't let me give you the news.' She paused, barely able to contain her excitement, and then said, 'I'll tell you all the details when I see you. But you won't believe what's happened here at the hall this morning. They've found Philip McKeith's body in the lake.'

21

'I don't suppose it occurred to you to break it to him gently?' There was a distinctly icy tone in Kathryn's voice and it took Ennor Price completely by surprise. They were striding out across the terrace, away from the house, Kathryn taking the lead and Ennor keeping up behind. 'He's an old man, he's just lost his granddaughter, and Philip was like a son to him.' She was making no attempt to hide her exasperation.

'I'm trying to solve a murder case, Kathryn. Richard Lancefield promised me every assistance. When I asked him if there were any keys to the leg irons that had gone missing from the storeroom, I thought I might get an answer. I didn't expect him to just get up and take the damned dog for a walk.'

She stopped in her tracks and turned to face him. 'I was there, remember? I heard.' She gave a frustrated shake of her head. 'What I heard was "I can confirm the body is that of Philip McKeith. And I have to ask you if there are any keys for the leg irons that are missing from the storeroom." Richard isn't an idiot. He's perfectly capable of putting two and two together and coming up with "I've lost my boy" and "If I'd been more careful with the contents of the storeroom he might still be alive".'

'I wasn't accusing him of anything.'

'You didn't have to. He's just the sort of man to blame himself.' Kathryn turned away and started walking again, taking the few short steps to the storeroom door. The door was padlocked and she turned to Ennor with a cynical eye. 'I can confirm that the storeroom door is locked. And I have to ask you if there is a key for the padlock.'

'Don't be facetious, Kathryn. It doesn't suit you.'

'How would you know what suits me? You hardly know me.'

There was no answer to that. No two and half minute ice-breaker over a glass of wine could have hinted at what lay beneath the surface of Kathryn's outwardly placid demeanour. Ennor fished in his pocket and brought out a small steel key, and held it out to her with what he hoped was a sheepish look. 'I do appreciate what you're doing to help.'

She took the key from him, rattled it into the padlock, and pushed the door open without a word. The bare electric light bulb that hung from the ceiling was still switched on and if the previous day's search of the room had been as thorough as DS Parkinson had claimed, then the search team had made a very discreet job of it. To his meticulous investigative eye, everything still looked very much as it had the first time he had seen it.

He watched as Kathryn walked into the room and circled slowly around, examining the packing crates, eyeing up the contents of each as she went, as if trying to remember what she had found on a previous sweep of the goods. She paused by what looked like an old tea chest, bent down to it, gave a shake of the head, and moved on to the next one. This time she dropped a hand into the case and pulled out a small metal tea caddy. She pulled off the lid and peered inside. 'This one.' She pushed the lid back on and held it out to Ennor. 'I can't promise that any of these keys will work, but they're the only keys I found while I was photographing the contents of the crates.'

He took the tin from her. 'I'm sorry if I've offended you.'

'And I'm sorry I snapped.' If that were true, then it would be hard to tell from the brittle edge in her voice. 'Richard isn't without feelings, Ennor. Sometimes people are aloof or seem cold, but inside they are just as vulnerable as the rest of us. Sometimes more so. Sometimes that aloofness is the only way they have of protecting their feelings.'

'I understand that.' He gave an unconvincing nod. 'But to be honest, Kathryn, the sight of that body shackled with those leg irons left me rattled.' He leaned back a little and rested against the edge of a packing crate. 'I admit that I probably played it wrong this morning. My first thought was to ask Richard if there might be a key, in case the pathologist wanted the irons off the body while it was still in the water. But then I thought it would upset him, so I told her that we'd have to bring the body up as it was. When I saw it hanging there, dripping with water and still manacled, it made me angry. No human being should ever be shackled like that.'

'Well amen to that.' Kathryn's tone had softened a little. 'But if Philip McKeith decided to weigh himself down with the irons so that he could commit suicide, that's hardly Richard's fault.'

Ennor blew out a breath. 'Maybe not. But this isn't a normal death, and the Lancefields are not a normal family. A normal family, with normal sensibilities, wouldn't even own such horrific items.' He looked down at the tin of keys and gave it a gentle shake. 'At least there's a possibility now that the pathologist will be able to unlock the cuffs rather than trying to cut them off.'

'They may have rusted. Old iron like that, it's possible you may not get them off easily, even if you do find the right key. They must be around two hundred years old.' Her anger was subsiding. 'And they are destined for a museum, so I'd be grateful if you would treat them carefully and avoid any further damage.'

Ennor gave a spontaneous laugh. 'Are you serious? You're going to put them in a museum after they've been used to weigh down a dead body?'

Kathryn's eyes narrowed. 'I think, given the nature of the object, it's highly unlikely that this is the only time that's occurred.'

It was one snipe too many. 'Who had access to them, Kathryn?' Ennor's tone sharpened. 'Who knew they were there?'

'As far as I understand, the room was never locked. At least, not until the police came on the scene. As to who knew they were there, I should think anyone living on the estate who'd ever bothered to come and look around.'

'Would it have taken two people to carry them?'

'I don't know. Perhaps not. They're made of iron, and they're heavy. But a strong person could have carried them, or possibly dragged them, if they had the will.' She thought for a moment. 'You're wondering if Philip McKeith could have carried them to the lake and attached them to his ankles before going into the water?'

'No, not that.' He eyed her sternly. 'I'm wondering whether it would take one person or two to carry them across the lawns and attach them to his body, to make sure that he stayed at the bottom of the lake.'

*

Richard Lancefield opened the door of the orchid house and stepped over the threshold into the hot, moist, breath-suppressing heat. The heat brought with it a familiar sense of peace, and he closed his eyes for a moment and imagined the door of an aircraft opening, the buzz of other passengers behind him on the plane, the bliss that always overcame him as the door opened to reveal the clear blue skies, and the searing, stifling heat of St Felix. It had been eighteen months now since he'd flown to the Caribbean, but the change of habit hadn't been a personal choice. It had been the doctor who had suggested that it might be unwise, a recommendation that Richard had accepted with the heaviest of hearts.

He opened his eyes reluctantly and bent down to

retrieve a small dog basket from under the right-hand staging, and turned to place the basket just outside the door. 'There you are, dog. There's your bed.' Samson, wary as always of the extreme heat, eyed him gratefully and curled up obediently on the warm cotton cushion in the basket, staying close, and keeping watch.

Inside the glasshouse, two long benches of precious orchids were nodding gently in the soft Cornish breeze that was blowing in through the open door. Richard smiled at the sight and closed the door gently behind him, then ran his eye slowly along the left-hand bench. The plants were in fine fettle and most of them in flower. These were the orchids that he and Philip had grown together, and there was no doubt in his mind that these would be the flowers he would place on top of Philip's coffin when the day came to bury him.

The thought disturbed him. He knew that Philip's burial would cause gossip in the village. He knew some believed that Philip was his natural son. What fools men are, he thought, to waste time looking around for rational explanations where none were needed. He'd needed no illicit blood tie to explain his friendship with Philip McKeith. The boy was a talented naturalist and a decent human being. Richard would have admired him for the former attribute alone. The humanity was just an added bonus.

He reached up to a window in the sloping roof and opened it to let in some air, then turned his attention to the right-hand bench and inspected it with satisfaction. The secondary plants were coming along nicely. They wouldn't win prizes at the autumn show, but they would create a presence. And this year there would be a new prize on offer, the Philip McKeith Trophy. Nothing too fancy, he thought. Something modest and workmanlike, to celebrate the man himself.

There was a Lloyd Loom chair beside the door, a battered old thing that had seen many summers and winters of orchid growing, and Richard sank into it, thankful for the moment's privacy and peace.

Chief Inspector Price meant well. Richard was sure of that. But the man must be under pressure. Despite his protestations that he would never take the easy option, it would wrap the case up for him neatly to assume that Philip murdered Lucy, and then drowned himself in the lake in a fit of remorse. But Philip was made of stronger stuff. And the young man had known Lucy for far too long to be bothered by her selfish, thoughtless ways. He might have chastised her, perhaps even tried to humiliate her in a small way if he'd thought it would bring her to heel. But he wouldn't have hurt her physically, any more than he would have committed suicide. There would be no easy solution for Detective Chief Inspector Ennor Price here.

And no easy solution for himself.

He rubbed at his forehead with an arthritic finger, hoping to ease the growing tension. Philip McKeith's death had robbed Richard Lancefield of more than a gardener and more than a friend. It had robbed him of a contingency. It had been one thing to consider disinheriting his son and his granddaughter and trust the future of the estate to more reliable hands than theirs. It was another thing altogether to have that choice taken away from him.

Of course, it had not been his intention to leave David and Lucy with nothing. David had been bequeathed the right to live in the Dower House for his lifetime, and the continuation of the annual allowance from the estate that he already enjoyed. And the right to live in Salvation Hall itself had been written for Lucy and her heirs in perpetuity, along with a generous income from the estate. But neither could be trusted with the estate itself. There had been no other option open to him.

The creation of a trust, with Hugh Ferguson and his son as financial trustees, and Philip as trustee for the care of Salvation Hall and Woodlands Park, had been the only way. The Fergusons would ensure that the estates remained profitable. Philip would have ensured that they retained their natural beauty and heritage. David would spurn the opportunity to live in the Dower House and see out his days in Edinburgh, leaving Lucy's continued residence to ensure that a Lancefield still lived at Salvation Hall. And Kathryn's work would be the icing on the cake – everything documented and curated to ensure that the family's history and heritage would never be forgotten.

He lowered his head into his hands. In barely thirty-six hours he had lost the one man he could trust to care for everything beyond money that mattered to him, and the one Lancefield whose vanity he knew would tie his descendants irrevocably to the luxuries of Salvation Hall. Only in gaining Kathryn was there a glimmer of hope that something could be salvaged out of the mess. He needed her assistance to find another line of heirs within the family, but in testing the water this morning he had found an unexpected streak of resistance that he would have to work hard to overcome.

He lifted his head and smiled to himself. Kathryn didn't strike him as the sort of woman who could be pressured into a course of action that didn't suit her. But then again, her interest in the heritage of the estate might be reason enough for her to at least consider his proposals.

His smile deepened. He had seen her on a mission barely thirty minutes before, feistily leading the unfortunate Chief Inspector Price to the storeroom in search of a set of keys. Even from a distance, as he and Samson had paused to take a breath during their walk, he could sense her spirit, her dissatisfaction with the chief inspector's arguments. She had looked magnificent as she rallied to the cause. As she had rallied to *his* cause.

And what a damned shame it was, he thought, that his son had nailed his colours to the mast of a troublesome, skeletal witch like Stella Drake instead of marrying a splendid and spirited creature like Kathryn.

*

'I'll be back around four o'clock. I'm meeting Marcus for lunch, and then I have some shopping to do.' Stella was inspecting herself in the drawing room mirror. She leaned over the fireplace to get closer to the glass and pretended to examine the line of her lipstick, pulling down on the flesh of her chin with a finger to make it look convincing. In reality, she was watching her husband. David was sitting behind her on the sofa and, reflected in the mirror, she could see the scowl on his face, the weary dissatisfaction in his eyes.

She swung around to face him. 'What are you going to do with yourself while I'm out? I hope you're not just going to sit here moping. Really, darling, you can be so morose sometimes.' She huffed a sigh. 'I suppose that's the melancholy temperament of an artist.'

'Or perhaps just a symptom of losing my only daughter.'

'Ah. That again.' Stella crossed to the sofa, took hold of David's hand, and squeezed it. 'Darling, you weren't close to Lucy. And it is just a teeny bit hypocritical of you to play the grieving father now.'

David turned to his wife with a contemptuous snarl. 'I want my daughter's killer to be found and brought to justice.'

'He has been found. Philip has been found in the lake.' She leaned back a little and regarded him with a critical eye. 'The dead are the dead, David. One has to give thought to the living.'

'I'm sorry about Philip McKeith. And for once in my life, I have to agree with my father. He wasn't the sort of man to commit suicide, any more than he would have hurt Lucy. He cared about her.'

Stella's green eyes narrowed. 'How typical of you to

make something romantically tragic out of something so sordid. Lucy and Philip made a fool of my boy. They humiliated him with their public carryings-on.'

'Your boy made a fool of himself. If Marcus had any backbone, he would have broken off the engagement instead of hiding away in his room sulking.'

'How do you know how Marcus has been behaving? You haven't been here?'

He hesitated and looked away. 'I heard…' He was choosing his words carefully. 'I heard that…' Behind him, the drawing room door opened, and his attention flashed up to the mirror above the mantelpiece and the reflection of Nancy framed in the doorway.

'Your taxi is here, Stella. I've asked him to wait.' Nancy smiled at David through the mirror. 'I was just about to make some lunch for myself. Can I make something for you? A ham sandwich, perhaps? Or there's roast beef, if you would prefer?'

'That's very kind of you, Nancy.' David drew his hand away from Stella's clasp and returned Nancy's smile in the mirror with uncharacteristic warmth. 'A ham sandwich would be appreciated. And there's no need to bring it through, I'll come and join you in the kitchen.'

Stella pursed her lips and turned her head away from her husband. 'My God, you *are* a hypocrite, David. You object to your family's heritage, but you're happy for it to make you a sandwich for lunch.'

Nancy's gentle face flushed. For a moment she froze in the doorway, and then she nodded, a gracious bow of the head, and backed out of the room.

David turned angry eyes towards his wife. 'That was an unforgivable thing to say. Nancy is a part of the family. A much-loved part of the family. And you would do well not to forget it.'

'A part of the family?' Stella leaned over to the far end of the sofa and picked up her jacket and handbag. 'And what is my son, if he isn't part of the family?' She shook her head. 'Really, David, I'm beginning to think you're as bad as your father. That girl has both of you eating out of her hand.' She walked to the door and then turned to look back at him. 'Nancy is part of that heritage that you despise so much, part of that all-encompassing Lancefield family that you claim to deny. And my son Marcus, your stepson, is being excluded from that heritage and family. Lucy died because she pursued the cheap thrills of playing slut to the family's gardener. Nancy is the product of your family's disgraceful heritage in the Caribbean. Your father would rather walk the dog and tend to his bloody orchids than sit here and discuss the family crisis with his son.' Her voice crackled with emotion. 'And my son Marcus, a boy with a strong work ethic and decent morals, making his own living, and faithful to Lucy in spite of her cruelty and deceit, is considered unworthy to be a part of the family.'

Stella's anger appeared to touch something within him, and for a moment David looked remorseful. 'Stella, I didn't mean…'

'Don't waste your breath.' Stella eyed him with utter contempt. 'I am going to take Marcus out to lunch. And when I return, I will speak to Richard about the abysmal way this family has treated my son. And I shall ask your father what he intends to do to make amends.'

22

Ennor Price found Kathryn sitting alone on a wooden bench at the far end of the garden.

The bench was pushed back between a pair of substantial hydrangea bushes, and he almost missed her as he walked past, just catching a glimpse of slim, tanned ankles and gold lattice-work sandals out of the corner of his eye as he strode along the path. He turned to glance under the boughs of gently-nodding lilac flowers with a smile of recognition and only then, as their eyes met, did he realise that he'd actually been looking for her.

He hesitated for a moment, waiting to see whether his smile would be returned, and then stepped forward to join her when it was. He sat down next to her without speaking and surveyed the scene in front of him. They were at the outer reaches of the garden, and beyond the path the land fell away sharply into a small ravine overgrown with lush foliage, the sharp, pointed leaves of Cornish palm trees vying for space against blossomless rhododendrons and magnolias. On the other side of the ravine Salvation Hall could be seen, its mullioned windows and grand gables rising beyond the manicured lawn that surrounded the ornamental lake. He turned to look at Kathryn. She was gazing out across the grounds, her eyes fixed on the house, her expression unreadable. 'What do you see?' He asked the question quietly.

'I see history.' She smiled, the now-familiar enigmatic curl of the lips, her eyes still fixed on the view. 'I see the Lancefield family, generation after generation, and a house that's never left the family's possession. I see the blind ambition of those first adventurers who went out to St

Felix in pursuit of wealth, and I see the reward that all their endeavours brought about. And however much I look at it, I can't help wondering how something so magnificent could result from something so horrific.' She turned to look at him. 'How could something as beautiful as this house and its gardens grow from the horror of the way these people made their money? This could have been one of the great gardens of Cornwall – it probably is one of the great gardens – but Richard won't let the public in. He won't let the public see the family's history. At least not in this country. He knows that people just wouldn't understand.'

'Do you understand?'

'No, of course not. Sometimes I think I do. I've read book after book on the subject, but cold facts on a page can't prepare you for the human element. This house has been with the family for hundreds of years. Every room, every brick is steeped in their history. It's a living history. The documents I've been given to study aren't library pieces, they belong to the family. They mean something to the Lancefields on a personal level. The artefacts inside, the furniture, the books, the paintings. They aren't museum pieces. They belong to the family too, and the family use them. The place is magnificent.' Her smile faded and her voice quietened to almost a whisper. 'And yet it's all so bloody dysfunctional.'

Ennor felt a sudden pang of sympathy. 'This place has really got under your skin, hasn't it?'

She shrugged. 'The place, the history, the family.' She looked for a moment as if emotion might overcome her. 'I came out here for a walk to clear my head, and I walked farther than I meant to, found this bench, and decided to just sit for a while. I didn't know I'd find myself looking back at the house. The more I look at it, the more I feel bewitched by it and by everything it stands for. But it doesn't feel like a benign enchantment.' She turned to look at him, her face solemn now. 'I'm not making much sense, am I?'

'I don't think sense comes into it. I think it's a dangerous seduction. I think you care very much about the history of this place and the family, and I think you want all sides of that story to be known. But you can care without getting involved. You know' – he leaned a little closer to her – 'it's one thing to come here and curate the family's history. It's another thing altogether to let yourself be drawn into that history.'

Kathryn took in a breath. 'There's a family dinner this evening and I've been invited. Richard has begun to hint that he wants to locate his wider family. He's tired of David's intransigence when it comes to the family's heritage and I think he wants to find someone else to pass that heritage on to.' She looked uneasy now. 'I think he's going to tell them of his plans this evening, and I don't think it's going to go down well.'

'Who else is going to be there?'

'David and Stella and Marcus. And Nancy, of course.'

Ennor was eyeing her closely now. 'Are you afraid, Kathryn?'

'Afraid?' She seemed confused by the question, and then she smiled. 'I don't like confrontation. And I like being the reason for it even less.'

He let out a spontaneous laugh. 'You didn't mind confronting me this morning.'

She had the grace to blush. 'I'm sorry about that. But I was concerned about Richard. He is upset about Philip McKeith's death.'

'Is he more upset about Philip's death than Lucy's?'

'Yes, I think he is. I wondered if it was because Lucy didn't share his values. She didn't care about the history that means so much to him. But Philip did. At least, he cared about Salvation Hall. I think Richard feels that in losing Philip he's lost his only ally.' She turned away from Ennor, and looked back across the ravine towards the lake.

Ennor followed her gaze and tried to see Salvation Hall

through her eyes, but where she saw history he could see only a beribboned crime scene, a watery grave for two bloated and undeserving corpses, and a scattering of uniformed officers searching for the weapon that might have bludgeoned one of those victims on the back of the head before he slid lifelessly into the water. 'Could you imagine one of the family murdering Philip McKeith?'

Kathryn, troubled now, turned to look at him. 'You think that Philip was murdered? I thought he committed suicide?'

'Suicide was our working assumption.' He didn't want to say too much. 'We'll know for certain by the end of the day, but until then all I can say to you is this – there could be a killer amongst the family. That killer has murdered one and possibly two people, and won't hesitate to kill again if they have to defend their position. If you suspect anything, then don't give it away.' He stretched out his arm and took her hand firmly in his. 'Please be careful, Kathryn. If you hear or see anything that leads you to suspect someone here at Salvation Hall, confide in no one. Only me. You have my number. Call me any time, day or night.'

She was pale now. 'Are you asking me to spy for you?'

'No, of course not. I don't have to. I know that if you saw or heard anything that the police should know about, you wouldn't hesitate to pass that information on.' He squeezed her hand. 'I'm asking you to be *careful*. I want to find the killer. But the last thing I want on top of everything else is to have your safety on my conscience.' He let a gentle smile curl the corner of his lip. 'And in any case, I only have a limited budget for bribery these days. If I was going to hire a copper's nark, I think it would have to be one that didn't have a healthy appetite for lobster.'

*

'I still don't see why we couldn't have lunched at The

Zoological. I had a marvellous fillet mignon the last time.' Stella made no attempt to keep the disdain from her voice.

But Marcus had no intention of explaining how much he wanted to keep her away from the sanctuary he'd created for himself at the hotel. Bringing her to Morrab Gardens for an al fresco lunch had been a carefully considered manoeuvre, a ploy intended to keep her at a distance from the new life he was planning to build for himself. The gardens were a tranquil oasis in the centre of town, a magnet for young mothers and their toddlers, office workers escaping their desks, and the occasional stray tourist looking for a shortcut to the harbour. And they were neutral territory.

He dipped a hand into the picnic basket between them on the bench and pulled out a box containing smoked salmon sandwiches. 'It's too nice a day to waste indoors. I thought you would enjoy the fresh air.' He offered her the box. 'These are made with the best gravadlax. Ian bought it in for a corporate buffet we're hosting tomorrow. I think it's wasted in a sandwich, but Ian said it's not a waste if it pleases you.'

The flattery fell on deaf ears. 'Marcus, darling, it must be seventy degrees out here. You know how damaging the sun is to my skin.' Stella waved away the sandwich box with a dismissive hand, and then lifted the hand higher to shield her face from the sun. 'And so many little ones running around.' Her pained expression conveyed complete contempt for anything remotely child-shaped.

Marcus dropped the box back into the basket and helped himself to a sandwich. 'If you change your mind there are other things to eat. Olives, cold chicken, grapes.' He turned his head away from her and looked out across the lawn to the bandstand where a small group of boys were playing hide and seek. His mother had never liked children, not even her own, a disposition that had more or less robbed him of any opportunity to experience childhood. But today wasn't about what Stella liked. '*I* like it here.' It felt strange to him to place emphasis on the personal pronoun.

Beside him, Stella was still sulking. 'I do wish you would come back to Salvation Hall. You have no idea how awful it is for me to be there without you.'

'And you evidently have no idea how awful it is for me just to be there, now that Lucy's gone.' He paused, and then added, 'Or how awful it's been for me to lose Lucy at all.'

'My poor boy.' Stella laid a hand on his knee and patted it. 'That girl was making such a fool of you. I just don't know how you could bear it.'

'I could bear it because I loved her.'

Stella stiffened and then turned to regard him with a cynical eye. 'Loved her? Darling, she's gone now. I've already told you that you don't have to lie about it. And especially not to me.'

'I'm not lying.' It was the truth, but there would be no point in trying to explain that to his mother. He wasn't even sure he understood the feeling himself, that love had come as Lucy had died.

'Well, I won't mourn her passing.' Stella shrugged and dipped her hand into the picnic basket to pull out a solitary grape. 'Still, it presents an opportunity. Lucy and Philip played a dangerous game, and now they are both dead. They only have themselves to blame.' She held the grape up to her eyes and examined it closely. 'You are David's heir now, and I think it's time for you to come home.' She popped the grape into her mouth and turned to look at her son with imperious eyes.

'I'm not David's heir.'

'Of course you are. You're David's stepson. And God knows we won't be having any children together, so you're the only heir he's ever likely to see.' She coughed on the thought. 'There's a family conference at Salvation Hall this evening, and Richard wants you there. You must come, Marcus. Otherwise, you'll be letting Richard down. He needs you now, and if you're skulking away here in Penzance then you're not there for him.'

'Richard doesn't need me. He has David. And he has Nancy.'

Stella sucked in her cheeks and pouted. 'That girl is fawning all over David, and all over Richard. It's quite nauseating to watch.'

'She cares about them. And this is a difficult time for her too, you know.'

'I don't see why. She's only Richard's secretary.'

'She was close to Lucy. And she's known Philip for a long time.'

'Yes, but they are both gone now.' She frowned. 'I will admit that Philip's suicide appears to have hit Richard very hard. I suppose if anyone were to give the gardener any credit, one might say that at least he did the decent thing after he'd murdered her.' Stella sucked in her cheeks. 'Or then one might say that he took the coward's way out. I suppose it all depends upon your point of view. Either way, darling, it has cleared the path for us.'

'You really mean that, don't you?' He turned his head to look at her with a vague, unseeing gaze. 'Have the police confirmed that Philip murdered Lucy, and then took his own life?'

'I believe they intend to confirm with Richard and David when they have the results of the post-mortem later today.' Stella smiled at him and placed a hand on his arm. 'But it's only a matter of formality. Everyone knows that's what happened.'

Marcus blinked and then forced a smile. 'Well, if you really want me to come to Salvation Hall this evening, then I'll come.'

'Darling, I knew you would come round to my way of thinking.' Stella squeezed the arm beneath her hand. 'You know, all this talking has given me quite an appetite. Perhaps I will try one of those sandwiches after all.' She peered down into the picnic basket. 'You've quite spoiled me with all this choice, and I've been so very ungrateful.' She took a sandwich out of the box and lifted it to her lips with a smile. 'But I knew that you wouldn't let me down. After all, you know that I'm only thinking of your best interests.'

Marcus watched as she bit into the sandwich, and his smile warmed. For the first time in his life, he realised, it didn't matter to him whether his mother was lying or not. Because for the first time in his life, he was also thinking only of his own best interests.

23

DS Parkinson perched on the edge of the armchair and leaned forward. He rested his forearms on his knees and tried to look into Becca's face, but she was avoiding his gaze, still absorbing the news that she'd been dreading. He glanced to her right, and into the face of her brother. Robin looked drained, tired of the drama, his young, thin face grey with worry. But he hadn't shut down. He returned Parkinson's glance with an almost imperceptible nod as if granting the policeman a wholly unnecessary permission to speak.

Parkinson clasped his fingers together and looked down at them. 'We've had an initial post-mortem report on the body. And I have to tell you that Philip received a blow to the back of the head before he went into the water. We think it's unlikely that the blow killed him. But we believe that it might have rendered him sufficiently unconscious to be unaware that he was in the water. The pathologist is running further tests, and we'll know in the next twenty-four hours whether the blow killed him, or whether he drowned without regaining consciousness.'

'Will you know whether he tried to free himself from the leg irons?' It was Robin who spoke, his voice quiet and calm.

'We will, yes. There will be evidence if he'd tried to free himself.' Parkinson himself couldn't bear to think about the possibility. 'Becca, I need to ask you to confirm that you understand what I'm going to say to you now.' She was still looking away from him. 'There is a possibility that Philip might have been murdered. Do you understand?'

Robin put an arm around his sister. 'Becs, the sergeant

needs you to answer him.'

Becca pulled a grey and crumpled tissue from the pocket of her cardigan and dabbed at her eyes with it, then turned them, dull and desperate, onto DS Parkinson's face. 'What is there not to understand?'

'If Philip's death wasn't suicide, then we'll be looking at a double murder investigation. Which means we'll be looking for a suspect who bore a grudge against both Lucy and Philip.'

'Against them both? You mean Marcus?' For a moment she considered the possibility, and then she pouted her dismissal of the idea. 'Why would he do that? He's put up with them carrying on for so long.' She turned to her brother. 'He wouldn't do that, would he?' She seemed to be looking at Robin without really seeing him, without noticing his stern look of concern. And then it registered. 'What? What is it?' She swung her gaze back to Parkinson. 'That is what you meant, isn't it?'

Parkinson felt his face settle into a mask of inscrutability. 'Did you and Marcus ever discuss Lucy and Philip?'

Anger flushed into Becca's face. 'Discuss Lucy and Philip? You think Marcus would ever lower himself to have a conversation with me? Like we ever had anything in common?'

'You had Lucy and Philip in common.' Parkinson was keeping his voice as level as he could.

'You *bastard*.' She spat the word at him. 'I thought you were alright. I thought you understood.' She wriggled violently and tried to break free from her brother's grasp.

Robin tightened his grip. 'Shut up, Becca.'

'Shut up? Why the hell should I?' She squirmed again and tried to push him away with hands that were balled tightly into fists, but he held her firm.

'Because he's trying to trip you up.' Robin shot an almost apologetic glance at the policeman. 'I'm sorry, sergeant, but I've got to tell her.' He turned back to his sister. 'You're a suspect, Becs. Can't you see that? It isn't just Marcus Drake who had a grudge against them both.'

'He wouldn't.' She swung her eyes round to Parkinson, and he felt them burn into his face, melting the mask of inscrutability. 'You wouldn't do that? What about the texts? You know that I got those texts from Philip's phone.'

'You could have sent those to yourself.'

'To myself?'

Parkinson kept his gaze fixed firmly on her face. 'How well do you know Marcus Drake, Becca?'

It was the final push he needed. Becca struggled to her feet and broke free of Robin's grasp. She lunged towards the policeman and began to beat the balled fists against his shoulders, but her brother was only a split second behind her. He wrapped his arms around her waist and carried her kicking and screaming out of the living room and into the kitchen, then kicked the door closed behind him with his foot.

Parkinson blew out a long breath and put his hand up to his head to rub at his forehead. Ennor Price had been sure that Becca had a temper, and that it wouldn't take much of a push to light the fuse.

And, not for the first time, Ennor Price hadn't been wrong.

*

Nancy took the piece of paper from Kathryn's outstretched hand and laid it gently down on the library desk. She leaned forward to study it, her dark eyes sweeping back and forth over the hand-sketched family tree, and her lips moved silently as she mouthed the names written in the boxes. Occasionally, she gave a tiny nod of the head as she recognised a piece of information, and now and then the dark eyes narrowed as she came across something new and hitherto unknown.

Kathryn watched her from the other side of the desk, and could only wonder at the thought processes that lay behind the nods and narrowings. Nancy had come late to the library, her day so far consumed by the tedium of catering to the household, and there was an uncharacteristic brittleness to her. The growing bond between them, forged the day before in the fires of a common interest in the Lancefield family heritage, seemed somehow to have developed a hairline fracture. Where previously Nancy would have offered to help with whatever task it pleased Kathryn to pursue, this afternoon she had set out her stall at the start, asking to see the family tree that Kathryn had drafted for Richard.

The mood in Salvation Hall was shifting.

Eventually, almost reluctantly, Nancy drew her attention away from the document and lifted her head to smile at Kathryn. 'There's no wonder Richard is so pleased with this. I know he's worried that David will be alone in the future, now that Lucy is gone.' It was a question veiled as a suggestion, a stab in the dark, Kathryn thought, to flush out the real reason for the exercise. What Nancy really wanted was for Kathryn to say "Oh, that's not why we're doing it. We're doing it to find another heir for the estate."

But that wasn't going to happen. Kathryn was still troubled by Ennor's words to her in the garden – *there could be a killer amongst the family* – and for a moment she was acutely aware of just how much Lucy's death affected Nancy. Nancy, who came from St Felix to work as Richard's secretary. Nancy, who claimed to love the family's heritage as if it were her own. Nancy, who shared Richard's frustrations that neither his son nor his granddaughter would agree to uphold the family's traditions. 'Nancy, what was Lucy like?' Kathryn tried to sound nonchalant, as if the question were just a passing interest.

'What was she like?' Nancy smiled. 'Well, she had crazy

ideas about Salvation Hall, and she drove Richard to distraction. And people outside the family thought she was just a spoiled little rich girl. But at home? No. Lucy was just one of us. She loved Salvation Hall in her own way, and I think she really believed that Richard would settle the estate on her because David wasn't interested.'

'Surely she didn't expect Richard to be happy with the idea of turning the place into a hotel?'

'She wasn't doing it to make Richard happy. I think she was doing it to make it acceptable to herself.' Nancy leaned her elbows on the desk and rested her chin on her hands. 'Lucy grew up in England. She looked at the family's heritage through English eyes, just like David. But where David chose to distance himself from it, to deny his connections, Lucy wanted to transform it. I think perhaps she was trying to wash away the family's sins. And I suppose it's possible she might have succeeded. The plans she had drawn up were quite extensive. Perhaps if the new buildings had outweighed the old.'

'She had plans drawn up? Even though the house didn't belong to her?'

'Lucy wasn't the sort to let a small thing like ownership stop her. Her sense of entitlement was too strong for that. She had money of her own that she'd inherited from her mother, and she engaged a firm of architects to put a proposal together. They suggested leaving the main house intact as a reception suite and common areas, extending the Dower House to provide accommodation for the family, and then building a new block at the other side of the lake to accommodate guests.' Nancy paused and thought for a moment. Then she said, 'Lucy thought the plans were marvellous. She was so proud when she showed them to Richard.'

'But he wasn't impressed?'

'What do you think?' Nancy was laughing again. 'I think his actual words were "over my dead body". Of course, Lucy being Lucy she just laughed and said "that was the general idea".'

'And how did you feel about it? I mean, this is your home too, isn't it?'

'Oh, I couldn't take it too seriously. I knew Richard would never permit it.' Nancy frowned again. 'I was part of the elaborate plans though. She was always telling me that I was the natural choice for hotel manager.'

'Wouldn't that be her role?'

'Hell, no.' Nancy balked at the thought. 'That wasn't Lucy's way. There always had to be someone to carry the load while she enjoyed herself. Me, usually. Or Marcus. Lucy would have carried on lunching and shopping, and taking holidays.'

'Did she holiday at Woodlands Park?'

'Not if she could help it. She preferred the Mediterranean to the Caribbean. She was definitely more St Tropez than St Felix.'

Kathryn leaned back in her chair and folded her arms across her chest. 'I suppose that threat has gone away now.' She was watching Nancy's face and didn't miss the slight arching of an eyebrow. The threat for Richard, and for Nancy, had gone away. There would be no more talk of turning Salvation Hall into a hotel. But for someone else? Kathryn examined her fingers. 'I can't imagine how Marcus must be feeling about all of this. He's lost his fiancée and his future all in one go.'

Nancy's eyes narrowed. 'Richard thinks that Marcus was using Lucy.'

'Do you?'

'I think that they were using each other. Marcus is quite sweet, really. But I think he was marrying Lucy because it's what his mother wanted. And I think Lucy was marrying Marcus because he was her idea of a husband.' Nancy looked at Kathryn for a sign of understanding and seeing none added, 'It suited Lucy very well to have someone capable and practical, but also pliable. Someone who would do as he was told.'

'And that was Marcus?'

Nancy's smile was subtle. 'I think Marcus grew up doing as he was told. But he didn't seem to mind. He and Lucy had a way of working together.'

'And Philip?'

Nancy laughed again. 'Lucy and Philip were lovers. Marcus was the man she was planning to marry.'

'But which of them did she love?'

'Neither. I don't think love ever came into it as far as Lucy was concerned.'

'And what about you, Nancy?'

A slight blush made its way into the chiselled cheeks. 'What about me?' She sounded unexpectedly cautious.

'How did you come to be here?'

'It was an opportunity I couldn't pass up. You know I was born at Woodlands Park. It was such a privilege to train as Richard's secretary. I've been here almost ten years now.' Her smile had warmed with genuine pleasure. 'And Richard is wonderful. Every year we go back to St Felix for a five-week holiday. Except for this year, of course. Richard was unwell in April, but he wouldn't hear of my staying here with him. He sent me back to St Felix for a holiday just the same. I had a wonderful time.' She pointed towards the pile of papers on the desk in front of Kathryn. 'And I brought more documents back with me.'

Nancy's evident pleasure at the way her life had unfolded left Kathryn feeling uncomfortable with her suspicions. There was still an unspoken question hanging in the air, and Kathryn could barely bring herself to ask it. But it had to be done. She licked her lips and smiled at the glowing girl. 'What do you think will happen, Nancy, if there is no heir to the estate now, other than David?'

Nancy looked curiously discomfited. 'I think Richard is hoping that David might change his mind. It's one thing to say that he doesn't want the estate, it's quite another to have the estate denied to him.'

'And if he doesn't?'

'Then I suppose David may still inherit, sell everything off, and retire on the proceeds. And I will go back to St Felix.' She turned wary eyes up to Kathryn's face. 'Richard doesn't confide in me about family matters. At least, not those relating to the estate. But I know he has concerns.' Her gaze wandered back to the family tree, still lying on the desk.

Kathryn reached out a hand and placed it on Nancy's arm. 'We must make time, while I'm here, to make a start on your own family tree.'

Nancy kept her gaze on the document in front of her, and didn't reply. But beneath her fingers, Kathryn felt the sinews of Nancy's arm tighten, her muscles tensing at the thought. And that was all the answer she needed.

*

'Nancy tells me that you've invited Marcus to join us for this evening's dinner.' David Lancefield pulled a chair away from the kitchen table and sat down on it sideways, leaning his right arm on the back of the chair. He regarded his father with a suspicious eye. 'I'd like to know why.'

Richard Lancefield smiled into his coffee and sipped. Conversations with his son were never easy. Why should this one be any different? 'I thought you would be pleased. Stella is always complaining that her son isn't included in the family discussions. If I include him, there will be nothing for her to complain about, will there?'

'Why do you always have to be so disagreeable?'

'Why do you?' The old man settled his coffee mug down on the table and wrapped his hands around it, as if for comfort. 'David, you and I have never had a good relationship. We have nothing in common except our genetics. And even then I have to wonder because you have no instinctive love of your family and its achievements.' The old man coughed out his disappointment with a contemptuous snort. 'But I can't judge you for that. A man is entitled to his opinions.'

'But not entitled to act upon them?'

'Of course you're entitled to act upon them. Why else do I tolerate you living hundreds of miles away in Edinburgh? Why else do I fund your artistic lifestyle from the estate, and tolerate your total lack of regard for the family home and business?' Richard gave a waspish smile. 'Why else do I tolerate your delightful wife?'

'What has Stella ever done to alienate you?'

'Apart from breathing?' Richard settled back in his seat, his gnarled hands still holding tightly to the mug. He pursed his lips and looked away, then looked back at his son. 'There is nothing to be gained by us sitting here trading insults. There is too much to be done. There are funerals to arrange, and matters of the estate to be settled. Until we have buried our loved ones, we must bury our differences. Putting his mother to one side, Marcus is a decent enough boy and he was Lucy's choice for a husband. It is only right that he is invited here to take part in any discussion about her funeral.' Richard blew out a breath. 'The family is in crisis, David. We must pull together against those forces that would harm us.'

'Forces that would harm us?' David sounded perplexed. 'I don't understand what you're driving at.'

'Then you should. Lucy's murder was not a crime of passion, and you should not assume that Philip McKeith sank himself into the lake in a fit of remorse.' Richard paused, waiting for his words to sink in. 'I received a visit from Chief Inspector Price earlier this afternoon. He has advised me that they have found a wound to Philip's head. They are awaiting confirmation of the time and cause of death before drawing any conclusions. But if Philip was murdered, then they will be looking for a double murderer.' He leaned towards his son and lowered his voice. 'And I believe that the first place they will look is at the family.'

What little colour existed in David Lancefield's cheeks

faded to a pallid grey. 'That's ridiculous. Who on earth do you think..?' He looked bemused and slightly panicked. 'It must have been an unknown assailant. A chance killing. Or an enemy of Philip's. Someone who bore him a grudge.'

'Philip didn't have any enemies.'

'How do you know? You don't know what went on in his life outside of Salvation Hall.'

'He didn't have a life outside Salvation Hall. Salvation Hall *was* his life. The gardens were his life. His home was here, his job, his partner, his child. All here.' Richard scowled. 'Even his mistress was here. And why would an unknown assailant murder Lucy?'

'Because she was with Philip when it happened?'

'And the leg irons?'

'Leg irons?'

'Philip's body was weighted down with a set of leg irons that were taken from the storeroom next to the potting shed. How on earth would this unknown assailant have known they were there?'

David opened his mouth but didn't speak. He thought for a moment and then said, 'It can't have been one of the family. You can't possibly think that Stella and I were involved? And in any case, we were in Edinburgh. That would mean it was you.'

'Chief Inspector Price has asked that we keep the news of Philip's injury to ourselves for the time being. You must tell no one.'

'It's too ridiculous. They can't imagine it was you. Or Nancy.' He shook his head. 'Becca? Surely they don't suspect Becca?'

'David, you're not listening to me. You must tell no one, not even Stella.'

'It can't be anyone else. Can it? They suspect Becca, don't they?'

'I don't know whether they suspect Becca,' Richard said calmly, 'any more than I know whether or not they suspect Marcus.'

24

It was almost six o'clock when Kathryn returned to The Zoological. The reception area was deserted, but music was coming from the direction of the bar and she pushed tentatively on the door to see if anyone was in there.

Ian was sitting alone at a table by the window, nursing what appeared to be a large Scotch and soda. He turned and looked up as she opened the door, and forced a smile. 'Care to join me?' He looked hopeful.

She glanced up at the clock behind the bar. 'I'd better pass, I'm afraid. I'm expected at Salvation Hall by seven thirty, and I need to shower and change. There's a family dinner this evening.' She saw the disappointment register on his face. He looked tired, troubled by some invisible burden.

'So I've heard.' He lifted his glass and sipped on the whisky. 'So you're part of the family now?'

The jibe spiked a flush of colour into Kathryn's cheeks. 'Hardly. I'm not sure why Richard wants me there.' The statement wasn't completely truthful, but for some reason she was still wary of trusting him. 'To be honest, I'm not looking forward to attending. But Richard is a client and he's having a difficult time. The least I can do is support him.'

'Well, whatever the reason, you're not the only one who doesn't want to be there. Marcus has been invited too, and he doesn't want to attend any more than you do.'

'So why attend?'

'I would have said to please his mother, but it would be more accurate to say he's doing it to avoid unleashing his mother's fury.' Ian leaned back in his seat and rested the whisky glass against his chin, contemplating. 'To be fair, I think they are planning to discuss the arrangements for Lucy's funeral, so I suppose we should be pleased that he's being included. Otherwise…' He turned to look at Kathryn. 'Have you met Stella yet?'

Kathryn relaxed a little and smiled. 'I haven't had the pleasure of meeting either of them yet, Stella or Marcus. I've spent most of my time closeted in the library working, or sitting in the grounds trying to stay out of the way of the police.'

'Are they any closer to solving the case?'

'I really don't know.' It was something she still didn't want to discuss with him. 'I'm doing my best not to know. But it isn't easy.'

'I shouldn't think this evening's dinner will be easy either.' He looked thoughtful now. 'Between you and me, Kathryn, Marcus is dreading it. It's been tough enough for him losing Lucy in such violent circumstances, but now his mother wants to pass him off to Richard Lancefield as a potential heir.'

'With no concern that the family is grieving the loss of two loved ones?'

'Stella doesn't believe in standing on ceremony. As you'll probably find out this evening.' He downed the last of the whisky and placed the glass gently on the table. 'It won't get her anywhere, of course. Marcus doesn't want to know. He's asked me if he can take an extended holiday after Lucy's funeral. He wants to go travelling. A university friend is studying for a PhD in Barcelona. Marcus is planning to visit for a couple of weeks, and then spend some time travelling around Spain. I've told him he can go. I'm not going to stand in his way. And I'll keep his job open for him. We'll manage for a couple of months.' Despite his words, Ian didn't seem convinced. 'I can always bring in a temp.'

'But?'

His lips curled into a resigned smile, and he tilted his

head. 'I can't help thinking that he's running away.'

'Running away from what?'

Ian hesitated, and then said, 'From losing Lucy. And from being a pawn in his mother's game.' For a moment it seemed like there was more to come, and then his eyes clouded, and he raised them to look out of the window. 'He's a decent lad, Kathryn.' There was something Ian was finding difficult to put into words. 'I'm glad you're going to be there this evening. I don't like to think of him in the clutches of those vipers. If you're there when Stella makes her pitch, you might be able to bring some humanity to the proceedings.'

'I can't promise to do that. But…' Kathryn was almost afraid to say too much, and then nodded to herself. 'I can't see that it would do any harm to put your mind at rest. For what it's worth, I don't think Stella will get very far with her plan, whether Marcus goes travelling or not. I think Richard already has plans of his own for the estate, and I don't think they include Marcus.' She had been hovering beside the bar since entering the room, but she stepped forward now and dropped her bag on the floor beside his table, and lowered herself into the chair opposite. 'Do you think Marcus will be upset?'

'Upset?'

'Not to inherit anything from the estate. I mean, he was planning to marry into the family. He must have harboured some expectations of benefitting from the family's wealth. Otherwise, why go through with it?'

'Perhaps because he loved her?'

Kathryn fell silent. It occurred to her now that earlier that day she had asked Nancy which of the two men Lucy Lancefield had loved, Philip McKeith or Marcus Drake. It had not occurred to her to ask which of the two men had really loved Lucy in return. Had she become so cynical that she had forgotten a man could marry for love? Nancy had suggested that Lucy and Marcus had been using each other, and Kathryn had found no reason to disbelieve her.

But what if Nancy had been wrong?

*

Tom Parkinson pulled his Audi onto the foreshore at Marazion and switched off the ignition. The car park was empty now, the mobile coffee bar nowhere to be seen, the causeway to St Michael's Mount long since submerged under water. He pulled on the handbrake, securing the car, and turned to look at Ennor Price. 'Are you sure you don't fancy a pint, sir?'

'I'd rather pass, if it's all the same to you, Tom. It's been a long day.' And a worrying one. He turned his head to look out of the car's passenger window towards the village. In the distance, he could just make out the strings of lights adorning the front of the restaurant where he and Kathryn had enjoyed their meal the previous evening. His brow beetled forward. He knew now that Philip McKeith had been murdered, and that the blow to the head had killed him before his body had gone anywhere near the water. There was danger at Salvation Hall tonight, a double killer in their midst, and it troubled him to think of Kathryn alone there with the family. He pushed the thought to the back of his mind and turned back to look at Tom Parkinson. 'Tell me about Becca Smith.'

'Well, you were right about her temper. It didn't take much to light the fuse. And it wasn't a one-off. I could tell that by the way her brother reacted. He jumped to restrain her. And he did it so quickly that I reckon he's used to doing it. It's not the first time he's stepped in to calm her down.'

'And what about the brother?'

'Robin? He looks twitchy, but he seems a decent enough sort. I think he regrets diving the lake, and he's still worried about some sort of reprisal from Richard Lancefield, even though you tried to reassure him. I think he's honest.' Tom settled back in his seat. 'But I suppose it's possible that he might have held a grudge against Philip McKeith. He seemed angry that McKeith had made a fool of his sister. And he was annoyed with Becca for not leaving McKeith and going home to her family.'

'If Becca was our murderer, would he defend her? Would he help her to dispose of the bodies?'

'He's definitely there for her. He came running when she called him last night. And he dived into the lake to look for McKeith and then sat with her all night until we arrived to recover the body. But if he knew about the murder, why go through the performance of diving for the body?'

'For the same reason that Becca might have sent those texts to herself. To make it look good.' Ennor Price turned his gaze out towards St Michael's Mount. The night was rolling in fast, and the outline of the mount was barely visible now, with scattered lights twinkling at random around its contours. 'Becca Smith and Marcus Drake both had the same motive for murdering Lucy and Philip. They both had the opportunity, both lived on the Salvation Hall estate, and both had access to the storeroom to take the leg irons. And neither of them has a cast-iron alibi because we can't get an accurate time of death for the victims. But at least we know now that Lucy was murdered first.' An unpleasant thought crossed his mind. 'We don't know whether Lucy was alone when she was murdered, or whether Philip witnessed the killing. If they were due to meet at the lake, it's possible that she arrived first, encountered the murderer, and then Philip arrived too late to save her. And he paid with his life for what he witnessed.'

'And the leg irons?'

'I asked Halliwell to help me with an experiment with those leg irons this afternoon. I could lift them, with enough effort, but she couldn't. But she could drag them. And she could lift them with my help.'

'So you could see Becca Smith dragging those leg irons

down to the lake and fastening them onto the ankles of the man that she loved?'

'She could have had help. Her brother could have carried them, or helped her to carry them. Or someone else could. It was a clever move, weighting the body down so that it wouldn't rise to the surface. We certainly jumped to the obvious conclusion. There didn't seem any doubt to begin with that Philip had murdered Lucy and then done a runner to escape being charged. We shouldn't blame ourselves for that. It's a fair enough assumption.' Ennor frowned. 'I take it there's been no trace of a weapon, nothing that might have been used to deliver the blow to the back of McKeith's head?'

'Sorry, sir. Nothing so far. It makes you think, though, doesn't it? Those leg irons, that those things were actually used on human beings. I can hardly believe that the family owns things like that.'

'Man's inhumanity to man knows no bounds.' The chief inspector let out a sigh. 'I'm getting tired of that inhumanity, Tom. I've had a lifetime of it as a policeman.' He tilted his head towards his sergeant. 'I'm starting to feel maudlin. It's time to go home.'

Tom Parkinson smiled and started the car's engine. 'What's our next move?'

'To wait and see. There's a family dinner at Salvation Hall tonight, and we have an independent witness. Kathryn Clifton is going to be there. And so is Marcus Drake. I think it's all going to kick off, and there's going to be some fall-out. And if there isn't' – he turned to Tom – 'then tomorrow morning we'll go back to Salvation Hall and we'll shake that Lancefield family tree until we see what falls out of it.'

25

Kathryn balanced uncomfortably on the edge of the sofa, a small crystal glass of amontillado in her right hand. Despite donning her most expensive outfit for the evening, a pale blue silk shift, matching pashmina, and a pair of ageing Manolo Blahnik shoes she had inherited from Moira, she felt quite decidedly out of her depth in the hushed and elegant atmosphere of Salvation Hall's gracious drawing room.

The place felt different in the evening, and she might have found the experience overwhelming were it not for the presence of Marcus. He was seated to her left, reclining in a generous armchair placed so close to the sofa that their arms almost touched. She leaned towards him with a tentative smile. 'Thank you again for sharing a taxi with me.'

'Not at all. It made no sense for us to travel out from Penzance in separate cars. And I think Ian was glad you were there to chaperone me into the lion's den.' He blinked, an almost wink of his right eye. 'I'm sorry it took so long for us to finally meet.' He was trying to put her at ease, but the strain was still showing.

Kathryn smiled her understanding. After waiting so long to meet the man that Lucy Lancefield had chosen as her ideal husband, she was finding Marcus to be an affable and socially charming young man. Undeniably handsome, with clear blue eyes and a disarming smile, he had an easy way of talking, and had introduced himself to her earlier that evening in a self-deprecating way as "the fiancé that didn't quite make it onto the family tree". She supposed it was a sly reference to the work she was doing for Richard, but she could hardly blame him if his good humour was forced. There was a sadness about him. Not grief, but a world-weariness, as if he'd seen everything that he wanted just inches from his grasp, and then by this cruel twist of fate had it snatched away from him by something that was utterly outside his control.

'Do you think Ian was right? That you need a chaperone?' She tried to make the question sound light-hearted.

'I think Ian always tries to do his best to look out for me. I've become something of a surrogate son since Laurence took up his job in London.' Marcus shifted a little in his seat, turning towards her. 'I've always been a bit too normal for the Lancefield family. I believe in working for my living, and I don't believe that privilege arises simply from an accident of birth. But I'm not afraid of the family, or in awe of them. They've always been gracious towards me, never unkind. So no, I don't think I need a chaperone.' He frowned at a private thought. 'Not to protect me from the Lancefields anyway.'

'From something else then?' Kathryn asked the question quietly, but before he could answer the door to the drawing room swung open.

'Marcus, my boy. Thank you for coming to dine with us.' Richard, resplendent in formal dinner dress, bustled into the room. 'And Kathryn, too. I hope Nancy has kept you both plied with sherry.' He turned to look behind him and gave a low whistle. 'C'mon, dog. In you come.' He waited until Samson had shuffled through the doorway, and then closed the door gently behind him, and lowered himself into a wing-backed chair beside the fireplace. It placed him beside Marcus, and directly opposite Kathryn. 'Well now, sad times are upon us. But, Marcus, I want you to know that you are still a part of this family. I don't want you to be a stranger.' He tapped on the arm of Marcus's chair with a crooked finger to stress the point.

Marcus looked down at his sherry glass, an embarrassed

flush in his cheeks, and then lifted his head and put out his hand towards his host. 'I won't be a stranger. But I want to tell you now, before my mother arrives, that I have no expectations of the Lancefield family. I hope you will understand if I say I would prefer us to be friends, rather than family.'

Richard shot a glance at Kathryn and smiled, then gave a little nod of satisfaction. He took the hand that Marcus had offered into his left hand and wrapped his right warmly over the top of it. 'Good man. I think we understand each other.' He let go and sank back into his seat. 'And now that we've agreed to be friends, I hope you will understand if I ask you to pop into the kitchen and see how Nancy is getting on with dinner, while I have a word with Kathryn here. Stuff and nonsense about the family tree she's building for me, nothing that would interest you, I think.'

Marcus laughed and turned to Kathryn. 'Richard has tried many times to interest me in the family's history, but I'm afraid he's never succeeded. History of any sort has never stirred a heartbeat for me.'

'Then I'm sorry we didn't meet sooner. Perhaps I might have changed your mind.' Kathryn waited until Marcus had left the room and then turned her attention to Richard. 'He's quite charming, isn't he? I don't know what I expected. But having met him, I can't help thinking that Lucy was on to something.' She caught an unexpected twinkle in Richard's eye. 'Oh goodness, I didn't mean in a romantic sense.' She put a hand up to her face to cover the hint of a blush. 'No, I meant that he's a decent, practical sort. I can see that he would have been an asset to her business plans.'

'I think that young man would be an asset to anyone's business plans. There is an old-fashioned decency about him that I'm ashamed to say I failed to spot. I suspect that his mother is not going to be pleased when she hears that Marcus and I have already come to an understanding. Nor is she going to be pleased when she hears of the conversation I have had with David this afternoon.' Richard leaned forward. 'Now Kathryn, I want to brief you on that conversation, before David joins us and the harpy descends, but we don't have long before dinner will be served. Why don't you move over into this armchair next to me, so that we can put our heads together and not be overheard?' He leaned back again and then started, sitting upright in his seat. 'Whatever is that noise?' He grumbled his irritation at the disturbance. 'Where is Nancy? Someone needs to answer that damned door.'

Outside the house, an unseen hand was battering loudly on the oak front door, and the doorbell chimed with infuriating persistence as if someone was leaning on it. Kathryn turned her head towards the drawing room door. Through it she could hear Nancy's voice as she walked across the hallway, the sound of an iron bolt being drawn back, the creak as the heavy door swung open. Nancy's words were indistinct when she spoke, but she sounded flustered. Then she cried out. 'No!'

Kathryn instinctively rose to her feet and stood between Richard and the drawing room door, and as she did so the door flew open and Becca almost fell into the room. She flung out a hand to steady herself against the door frame and scowled at them with venomous eyes. 'Look at you,' she hissed, 'all dressed up and swilling sherry, like nothing out of the ordinary has happened. And my Philip, lying cold on a slab in the mortuary. And none of you give a damn.' Her lips folded inwards to suppress a sob, and she crumpled forward in her grief.

Behind her, Nancy was framed in the doorway. 'I tried to stop her.'

'Please take her away and calm her down.' Richard turned away with a scowl.

Nancy stepped forward to follow his instruction and tried to put her arms around the sobbing girl, but Becca shook herself free and turned her anger back towards the old man. 'I don't want your pity. You said you cared about him. You let this happen to him.'

Richard turned an anguished face towards the grieving girl but found no need to speak. Marcus was behind her now, his hands on her shoulders, his face close to her ear. 'This isn't the way, Becca.' His voice was calm as he gently turned her towards the doorway. 'You don't want to do this. Not to Richard.' He spoke to Nancy as he guided Becca out into the hallway. 'I'll take her back to the cottage. Don't wait for me for dinner.'

Back in the drawing room, Richard sank back into his chair with a groan. 'My God, is this nightmare ever going to stop?'

'It has to stop sometime.' Kathryn's mouth was dry, her rapid heartbeat reluctant to slow. 'But she's gone now. Marcus will look after her. You said yourself that he's a decent sort.'

'Who is a decent sort? And what on earth was all that awful racket?' The question was asked by a voice not familiar to Kathryn, and she turned to see a gaunt blonde framed in the doorway next to Nancy. The blonde flashed supercilious green eyes at her and then turned them back to Richard. 'My God, Richard darling, you look truly awful. Have I missed something?'

*

Ennor Price pulled a clean sheet of paper from the in-tray on his desk, picked up a pencil, and neatly jotted the name "Richard Lancefield" at the top of the page. It was his custom, during an investigation, to sit down in his study every evening and write out the key facts of a case from scratch on a clean piece of paper, always beginning with the list of people involved. But today he had a fancy to take a slightly different approach. He drew a box around Lancefield's name, then added another box underneath, into which he wrote the name "David Lancefield". He connected the boxes with a single line, tapped his pencil on the paper thoughtfully, and then added "Stella Drake Lancefield" in a box next to her husband.

Ennor had never before sketched out a family tree, but he found the subtle nuances of slowly drawing out the relationships between the players in his latest drama curiously thought-provoking. It didn't take long to complete the exercise, maybe five minutes at most, and once he'd finished he couldn't help feeling rather pleased with the result. He had attached Philip McKeith to Lucy Lancefield as a virtual spouse and, in turn, linked Becca to Philip on the same basis. And where every player was linked to another, he noted along the link the relationship that bound them together. There were only two people he couldn't attach to the tree. Kathryn Clifton he considered irrelevant to his case, except that she made an exceptionally useful source of information. Nancy Woodlands, on the other hand, he couldn't dismiss so easily. She had no relationship tying her to Salvation Hall other than her role as Richard Lancefield's secretary. And yet she was considered a part of the family.

He dropped the pencil onto the desk and leaned back in his seat. He was sure that either Becca Smith or Marcus Drake was at the root of this crime, but he couldn't for the life of him work out which. Or perhaps they were working together. It occurred to him that he felt curiously sorry for both of them – Becca besotted with the unfaithful Philip, and Marcus cuckolded by Lucy's carryings-on. He knew how that felt. Seven years on he was still nursing the scars of his own wife's infidelity. He brushed the thought away. It was time to move on. It had been time to move on for a long time. He turned his attention back to the paper on his desk.

Somewhere on that tree, he thought, is a killer. And everyone on that tree is in the house or grounds of Salvation Hall tonight. And that's where Kathryn is. In close proximity to a killer. Should he be worried about her? He didn't think so, as long as she would heed his instructions. He was still inclined to think that passion and jealousy lay at the bottom of the crime, and that was nothing to do with Kathryn. All she had to do was stay detached and keep her thoughts to herself.

He picked up the pencil again and began to doodle random thoughts around the sketch as they occurred to him. Lucy Lancefield died first. Philip McKeith was dead before he went into the water. Could Robin have assisted Becca by carrying the leg irons to the lake? Did Drake even know the leg irons existed? Price doodled a mobile phone between Becca and Philip. Who sent the texts to Becca?

Thoughts were coming to him thick and fast now. What was Drake going to do now? Would Becca stay on at Salvation Hall? Who would inherit the estate? And what would happen to Nancy?

That particular thought intrigued him. What *would* happen to Nancy? He doodled her name in a box beside Richard Lancefield and stretched a dotted line between the two of them, jotting the word "secretary" above it. Another dotted line he stretched between Nancy and Becca – colleagues. Nancy and Kathryn – acquaintances. He rubbed at his temple. Where was this taking him? He let the pencil guide him this time. Nancy and Lucy – friends. Nancy and Marcus – alibi.

Alibi?

The word startled him and he drew back the pencil and looked more closely at what he had written. Nancy was the closest thing that Marcus had to an alibi. She had prepared him a meal, seen that he'd eaten it, then kept him company while Lucy was supposedly out enjoying an evening with friends. Had Nancy been more than an alibi, as Tom Parkinson suspected? She had already admitted to Price that it would break her heart to discover that Philip had murdered Lucy. What did she mean by that?

He dropped the pencil on to the desk a second time

and stretched out a hand to pick up his mobile phone. He flicked at the screen until it filled with a colourful, striking image, the photograph he had taken of the framed print hanging on the wall of Lucy Lancefield's room. The portrait attributed to David Martin showed two young women exquisitely dressed in Georgian satins and silks, their smiling faces turned towards the painter. On the right of the picture, Lady Elizabeth Murray, elegant in a soft pink dress, was stretching out a slim, pale hand towards her companion. On the left, a beauty of mixed race in a white gown and turban was pointing to her face with a wry and teasing smile. Both girls were nieces to the Earl of Mansfield, a significant figure in the abolition of the British slave trade. Elizabeth Murray was born easily into a privileged British life. Her cousin Dido Belle was born into slavery, claimed by the British naval officer who fathered her, and raised as a British gentlewoman.

Ennor had asked Kathryn about this picture the evening before, and had felt foolish for not already knowing what it was. He found the image beautiful and terrifying at the same time – its portrayal of two elegant young women ahead of their time, their blood bound across continents, their ease with each other so evident in the poses they adopted. Looking at it again, he could see why Kathryn had laughed and declared that she found the study to be a kind of family joke. There's a way of looking at it, she had said, that will lead you to see Dido pointing at the colour of her skin with mischief in her eyes, and Elizabeth not so much reaching out to touch her cousin as pushing her away, as one might lightly push away a friend who is trying to make you laugh when you are trying to be serious.

But Ennor could find nothing to laugh at here. Lucy Lancefield had disowned the heritage of her sugar-growing, slave-owning family, and eschewed it so strongly that she planned to remove all traces of it if the estate fell into her hands. So why would she hang a copy of David

Martin's famous painting in full view where she would be reminded of it every day? The question perplexed him, and he was still musing on the answer when his phone vibrated with an incoming text. He scrolled down the screen to reveal the message, squinted at it, and nodded to himself with a smile.

It had only been a matter of time.

26

Richard dropped his hand to the side of his armchair to ruffle Samson's coat. 'I hope you enjoyed your supper this evening, girl. I'm afraid I'm about to ask you to earn it.' The remark was addressed to Kathryn. 'Now that we've dined, I'm hoping to explain to David and to Stella why your work must continue, despite the sadness that currently hangs over our unfortunate family. And I think you can add weight to my arguments.'

Kathryn looked across at David and Stella, and could only conclude that they didn't share Richard's enthusiasm. She turned an awkward smile to Richard. 'I enjoyed supper very much, and I'm more than happy to earn it. It's quite a privilege for me to have this opportunity.'

Stella turned her gaze down to the drop of burgundy remaining in her glass. 'And quite an opportunity for you to be given the privilege.' Her voice was surprisingly quiet, but her tone beyond icy.

David Lancefield nudged his wife's foot with his own in silent reprimand. 'I think what Stella means, is that for you as a writer, accessing the family's material presents… a unique opportunity to, er, find evidence of…'.

'Oh for heaven's sake, David.' Stella, irked by his prevarication, clattered her now-empty wine glass down onto a small side table. 'I'm sure Kathryn fully understood what I meant.' She turned cold eyes towards Richard. 'I really do think this family history nonsense should stop now. And so does David.' She turned back to her husband in search of support, only to be piqued still further when he turned his head away.

Richard let out a heavy sigh. 'You must forgive Stella,

Kathryn. She sometimes forgets that she is only a member of this family by marriage and that the family's history – and its legacy – have nothing to do with her. Only my son. And he, sadly, is ashamed of the family heritage and has tried to distance himself from it. Until today he has made no secret of his plans to sell off the estate, buy a home in the south of France, and see out his days on the proceeds, drinking cheap wine and painting overweight nudes. He has been as keen to see the estate dispersed as I have been to ensure its survival.' Richard took a breath. 'Unfortunately for David, as I am the present owner it is up to me to decide whether he inherits the estate in the first place.'

Stella hissed. 'That's an unforgivable thing to say in front of a stranger.'

'Kathryn isn't a stranger, Stella.' Richard met the rebuff with an easy smile. 'Kathryn is, I hope, a friend of the family.'

Kathryn felt a flush of embarrassment colour her cheeks. 'I would like to think so. But that doesn't make me a member of the family, only a friend to it, and perhaps Stella is right. Perhaps these are matters that should be discussed in private.'

'How would you resolve the issue?' David Lancefield appeared to have woken up, and he leaned towards Kathryn, his brow furrowed in concentration. 'I mean, surely you can see why I would be ashamed of the family's heritage? And why I might want to disassociate myself from it?'

'Perhaps. Perhaps not. Colonialism, sugar production, the slave trade, they all happened. Whether we like it or not, however they make us feel, we can't re-invent history. And I don't believe we should try to bury it. However horrific the acts of the past, we can learn from them. We can learn not to make the same mistakes again. And we can honour the past, honour those affected by it, and ensure that they are never forgotten. Perhaps you could look at this thing the other way up, and consider using the estate to bring about something good?'

An uncomfortable silence settled on the room and Kathryn felt all eyes fixed on her face. David was regarding her with a strange curiosity, as if he didn't quite understand the point she was trying to make, but felt he ought to. Stella was looking at her with nothing short of disgust. And Richard…

Richard's gaze was burning into her cheeks and for a moment she couldn't help wondering if she had overstepped the mark. And then he smiled and rubbed his hands together. 'Tomorrow, David, I would like Kathryn to talk you through the family tree she is drawing up for me. I think you would be interested. But now, I think we should turn our attention to the police investigation into Lucy's and Philip's murders.'

'Richard, darling, before we discuss any of that, I really feel that we need to discuss how the events of the last few days have affected Marcus.' Stella blinked at her father-in-law, the cold, piercing eyes now widening with feigned humility. 'Marcus has lost everything with Lucy's death. His fiancée, and his future.'

Richard tilted his head, birdlike, and regarded her with a smile. 'Marcus and I have already discussed his future, Stella. I'm quite sure you will be as delighted as I am to know that he and I have shaken hands on an agreement of friendship. Marcus knows I am here for him if he needs me. But it would appear that for the immediate future he has plans of his own which don't include the Lancefield family.'

Stella shot a bewildered glance at David but he turned his head away to avoid her gaze. She turned her attention back to Richard, and her brittle voice sweetened with a hint of honey. 'Marcus is unwell at the moment. He doesn't know what he wants. We all know that he belongs here, at Salvation Hall. He may no longer be Lucy's fiancé, but he is still David's stepson. And David has every intention of leaving everything to him in the future. Don't you, David?'

'Everything that I may not inherit?' David swung his head around to glare at her. 'Where is Marcus, anyway? Couldn't we expect him to be here with us now if he was that interested in the affairs of the family?'

The delicate balance of the evening's good humour, so carefully nurtured through a summer soup, a roast rib of beef, a selection of Cornish cheeses and a lemon and passionfruit trifle, was beginning to fall apart. Kathryn, quietly watching the proceedings and keeping her own counsel, found herself wishing that she were anywhere but Salvation Hall. Her mind had wandered to the text she had sent to Ennor Price earlier in the evening. If she had hoped that he might appear to rescue her from this latest burgeoning nightmare, then the hope appeared to be a forlorn one.

But David's mention of Marcus had given her a glimmer of opportunity, a chance to remove herself from the escalating family squabble. 'Would you like me to go and look for Marcus? If he's back from the cottage, then he might be in the kitchen with Nancy.' She was on her feet and heading for the drawing room door before anyone could answer.

Out in the hallway, she could hear raised voices behind her; David admonishing his wife for her rudeness, and Stella defending her position. With a shake of the head, she crossed the hall to a leaded window that looked out over the garden and lifted the latch to open it wide. The cooling air was irresistible and she pushed her head between the glass and the frame to feel the breeze blow softly around her face and neck and shoulders.

The terrace outside was bathed in moonlight, and it was impossible to miss two figures sitting close together on the bench, their heads tilted and almost touching. Marcus and Nancy were looking out across the lake, to the spot where Lucy's body had been found beneath the water lilies. Kathryn caught her breath and drew back, afraid to intrude upon their privacy, but not quickly enough to avoid hearing their conversation.

'You have to stay strong now, Marcus. No one must know.' It was a malicious breeze that carried Nancy's words back towards the house. 'And when I say no one, then make no mistake. I mean *no one.*'

*

Ennor Price pushed his hands deep into the pockets of his jacket and set off briskly down the path from Becca Smith's cottage, towards Salvation Hall. Behind him, a single blue light from the dashboard of Tom Parkinson's Audi was flashing intermittently into the night sky. He knew that inside the cottage Tom was still refereeing the contest between Becca and the contrite uniformed officer who was meant to be keeping an eye on her. It was a silent match, both women reluctant to reveal how Becca had given WPC Halliwell the slip and managed to gatecrash the Lancefield family's dinner, but if pushed to the point his money would have been on Becca to hold her tongue the longest.

The air was cool, as befitted a mid-September night in coastal Cornwall, and Ennor shivered a little against its bite. The optimist in him always hoped that any situation would turn out to be more accommodating than he could reasonably expect. That had proved to be the case already that evening, finding the gates to Salvation Hall carelessly left unlocked, so that he hadn't had to alert the family to his unexpected arrival. But the Cornish weather had not been so obliging. Considering how often his optimism on that score turned out to be misplaced, he should have known by now that a thicker jacket would be required on a night like this.

The path from the cottage was gently undulating and lit by moonlight, and he moved swiftly along its ups and downs, navigating its occasional bends with ease. This was the rougher part of the garden where rhododendrons, hydrangeas and other overgrown shrubs vied for space, screening the house from the road outside during the day, and providing cover for rabbits and foxes and the odd domestic cat during the night.

But it was a short walk. He followed a sharp bend in the path to skirt a particularly large magnolia and there in front of him was Salvation Hall, proud and inviting, lights at every window, drawing him in. Before it, the ornamental lake lay bathed in moonlight, the closed water lilies eerily still in the ghostly glow. He paused, and for a moment fixed his eyes upon the spot where he'd first looked down at Lucy Lancefield's lifeless bloated body lying shallow in the water. It was the only spur he needed.

He strode on along the path, downhill now, curving around the lake and the manicured lawns, gathering pace until he found himself in sight of the oak front door, clammy from the exertion and the damp night air, and slightly out of breath.

The front door was open and a taxi was standing on the gravel drive, its engine still running, the driver tapping his fingers impatiently on the steering wheel as if he had so many things he would rather be doing with his time than picking up a fare. As Ennor drew closer a woman's voice carried out of the doorway. Kathryn was taking her leave of the family, thanking Richard for an enjoyable evening, promising that she would be back at the house to see him early tomorrow morning. Ennor walked past the taxi, ignoring the driver's enquiring gaze, and walked uninvited into the house.

Four people were standing in the hallway: Nancy hovering by a console table next to the drawing room door, Marcus Drake beside her, and Richard holding onto Kathryn's hand as they made their farewells for the day. As Ennor entered the house, all four of them turned to look at him.

'I'm sorry to intrude.' He did his best to look apologetic. 'But I thought I should let you know. We're taking Becca Smith in for questioning in relation to the murders of Lucy Lancefield and Philip McKeith.'

In the ominous silence that followed, Ennor looked at each face in turn. Nancy's beautiful features had settled into an inscrutable mask, while Marcus had turned pale. Richard Lancefield, standing without his stick, looked dumbstruck. He crumpled forward, grasping the table to steady himself, and Nancy darted forward to catch him. Kathryn, whose face had been turned partly away from Ennor, spun around on her heel and showed him the same expression of annoyance he had seen that morning in the storeroom.

She was breathing heavily, and her eyes were flashing with displeasure. He had upset her that morning, when he clumsily broke the news of Philip McKeith's death to Richard Lancefield. It looked as though he'd scored another direct hit this evening. He gave an almost imperceptible nod as if to say he understood. But he couldn't help feeling that this time the reprimand wasn't completely deserved.

After all, if Kathryn herself hadn't sent him a text just a couple of hours earlier, telling him that Becca Smith had barged into the house and accused the family of being complicit in Philip's death, Tom Parkinson wouldn't be at the cottage now trying to shoehorn Becca into his Audi, and Ennor Price himself would be still cosy in his study, enjoying a second bottle of the best Cornish ale.

27

'Have you heard anything more from the police?' David, blinded by the unexpected intensity of the Cornish morning sunlight, put up a hand to shield his eyes as he strode across the terrace.

Richard, sitting quietly on the bench with Samson in his lap, answered the question without turning to look at his son. 'No, nothing yet.' The old man went on gently stroking the dog's neck. 'I'm finding it very hard to believe Becca capable of such a terrible crime. But if that is what the police think, then we will have to honour their views.' He hoped that his judgement of Detective Chief Inspector Price had been a sound one, that the man was capable of identifying the killer, and that he could be trusted to get it right.

There was no denying that it would be a very convenient truth for the Lancefield family if it transpired that Becca was guilty. The family would be able to move on, to recover from their loss. Lucy and Philip could be buried without too much more delay. And he could turn his attention back to more important business. There was a new will to confirm, and Kathryn's work to continue so that a broader family could be found to support David. To support his son. He leaned his head back a little, and patted the bench, inviting David to sit next to him.

David hesitated and then skirted the bench to sit down next to his father. 'What will you do if Becca is charged?'

Richard shrugged. 'Provide her with legal assistance. And keep an eye on little Francesca. The child would probably go and live with her extended family, but we could make sure that she was provided for. It would be the least we could do for Philip.'

If only he could be sure that she *was* guilty. It wasn't enough to have the motive, or the temper to lash out in anger. This killer needed the sang froid to drag not one but two bodies into the lake and leave them there. To attach those leg irons to Philip. And he couldn't see that in Becca.

He tilted his head towards his son. 'I don't know how she would have known about the leg irons. I can't remember any occasion when she was asked to clean out the storeroom. She had no reason to go in there. Even Philip wouldn't go in there. When the last crates of objects were shipped back to the estate, I asked him to help me arrange them in a way they could be easily accessed, and he didn't want to do it. He didn't refuse, you understand. Philip was a sound man in that respect, he wouldn't refuse to help. But I could see that it made him uncomfortable.'

'If the room wasn't locked she could easily have gone poking about in there at some point without being seen. And she might not have been alone.' David raised an eyebrow. 'Her brother went into the lake without asking permission. Who's to say the two of them haven't been poking about in the storeroom, or the potting shed, or any other place on the estate, as and when they felt like it?'

'Perhaps.' Richard wasn't convinced. He knew it would be an unspeakably selfish thing to do, to deem Becca guilty, whether she committed the crime or not. To make her out to be the villain of the piece so that no one would have to consider the alternative. He took in a steadying breath. 'How is Stella this morning?'

David's face contorted as he tried – and failed – to suppress a smile. 'Unbearable.' He gave a low chuckle. 'Smug. Self-satisfied. Not quite yet exultant, but it will come. You know' – he shifted his posture to turn towards his father – 'Stella isn't quite as tough as you think she is. That smug satisfaction, it hides her relief. Whatever you think of her, she is acutely aware that Marcus also had a motive for the murders. And no one wants to think that of their child, to think him capable of taking someone's life.' David adopted a more sombre expression. 'This latest development has put her mind at rest.'

'And how long, would you think, before she is berating me again about Marcus having a role within the family?'

'I don't think she will. She was talking this morning about encouraging him to travel now. She thinks it would do him good to get away for a while.'

'That may be a point on which your wife and I finally agree. Do you think he would go to St Felix?'

'St Felix?' The unexpected question left David silent for a moment. And then he said 'I don't think it would occur to him.'

'I didn't mean by choice. I meant, would he go to St Felix if I asked him to? Would he take on a role for the family, a management role? It would be a fresh start for him. He's a capable boy, and I think perhaps I may have underestimated him.' Richard turned to his son with the beginnings of a smile. 'I don't know, of course, what his true feelings are about the family's heritage. He claims he has no interest in our history, but I've never heard him stand in judgement of it. He was prepared to work with Lucy on rebranding the family's image. Do you think he may consider it? As a business proposition? He could draw a decent salary from the estate, see something of the world.' Richard's smile took on a mischievous edge. 'It would get him away, a long way away, from his mother.'

David's eyes widened and then creased with barely suppressed amusement. 'We really shouldn't make fun of Stella. If only you would spend some time with her, then perhaps you might see what I see.'

Richard put a hand up to his face and wiped a mirthful tear away from the corner of his eye with the cuff of his shirt sleeve. 'Perhaps, when all of this is over. But for now, we must observe the proprieties. Poor Becca is assisting the police but, as far as I know, she has not been charged. And if she *is* charged, then we must display a silent dignity.

I will not permit there to be any celebration of her misfortune.' His other hand was still resting on Samson's neck, and he wrapped the fingers gently around the dog's shoulder, and rubbed at his coat, as much to calm himself as to caress the dozing dog. It had been a long-forgotten pleasure to share a joke with his son, but this newfound levity was coming too soon.

They were still a very, very long way away from having cause to share a celebration.

*

Ennor Price reached for his mobile phone and then thought better of it. The coffee in the station canteen wasn't up to much by Marazion standards, but Tom Parkinson was still angry with him. It would probably pay dividends to give his sergeant the time to linger there for one more cup before suggesting that the two of them pay a return visit to Salvation Hall.

It occurred to him that he seemed to have the knack of making people angry at the moment. Parkinson's anger came from the simple act of bringing Becca Smith in for questioning, just because she had the clearest motive for the murders. The sergeant seemed to be developing a soft spot for the girl that was beginning to cloud his judgement. It might be time to remind him that he had a wife at home who might not take too kindly to his sympathies extending that far towards another woman.

For his part, Price was sure that bringing Becca in had been the right thing to do. Apart from motive and opportunity, she had a growing antipathy towards the Lancefield family that was veering dangerously close to harassment. He could hardly be blamed for wanting to mitigate any consequential risk. At the very least, he thought, putting her out of harm's way while she calmed down might have been in her own best interests. That temper of hers needed curbing before it led her into serious trouble.

He leaned back in his seat and folded his arms across his chest. He'd been grateful to receive Kathryn's text the evening before, although gatecrashing a family dinner wasn't actually a crime in itself. It had interested him greatly to hear that Marcus Drake had comforted the angry girl and taken her back to the cottage. That would be the Marcus Drake with whom she claimed to have had no previous dealings. Was Drake just being kind, Price wondered? Was Becca telling the truth when she said it was the first time Lucy Lancefield's fiancé had given her the time of day? Or was there more to it, some unknown arrangement or previous assignation that was yet to come to light?

Price had hoped that a few sleepless hours of answering questions might have taken him a bit closer to the truth. But two hours in, he had realised the effort was going to get him nowhere. Belligerent when arrested, a trip to Penzance under blue flashing lights had taken the wind from Becca's sails, but left her morose and scowling. She's an angry little baggage, he thought with a wry smile, and it doesn't take much to light the fuse. She could have killed in anger, he had no problem with that idea. But it would have taken cool thinking to slide Lucy Lancefield's body into the water, and even more to collect the leg irons, attach them to Philip McKeith, and consign him quietly to the deepest part of the lake. She was too hot-headed for that. But someone else could have done it for her. Someone who cared about her, someone who didn't want to see her go down for double murder. Maybe the brother, who saw it as his role to protect her.

Or maybe someone for whom the double murder already committed might have provided an easy solution to a painful situation that was growing too difficult to deal with.

Like Marcus Drake.

The evening before, Marcus had taken care of Becca,

drawn her away from the family, and taken her back to the cottage. Maybe, in the past, he hadn't given her the time of day. But could something have happened that week to bring her unavoidably into his field of vision? Perhaps on Tuesday evening he had been out in the grounds of Salvation Hall, possibly even looking for Lucy, and somehow come upon Becca and the bodies out beside the lake. Lucy's murder would have been a terrible blow to him. But the chance to frame Philip McKeith for it? That opportunity might have been too much to resist.

What if Drake had picked up the pieces of Becca's vengeful crime? What if he had come up with the idea to put the bodies in the lake, and make it look as though Philip had murdered Lucy? Becca had loved Philip, but faced with the alternative to such a plan – her crime reported to the police by Marcus, followed by a long stretch in prison away from her daughter – it could have looked tempting. Maybe she had gone along with such a suggestion. Maybe she had even been persuaded to take Philip's phone and send those texts to herself, to keep up the pretence. And maybe that was why her anger now was so raw, so visceral. Maybe the guilt was eating away at her.

And maybe Price himself was just clutching at straws. Because right now, straws seemed to be the only thing he had.

He leaned wearily forward to rest his forearms on the desk. There was a folder of papers to his right, jottings from the previous evening that he had brought into the office with him that morning, and he reached into it and pulled out the top sheet. It was the Lancefield family tree that he had sketched before Kathryn's text had alerted him to Becca Smith's arrival at Salvation Hall.

He looked at it through intolerant eyes. What a spoiled, arrogant bunch of people they were, out of touch with the real world: Richard Lancefield unable to see the horror of his family's heritage and David Lancefield thinking only of how people would judge him if they knew. The hypocritical Stella Drake Lancefield, bleating about the errors of the past, while cheerfully setting out her stall to inherit as much of its wealth as she could. And the late, unlamented Lucy – spoiled, entitled, taking what she wanted whenever she wanted it, laying claim to the estate, sleeping with another woman's partner, marrying Marcus Drake, and for what?

What did Lucy get out of marrying Marcus? A willing servant, a lap dog to do her bidding? Didn't she have that in Nancy Woodlands? Nancy, whose sole aim in life appeared to be to serve the Lancefield family, whatever their wish?

He looked down again at the family tree. What was he missing? Did no one else benefit from Lucy's death? He reached again for his mobile phone and began to search for a number. There was only one person he could think of who might be able to answer that question for him, one person who was far closer to the Lancefield family tree than he could ever hope to be.

The number found, he glanced down at the phone to see the last communication that he and Kathryn had shared, an inbound text that said simply, "Please tell me that you didn't arrest Becca because I told you that she gatecrashed the party".

He let out a dispirited sigh. Tom Parkinson might be appeased by an extra twenty minutes in the staff canteen, but if past experience was anything to go by it would take more than an extra cup of coffee to placate Kathryn.

28

David closed the heavy oak door behind Kathryn and ushered her across the hallway. 'Nancy has gone into Penzance this morning.' He sounded nervous. 'I hope you don't mind if we have a chat first thing? I was planning to go into town myself later this morning. The funeral arrangements, you know?'

'Of course. If you think there is something I can do to help.'

'Indeed. I'm very confused now about this whole family heritage thing.' He hovered nervously behind her. 'By the way, I hope it's not impertinent of me, Kathryn, but another time, I really would like to speak to you about a portrait.'

'A portrait?' Kathryn paused at the library door and turned quizzical eyes back to him, before pushing it open with her shoulder.

'Yes. My father has never had much time for my art. But I think he would like it if I painted you. Your colouring is magnificent. Quite magnificent. You have a very strong profile, too. And there is a fierce independence in your eye. I think I could see you as Boudicca.'

'I wouldn't get too excited about that suggestion, Kathryn. He says that to every woman he meets.' The unexpected voice drawled out from the other end of the library. Stella was sitting on the window seat, her outline bathed in the morning sunlight, her gaze fixed firmly out of the window across the garden.

Kathryn crossed to the desk and dropped her bag onto the floor beside the chair. 'Good morning, Stella.' She smiled at David's wife, an amiable attempt to break the ice.

Stella ignored the greeting. She pushed herself to her feet, levering her slight frame against the firm velvet cushion and propelled herself past Kathryn's outstretched hand and off towards the open door. 'I find my husband's offer rather sweet, considering that you're a part of Richard's plan to disinherit him.' She lifted her hand to David's face and stroked her fingers down his cheek as she passed him. 'Don't be too long, darling. I was hoping to catch Marcus when we go into town. There's so much to be done now that the domestic has been arrested.'

As the door closed behind her, David turned towards Kathryn with an embarrassed smile. 'Please don't mind Stella too much. All this murder business has been very difficult for her. Marcus, you know? She was worried about, well, how it's affected him.'

So the possibility of her son's involvement in Lucy's and Philip's deaths had occurred to Stella, too. Kathryn lowered herself onto the leather chair beside the desk and settled her hands into her lap. 'How can I help you, David?'

He sank into a nearby armchair and crossed his arms defensively across his chest, ill at ease in the place that should have been his home. 'I don't know how much my father has discussed the estate with you, but you are aware that Lucy's death has put the family in a most difficult position. I am not wholly in my father's confidence, and I have no idea what his original intentions were, although he assures me it was always his plan that the estate should continue to provide an allowance for my living expenses.' David's eyes dropped to his knees. 'But he has put a proposition to me which, well, frankly what he suggests appears to me to be a test of my values. He knows my feelings about the family's heritage, but he proposes to make the whole estate over to me at his death. There are conditions, of course.' The reluctant heir lifted his gaze and forced an uncomfortable smile. 'In order to inherit, I must live at Salvation Hall, run the estate, and continue to run the plantation and distillery at Woodlands Park as a going concern. If I accept, there will be a covenant on the estate, that nothing can be disposed of for one hundred years after my father's death.' David narrowed his eyes. 'Which effectively means, not in my lifetime.'

'I see. So to inherit, you have to put aside your aversion to the family's history and heritage, and embrace it?'

'Yes. As I see it, I have to step into my father's shoes and walk in his path.'

'May I ask what will happen to the estate if you refuse to meet the conditions of the will?'

'You may. Indeed, I asked that very question myself. But my father refuses to tell me. He doesn't want that to be a factor in my decision-making. He wants to know that I took the estate because I wanted it, not because I didn't want to deprive someone else of it.'

'So there is an alternative legatee?

'Another question which I have already asked. He refuses to be drawn on that point. I am told that I will only discover the answer to that question if I refuse to adhere to the conditions and forfeit the estate.'

It was a cruel bargain by any standards. Kathryn looked down at her hands and thought for a moment. Then she smiled up at him. 'Have you discussed this with Stella?'

He replied with a curl of the lips. 'No. Not least, because Stella has her own views on the subject. She abhors the whole issue of slavery and will have no truck with it. Not even the legacy of it.' He sensed a question to come and put up his hand. 'Before you ask, I'm afraid my wife doesn't understand the concept of hypocrisy. And that is where we differ. I would prefer not to be a hypocrite and refuse the bequest if it means compromising my values, whereas my wife sees only the material gain.' He lowered his voice. 'Truth be told, Stella feels that you are somehow involved in assisting my father to find an alternative heir for the estate. She has convinced herself that your work centres on building the family tree to identify and secure another line of inheritance.'

'And is that what you think, David?'

He looked unsure. 'I don't know what to think. My father assures me that your work is to curate the family's heritage, but that since Lucy's death he has asked you to assist him in identifying other branches of the family so that I may be "supported".' David looked perplexed. 'I'm not sure quite what he means by that.'

'I think Richard is troubled by the fact that when he's gone, you will be alone.'

'I will be with Stella. And with Marcus.'

Kathryn's smile softened. 'Let me put it another way then. I think he is troubled that you will be the only Lancefield. You have no heir and no immediate family. Perhaps your father feels you should maintain some sort of connection with the Lancefield family. And by that, I don't mean the estate and its heritage. I mean your family of birth.' Her brow folded into a frown. 'Perhaps you are so used to thinking the worst of him that you can't see how worried he is about you.'

'He hasn't said so.'

'Would you expect him to?' She laughed at the thought. 'But that doesn't mean he doesn't care. He told me that some years ago you lost your sister in an accident, and now you've lost your daughter. There is no possibility, I suppose, of your having another child?'

'None.' David blushed, and an unmistakeable hint of sadness flitted across his face. 'And even if I did, that child wouldn't be Lucy.' He got up from the chair and walked over to the window to look out over the garden. 'Lucy and I were not close. In the way that my father and I are not close. But we did share some important values. Lucy shared my feelings about the family's heritage. I know that had she inherited the estate, she would have carried out her plans to erase the past.' His lips twisted as if suppressing a cry. 'I would not have had the strength to carry out such a plan.'

It was a curiously brave admission for a man who questioned his own courage. For a few moments, an embarrassed silence hung between them, and then Kathryn ventured a question. 'I've heard that Lucy had a print hanging on the wall of her room, a copy of the David Martin study of Dido Elizabeth Belle and Elizabeth Murray. Would it be impertinent of me to ask how that fitted in with her views on the family's heritage?'

'Honestly? She hated it. But the picture was a gift, meant as a gesture of friendship, I think. She mentioned it to me at the time. In fact, it was one of those very rare occasions when she sought my opinion.' He looked wistful. 'It was my suggestion that she hang it on the wall so that the giver might see that the gift had been valued. Good manners, you know?'

'She didn't want to hurt your father's feelings.'

'My father?' David gave a laugh of quiet astonishment. 'Good heavens, Kathryn, whatever makes you think that a gift like that would come from him?'

*

DCI Price cast his eyes around the drawing room. He'd been in the room before, on a previous visit to Salvation Hall, but until now he hadn't noticed its understated elegance. The room was large, long, and narrow with a vast bay window at one end, the glass running floor to ceiling, the frame unencumbered by drapes or shutters. Morning sunlight was flooding in, warming the cosier end of the room, the sofa on which he was perched, and the armchair occupied by a weary Richard Lancefield. Somewhere behind them, an expanse of empty floor space ran past the room's only door to a recess containing a grand piano.

He tried to imagine the room as it might have looked the previous evening, subtly lit by a collection of silk-shaded gilt table lamps, the family gathering for drinks before dinner, Kathryn Clifton seated amongst them. It would have been calm, he thought, genteel, the occasion oozing a subtle refinement. And then into that oasis of calm Becca had arrived, that angry little ball of venom, throwing her accusations wildly about until Marcus had appeared and steered her gently out of the door into the hallway. He glanced towards the door to get his bearings and then turned his attention back to Richard.

'Thank you again for seeing me this morning. I wanted to give you an update on the situation with Becca Smith.'

Richard lowered his head. 'Are you absolutely certain, Chief Inspector, that Philip McKeith was murdered?' His disappointment was evident. 'I hadn't wanted to believe him capable of Lucy's murder, but I had quite resigned myself to the fact. I had even resigned myself to the possibility that he had committed suicide. The suggestion that he was murdered brings with it a number of other possibilities which I am finding difficult to consider.'

'I'm afraid there is no doubt. The blow to the head was delivered with some force. He would have been dead before his body was put into the lake.'

Richard looked crestfallen. 'Two days ago I would have put money on Becca knowing where Philip was. But I must have been wrong. You know, I sent a text message to Philip, asking him to come home. I asked Kathryn to help me send it.' He smiled sadly. 'But I didn't receive a reply.'

The policeman cleared his throat. 'We are still questioning Becca, because at this stage we believe she has a clear motive for both crimes. We are also concerned that she may pose a threat to the Lancefield family.'

'Oh, come now, Inspector. Becca is a member of our extended family. If you're talking about her little outburst yesterday evening, then I agree it was unpleasant at the time. But I believe we must see it in the context of her grief, which must be unimaginable.' Richard's elbows were resting on the arms of the chair, and he lifted his hands and steepled his fingers. 'Do you remember, when we first met, I asked you to make me a promise? I asked you to treat every member of my household with respect.'

'Yes, I remember. And I can assure you that Becca *is* being treated with respect.' Price smiled. 'I also recall that you offered us every assistance with our enquiries. We have no hard evidence yet to charge her with the murders. And so I would like to ask you some questions about Becca which might help with the investigation.' He pulled a small notebook from the pocket of his jacket and flipped it open. 'If Becca was responsible, she would have needed help to get the bodies into the lake and to attach the leg irons to Philip's ankles. Can you tell me if she was familiar with the contents of the storeroom next to the potting shed? Would she have known there were leg irons stored in there?'

'I've been asking myself the same question this morning, Chief Inspector, and I can't remember any occasion when she was asked to clean in there. But the room wasn't locked.' His brow furrowed. 'The abominable use of those leg irons in this crime has led me to believe that Kathryn is quite right about the contents of that room. They should be in a museum, out of harm's way.'

Price wouldn't argue with that. 'Who else in the family knew about the contents?'

'Everyone. It wasn't a secret. Marcus and Lucy both knew but, to the best of my knowledge, they never went in there. They both avoided the family's heritage as much as they could. Of course, many of the contents were only brought over from St Felix this year.'

'Did Marcus get on well with Becca?'

'Well enough, I believe. I've only ever seen them together in the house, perhaps when Becca was cleaning or cooking and Marcus was at home. I don't believe that they interacted on what you might call a social level.'

'Who brought the items over from St Felix?'

'They were shipped by a private carrier. Nancy supervised the arrangements when she made her annual visit to St Felix back in April. I would have carried out the task myself, but sadly the doctor forbade me the trip for health reasons.'

'Might Nancy have discussed that trip with Becca?'

Richard shrugged. 'It's possible. They do get on quite well, but I don't know what they chat about. You would have to ask Nancy that.'

Price had been jotting notes in his notebook as they spoke, and now he stopped scribbling and looked directly into Richard Lancefield's face. 'Jealousy is a very powerful motivator in such things. I might even extend that motive to someone else in your household other than Becca.'

'To Marcus.'

'Yes.' Price cleared his throat a second time. 'But powerful or not, I'm beginning to wonder whether jealousy, in this case, is possibly too obvious a motive. Could you think of any other reason why someone would want to murder your granddaughter? I have to consider the possibility that Lucy was the intended victim and Philip was murdered because he witnessed what had happened.'

'You want to know if anyone bore a grudge against my granddaughter?'

'I'm wondering if the estate could have been a motive for the killing.'

At the mention of the estate, Richard's face clouded. 'As we speak, Chief Inspector, my son is in discussion with Kathryn about the estate. He is wrestling with his conscience and hoping to overcome his aversion to the family's heritage sufficiently to enable him to inherit its fortunes without burdening himself with any unpalatable guilt. Lucy herself made no secret of her plans to erase the family's heritage, if and when she inherited. And if you are thinking of Marcus, then surely he would have murdered Lucy after they had married, when there was some chance of inheriting her fortune?' He shook his head. 'We have no other immediate family who would stand to inherit in the case of Lucy's death. So, Chief Inspector, if you think the Lancefield fortunes lie at the heart of these unspeakable crimes, then I'm afraid that, like my dear companion Samson is often wont to do, you are barking up the wrong tree.'

*

Marcus pulled the BMW into a layby and turned off the engine. He rolled his neck around to ease the tension and then stretched out a hand to the jacket lying on the passenger seat. His mobile phone was in his pocket and he pulled it out and flicked at the screen to bring up a list of missed calls. Two from his mother, one from Ian, and a text message from David. He jabbed at the keypad and pressed the phone to his ear.

Voicemail messages from Stella were never an enjoyable experience. He listened patiently as she rambled incoherently about Becca, and the murders, and the relief of being able to move on, and nodded to himself as her tone became reproving, chastising him for walking away from Richard in his hour of need. He laughed to himself quietly, under no illusion that his mother's consideration of Richard's needs began and ended with the old man's cheque book. There was a beep at the end of the first message and then her voice began again, a disjointed jabbering about Kathryn Clifton and David painting a portrait, followed by an invitation to lunch at The Zoological.

He paused the messages and tipped his head back against the car's headrest, closing his eyes. Thankfully he had another client to see, this time in St Ives. He wouldn't need to invent an excuse to swerve lunch. He tapped at the phone's screen again without looking at it, and Ian's cheerful tones began to resonate around the car's interior with a warning about his mother's impending visit to Penzance, and a suggestion that he might like to bunk off and spend the afternoon in St Ives, at least until Stella was safely on her way back to Salvation Hall.

He opened his eyes, stared down at the phone, and tapped at the keypad again to open up David's text. He read it through once, and then looked up and out of the car's windscreen to stare into the distance, bemused. What kind of business proposition could Richard Lancefield be planning to put to him? He mused on the question for a moment, and then looked down at the message again, in case he had misunderstood.

There had been no mistake. David had extended his compliments, and those of his father, and asked if Marcus would be good enough to call at Salvation Hall to discuss a proposition, a proposal which Richard hoped would be to their mutual advantage.

It was a little late in the day now, Marcus reflected, for proposals to their mutual advantage. But he had to admit that the message intrigued him. He smiled to himself, and without any further delay set about tapping a reply to his stepfather.

29

Nancy balanced the shopping bag on the edge of the kitchen table and considered Kathryn with a smile. 'I'm sorry I wasn't here for you this morning. I would have been back sooner, but Richard's dry cleaning wasn't quite ready for collection, so I used the time to pop into the library and pick up some books for him.' She bristled with animated efficiency. 'He gets through books so quickly these days I can hardly keep up with him.'

Kathryn returned the girl's smile and sipped quietly on her coffee. She could detect a hint of something behind the effervescence, something at odds with the calm and usually effortless competence she had come to expect from Nancy. 'What does he like to read?'

'Adventure stories mostly, especially military ones. He's working his way through Douglas Reeman's books at the moment. He's read them all before, but it doesn't seem to stop him.' She pointed towards Kathryn's hands and the coffee mug within. 'At least my being out of the way has given you the opportunity to make yourself at home.' She laughed as she turned towards the fridge and began to unload the contents of the shopping bag into its cavernous interior. 'Now I can tell Richard that you can prepare his morning coffee and afternoon tea. That will be one less job for me while I minister to David's and Stella's needs, and plug the gap left by Becca's extended absence.' She paused, and half turned her head in Kathryn's direction. 'Has there been any news?'

'Of Becca? No, not that I've heard. But I've been closeted in the library all morning. David and Stella have gone into Penzance, and Richard has been busy with Chief

Inspector Price. I popped over to the Dower House to say hello, but his solicitor had arrived by then, so I came straight back over to the house.'

Nancy slid a final carton of milk into the refrigerator door, and let the door swing slowly shut with a muffled thud. She turned to look at Kathryn, her eyes slightly narrowed. 'His solicitor? I don't remember putting that in the diary.' She looked bemused for a moment, and then she smiled and lifted the kettle from its base, and set about filling it from the nearby tap. 'But there's been so much to think about this week. I suppose it must have slipped my mind.' She lifted a bone china mug from the draining board and spooned coffee and sugar into it. 'I don't mean to complain, Kathryn. Heaven knows I love my job, and I can't bear not to be busy. But this week? Two deaths, two *murders* even. Police all over the place, David and Stella descending on us, Becca unavailable to help with the domestic work, Marcus moving out, no one managing the maintenance of the garden…'

'And as if that wasn't enough, a genealogist under your feet, cluttering up the library, leaving piles of papers lying everywhere.'

Nancy placed her mug down on the table and sank into the seat next to Kathryn. She placed her hand on Kathryn's arm and squeezed it with a smile. 'Your being here is the only thing that is bringing any normality to Salvation Hall. Richard was right. Your work gives us something to hold on to, something to keep us anchored to our day-to-day life.' She let go of the arm and picked up her coffee and sipped on it, closing her eyes for a moment and savouring the hot, sweet liquid. 'I've been fantasising about this coffee for the last hour.' She looked back at Kathryn. 'I don't mean to complain, but it is all getting a bit too much for a single secretary. Mrs Peel has been an angel. She normally only comes in when we have an emergency, but this week every day has been an emergency. She has risen to the challenge, but I know that she has responsibilities of her own. Her husband is an invalid, you know? A few hours' work for us here and there gives another dimension to her life, but I don't want to abuse her kindness. We can't ask her to keep stepping into the breach.'

'Isn't there anyone else you could reach out to? There must be some sort of domestic service in the area, a firm that offers cleaning and laundry services?'

'If only it were that easy, Kathryn. Richard is such a private man, he's afraid to let strangers come into the house in case his confidence is breached.'

'He doesn't seem to have an issue with me being here.'

'Because you understand the family. You understand the heritage. You don't judge us for our past. And, of course, you were recommended to him by Hugh Ferguson, who has already vouched for your discretion.'

Kathryn felt a silent expectation begin to settle across her shoulders. She understood the family and the sensitivities of their past. She was trusted, given the run of the house. And perhaps she wasn't giving enough back to them in return. She was still resisting the pull of the family's needs, trying to focus on the facts of their past, and yet staying aloof from them, trying to maintain a boundary between the personal and professional. Ian had thrown a dig at her the day before. "So you're part of the family now?" She had balked when he'd suggested it and she still didn't agree with him. The jibe had come too soon. But she knew the opportunity was there. She could feel Nancy's eyes studying her face, looking for an acknowledgement, some recognition of the unspoken invitation to become a part of the extended Lancefield family.

And then Ennor's words were in her ears. "You can care without getting involved." She could see no harm in offering to help, no danger in proposing that she – at least in the short term – could help Nancy to carry the load. 'In a way, it was quite useful that everyone was too busy to speak to me this morning. I managed to scan the last two boxes of documents, and I think I have enough now to be able to continue my work from home next week. There is one further task I would like to do in the library this afternoon but, apart from that, is there anything else I can do to help the family? Any errands I might run, or odd jobs that I could pick up?'

The dark eyes that had been watching her face narrowed almost imperceptibly for a moment and then filled with the glint of unmistakeable triumph. 'Kathryn, you are a Godsend.' Nancy bowed her head and drew her hands together, prayer-like, in a gesture of thanks. 'Richard will be so very grateful when I tell him.' She paused, and then said 'I wonder, would you come with me now, over to the Dower House? We could speak to him together, there may have been developments this morning. I need to know what to do about finding a replacement for Becca.'

'A replacement?'

'Goodness, yes. Of course, Richard cares about her. We all do. But she isn't going to be coming back here to work. Even if the police decide there isn't enough evidence to charge her with Lucy's and Philip's murders, can you really see any way that she could come back to be a trusted part of the family?'

*

'Is there anything in this village that doesn't belong to that damned family?' Tom Parkinson placed two pints of ale on the table, then slipped off his jacket and draped it over the back of his chair.

Ennor Price helped himself to one of the glasses and lifted it in a toast. 'I take my hat off to any family that has its own pub, Tom.' He sipped from the glass. 'And their ale is good. I might have to add The Lancefield Arms to my list of favourite haunts.' He turned his head in the direction of the bar and smiled at the barmaid, a bronzed blonde with expressionless eyes. She stared back at him for a moment, poker-faced, and then turned away towards the other end of the bar. 'Is it my imagination, or does she bear an uncanny resemblance to Becca Smith?'

'Would it surprise you? This is a very tight-knit community.' Parkinson lowered his voice. 'It's probably just as well that the place is empty. At least we won't be overheard.' He turned his attention towards the bar. The barmaid was deep in conversation now with a sandy-haired man carrying a middle-aged paunch. The man looked up from the glasses he was polishing, stared at the two policemen, and then turned back to her and nodded. 'It looks as though we've been rumbled. I suppose we stick out like a sore thumb. They can't get many people in during the day. It makes you wonder how they make a profit.'

'If the place belongs to Richard Lancefield, they probably don't have to. Anyway, I don't care what they think as long as the pie and chips come up to scratch. Tell me how you got on at Becca's cottage.'

Parkinson puffed out a sigh. 'We've taken the place apart with as much care as we could, and we've put it all back together again. There was no sign of Philip McKeith's mobile phone, and nothing else that might be useful to the investigation.' He coughed a sour laugh. 'But we've done Becca a favour. I think the place is cleaner and tidier now than it was before we began.'

'I don't suppose you had chance to follow up on Robin Smith's alibi for the time of Lucy's death?'

'I did, and it's watertight. He was at a birthday party for his girlfriend's sister. A group of twelve went into St Ives for a meal. They took the bus from Penzance at around five thirty and travelled back in three taxis just before eleven o'clock. I've checked with three of the party and they all confirm that Robin was there the whole evening. So if Becca is our killer and she needed help to dispose of the bodies, it certainly wasn't her brother.'

'And he couldn't have set up the alibis?'

'One of the witnesses I spoke to was the girl's grandmother. She's in her seventies. Not the sort of witness you could lean on. She travelled on the bus with him from Penzance, and shared his taxi back again.'

'And we know that Lucy's body was in the water by ten o'clock at the latest. So our only known possibility for an accessory is still Marcus Drake.' Price frowned. 'I tried to call him half an hour ago, but I'm just getting through to voicemail. I'll try again after lunch.' The policeman scratched thoughtfully at his ear. 'We can't discount the possibility that Marcus would use the opportunity to discredit McKeith and frame him for Lucy's murder. Whoever put those leg irons on the body didn't expect it to be found.'

Parkinson leaned back a little and rested his elbows on the table. 'What are we going to do about Becca?'

'Do about her?'

'Aren't you worried about her? She's become very subdued.'

Ennor Price spluttered out a laugh. 'It isn't our job to worry about her. It's our job to find a double murderer. And to prevent her from harassing the Lancefield family.' He sipped on his ale. 'It isn't doing her any harm to spend a bit of time at the station cooling her heels. You know, even this morning Richard Lancefield spoke to me of his intention to look after her, and still she carries on biting the hand that's feeding her.'

'We don't have any evidence against her.'

'We don't have any evidence against her *yet*. We had every justification to ask her to come in for questioning after her performance at Salvation Hall last night. She's a risk to the family, and she's a risk to herself. Anyway, Halliwell doesn't bear a grudge, even if Becca did manage to give her the slip last night. She's keeping an eye on her.' He looked closely at Parkinson's face, took in the concern in the sergeant's eyes, and softened his tone a little. 'If you're really that bothered about her, then after lunch you can go back to the station and talk to her again. Try a different tack. Ask her how well she knows Nancy Woodlands. And ask her if Nancy shared any information with her about the contents of that storeroom. Nancy was responsible for it being shipped back from the Caribbean. It may have come out in a casual conversation.' Price took in a breath. 'And ask her when the last text from Philip's phone came through. Richard sent a text to him and didn't receive a reply. It might be that whoever had the phone was fazed by receiving Richard's text, enough to stop the pretence. And check Becca's reply against the information we received from his phone provider. She might not be telling the truth.'

'And after that?'

'I want to let her go, but wait until I give you the nod, because I need to track Drake down first. I want to see his reaction when I tell him that she's been released. And we need to take steps to keep her away from the Lancefields.'

'I don't see how we can. Her job is with the family, and her home belongs to them.' Parkinson sighed. 'You know, even though we have nothing to charge her with, the family will still suspect her until we nail the killer.'

'Richard Lancefield wants to look after her. The real issue is whether or not she will let him. I'll have another word when I go back to Salvation Hall.' Price stared into the bottom of his almost-empty glass. 'I'm going back this afternoon to speak to Kathryn Clifton. I want to test the theory that jealousy wasn't the motive. It's a long shot, but you never know. Money is a powerful motivator too. This could still have been about the estate.'

'I didn't think there was anyone left to inherit, apart from David Lancefield, and I can't imagine him murdering his daughter to inherit an estate that he didn't want in the first place.'

'What about Stella Lancefield? What if she paid for someone to remove Lucy so that her husband became the only viable heir, and had to change his mind and agree to inherit the estate? If Philip McKeith witnessed the killing, he would have to be silenced. And that would give Marcus an opportunity to frame the man who made him suffer.'

Parkinson's smile was withering. 'I think your blood sugar level must be dipping.'

'I didn't say it was a cast-iron theory. But if you don't like that one, there's still the possibility of an unknown factor. Kathryn is putting together an extended family tree for the old man. I think it's worth asking if she's found anyone else on the horizon who might stand to benefit from Lucy being off the scene. It might not be a coincidence at all that Lucy Lancefield was murdered just as Kathryn Clifton appeared at Salvation Hall to start digging into the family's past.'

*

Kathryn lifted the faded box onto the library desk and ran a hand over the top to brush away some of the dust. She lifted the lid carefully and folded back the protective tissue that encased the burgundy leather binding of a large and elaborate book. Two words embossed in clear gilt letters graced the front of the Bible, two words spelling out a single name – Woodlands Park.

The plantation family Bible was one of two items she had carefully purloined from the storeroom before Ennor Price had sent WPC Halliwell to lock up the room with a large and sturdy chain and padlock. At some point, she supposed, she might have to admit to Ennor that she had taken them. But he had been clear in his instruction to her about the items in the room – nothing was to be removed after the room had been locked. He'd said nothing about any items she might already have moved. It was a small deception, but it still brought a smile to her lips.

In any case, she could see no value in the items in terms of the police investigation. One, a flat, round canister containing a reel of cinefilm, she had put to one side for Richard's benefit. A label on the tin had indicated that the film was shot on St Felix in 1937, three years after Richard's birth. She had no way of knowing just what was on the film, but Richard had been born on the island, and she was hoping for footage of Richard himself as a child, something worth digitising for him to keep, something to remind him of the early part of his life. The other item – the Bible she was now examining – she had purloined for Nancy Woodland's sake. She had promised Nancy that at some point they would work on the Woodlands family tree, and the discovery of the Bible in the storeroom had been an opportunity that she couldn't pass up.

She ran a thoughtful finger down the edge of the Bible's cover and wondered how many hands over how many years had removed the box's lid, turned aside the protective tissue, and then lifted the Bible's heavy front cover. She gently hooked her fingernail under the cover's edge and levered it up. The action revealed a title page bearing an illustration of the baby Moses hidden in the bulrushes, and details of the Bible's English publisher. She thought it unlikely that M. Brown of Flesh Market, Newcastle-Upon-Tyne, would have expected his Bible to end up on the Caribbean island of St Felix. But then again, as the tome had been printed back in 1801 when Caribbean trade was booming, perhaps it wouldn't have been so much of a surprise.

The date of publication was a momentary disappointment. Kathryn had been hoping to find more of Nancy's heritage in the Bible's pages, evidence of births and marriages and deaths going back to the beginnings of the Woodlands Park plantation, and that meant the late 1730s. But it only took a turn of the first page to alleviate her disappointment. A once-empty page on the left was heavy with fading ink, and she ran her finger lightly over the list of names and dates. Angel and Rochester married 1743, Nancy born 1745, Robert born 1748, Nancy and

Nicholas married 1763, Honeysuckle born 1764.

The discovery brought a broader smile to her lips. It was possible, likely even, that Nancy had looked inside the Bible at some point, but Kathryn would be able to add some context for her, to build the parts into a coherent whole. She had already noticed documents in the boxes she had sorted over the last few days – certificates of births, marriages and deaths that could be used to validate the information in the Bible.

Kathryn drew her finger back across the book to turn to the next page, but the box in which the book reposed was a deep one, and her finger wouldn't fit between book and box to lever up the paper. The Bible would have to come out of its box. She carefully wrapped her fingers around the edge of the box and tipped it gently forward so that she could lift the book up and onto the desk. It was an action that freed up more than the Bible itself.

At the bottom of the box lay a large vellum envelope that was tied with a neat, crimson ribbon. Underneath the ribbon, she could see a name written in a strong and scrawling script – Honeysuckle Moses Woodlands. The envelope intrigued her and, without another thought, she tugged at the ribbon to loosen it and then drew out the small sheaf of documents within.

One by one, she examined the papers. They all related to the same Honeysuckle Moses Woodlands. A birth certificate from 1959 showed that her mother was Angel Woodlands and her father was Addison Woodlands Moses, a master carpenter on the Woodlands Park estate. A marriage certificate for Angel and Addison showed that they were married at the church of St Felicity at St Felix, just two months before their daughter Honeysuckle's birth. Beneath the marriage certificate was a deed of settlement on Addison, a generous payment on the understanding that Angel's child, when born, would be known as his, cared for by him, and supported by him. The deed was fastened by a paperclip to a small fading photograph, and Kathryn detached the two and lifted the photograph to her face to take a better look.

The image showed a young man and a child, the man perhaps in his twenties, tall and lithe with a shock of blond, wavy hair. The girl was held aloft in his arms, her face twisted in a sullen pout beneath thick, dark curls as she struggled to reach out to someone outside the frame of the photograph. The young man was smiling and happy, unconcerned by the girl's reluctance to engage with him. Kathryn turned the photograph over. On the back, scrawled untidily in pencil, were the words "Richard and Honeysuckle."

She let the photograph drop to the surface of the desk and sank back in the chair, then closed her eyes and tilted back her head. She had sought out the Bible with the best of intentions and had opened Pandora's Box. She blew out a breath. Were these documents evidence that Richard had fathered an illegitimate child on the Woodlands Park estate? And if they were, did it matter? Was it really any of her business?

Perhaps it was. Kathryn's brief was to document the family's history. How could she do that without including this child, a child that might be Richard's? She opened her eyes again and looked down at the papers. For now, she would put them back where she'd found them. This wasn't the time to bring up such a sensitive matter. For some moments, she attempted to put everything back as she had found it, papers clipped, documents back in the envelope, ribbon re-tied as best she could. She lifted them off the desk and was about to drop them back into the box when a single sheet, still lying face down in the box, caught her eye.

The temptation was too much. She dipped her hand into the box and began to move the document, but somewhere behind her the library door opened and, from the doorway, Nancy's voice sang into the room. 'Kathryn? Richard is looking for you. He'd like you to go down to the orchid house.'

'That sounds marvellous. I could do with some fresh air.' Kathryn barely glanced over her shoulder. 'Just give me a minute to put these papers away, and I'll be right there.' She hesitated as Nancy closed the door behind her, and then took the final piece of paper without looking at it, and slipped it along with the others into the envelope. Her leather work bag was beneath the desk and she slipped the envelope into it for safety, zipping the bag tightly without a moment's further thought.

30

'For pity's sake, Stella, keep your voice down. Everyone is looking.' David Lancefield leaned across the restaurant table and hissed at his wife. 'I didn't say that I suspected Marcus, I said that the police might suspect him.'

Unpacified, Stella leaned back in her seat and regarded him with wounded eyes. 'You are unspeakable, David Lancefield.' She flashed her eyes angrily around the room, barely seeing the other diners, and then returned her gaze to her husband's face. 'You have no basis on which to make such a vile accusation.'

'I didn't say that I did. I said that he shared the same motive as Becca. He must have been jealous of Lucy and Philip. And he's been behaving oddly lately, even Nancy noticed it. She said he'd become very withdrawn in the last few weeks, staying in his room and not coming out to speak to the family.'

'Nancy?' Stella's voice rose by an octave. 'What the hell has it got to do with the hired help?'

David blushed, and turned towards the elderly couple sitting at an adjacent table. 'I can only apologise for my wife's behaviour. We've had a very difficult morning, a bereavement in the family, you know.' He said it loudly, in the hope that diners occupying the dozen or so other tables would overhear, before turning contrite eyes back in the direction of his wife. 'Please don't excite yourself. I brought you to The Zoological so that we could enjoy a pleasant lunch and, like you, I had hoped that Marcus would be here to join us. It's not my fault that he's working through lunch.' He put up a hand to discourage her from interrupting him. 'I only mentioned it because you seem to be assuming that Becca has been charged. And as far as I am aware, she hasn't. She hasn't even been arrested, only taken in for questioning. And unless and until she is charged, I would suggest that for your own sake you keep your thoughts to yourself.' He fell silent for a moment, and then put out a hand to stroke her arm. 'Listen, darling, I know how worried you've been about him. But Becca must be innocent until she has been proven guilty.'

Stella's lower lip began to quiver. 'It was a hateful thing to say.'

'It was a remark which you misinterpreted.' He pointed to her wine glass. 'Now don't spoil a perfectly good burgundy with unnecessary tears. As we have the hour to ourselves, I may as well speak to you about the estate.' He waited until she had lifted her glass to her lips and taken a sip. 'I've had a long conversation with my father this morning, and he is considering a change to his will to leave the entire estate to me.'

Stella stared into the wine for a moment, and then lifted her eyes to meet his with a look of suspicion. 'Unconditionally?'

'I didn't say that.' David shook his head. 'It wouldn't be a straightforward inheritance. In order to inherit, I would have to live at Salvation Hall, and run both the estate and the Woodlands Park as they are run today.' He saw the clouds begin to gather in her eyes and he held up an admonishing finger. 'Please let me finish. You know that nothing could be further from my wishes, but we have to be pragmatic. I sought Kathryn's views on the matter this morning, and we discussed her suggestions that instead of seeing the inheritance as something to be ashamed of, I should see it as an opportunity to do something good.'

His wife pursed her lips and turned her head away. 'I wondered when that woman's name would come into the conversation.'

'Kathryn has no axe to grind in this affair, Stella. My

father has a right to document his family's heritage if he so chooses. And surely you would agree that it's better to have her on our side than working against us? After all, she has an interest in persuading my father to part with many of the objectionable items in his collection. She would like to see them in a museum. And we would like to be rid of them.'

The suggestion seemed to go some way towards placating his wife. She sipped again on the burgundy, a long, slow, savouring mouthful, and nodded as she swallowed it down. 'I suppose it's possible that she may be able to advise us. The setting up of a charitable foundation, perhaps?' She mused on the idea. 'The Stella and David Lancefield Foundation. It has quite a ring to it. Perhaps something to benefit the arts?' She brightened. 'You've always wanted your own art collection. You could loan the items out to the more illustrious galleries.'

David suppressed a wry smile. 'We didn't discuss the particulars. I suspect she was thinking more along the lines of a venture that might go some way towards atoning for my family's sins.' He lifted the wine bottle from the table and topped up Stella's glass before topping up his own. 'I've also been giving some thought this morning to the idea of resurrecting Lucy's plans to convert the estate into a hotel. I know my father is against it, but there may be some possibility of compromise. It would give us the opportunity to rebrand the family.'

'But what would you do about Woodlands Park? Darling, it's too abhorrent to even think about taking control of it.'

He drew in a deep breath and braced himself. 'My father has thought about that too. He has suggested that Marcus might like to take over the running of the St Felix side of things. It would be a fresh start for him.' He saw the glimmer of opposition beginning to grow, and he grasped hold of her hand and squeezed it. 'I think it's my father's way of drawing Marcus into the family after all.

Even you must realise how dear St Felix is to the old man. I think it's quite a concession for him to suggest that Marcus take over something that's so precious to him. And you'd be able to go out there and visit him as often as you wish.'

Her eyes narrowed with renewed suspicion. 'Richard made it abundantly clear to me that there was no role for Marcus within the family. And now he's offering my son the opportunity to run his precious Caribbean plantation?' She gave a mistrustful shake of the head. 'Why on earth would he do that, David?'

'Well obviously, darling, the old man is not as impervious to your charms as you've always thought. So you see, he *was* listening to you yesterday. And you managed to talk him round. Clever old girl.'

He waited for a moment to see if she would take the bait and watched as her eyes widened and blinked, and then glowed with the familiar smirk of vain satisfaction. For the moment, at least, it looked as though David had got away with it.

*

Samson lifted his head to look up at Kathryn as she approached the orchid house, ventured a wag of the tail, and then struggled to his feet to climb out of his basket and greet her. She bent down and stroked him gently, running her hand over his head and down under his chin. 'Are you on sentry duty today, then, Samson?' She ruffled his wiry hair, and then straightened her back to peer through the doorway of the glass house. 'Richard?' She could see him at the other end of the bench, diligently removing an orchid from its pot, and she stepped over the threshold into the stifling heat.

He turned to look over his shoulder with a smile and nodded towards the shabby Lloyd Loom chair. 'Take a seat, girl. You don't mind if I potter as we talk?' He had taken an old, stubby shaving brush and was gently sweeping away bark chippings from the roots of the plant. 'The trouble with orchids is that they're very good at looking in the peak of health, but underneath they can be harbouring a nasty case of root rot. And you have to cut it out, get rid of it to make sure that plant can get back to a healthy state.' He picked up a small pair of sharp, pointed snippers and began to clip away at the rotting roots. 'Thank you for coming over here to see me. I wanted to have a private word, to thank you for offering to give the family your assistance.'

Kathryn felt her cheeks grow warm and hoped it was down to the heat in the glass house. 'I'm sorry I didn't offer sooner. I didn't like to overstep the mark'

'Not at all.' He put down the orchid and picked up a pot, and tipped a little clean bark into the bottom. 'I suspect that when you fell victim to Nancy's persuasion, you intended to give us some help with the day-to-day issues that we are facing at the moment. Nancy mentioned to me that you might be called upon to help us find replacements for Becca and Philip.' He let out a sigh. 'It is my hope that we won't have to replace Becca at all. Unlike my son and his wife, I do not believe Becca guilty of the murders, and I don't think it will be too long before she is released. And unlike Nancy, I prefer to believe that our relationship can be healed.' He manoeuvred the orchid's roots into the pot and held them there. 'I wondered if you would be prepared to help me with that task? To bring Becca back into the fold, as it were?'

'Do you think I would be the right person to do that? I don't really know Becca.'

'I think that is why you would be my best opportunity. You have no previous history with her. She has no reason to dislike or distrust you. And I think if we could make you her point of contact for all things domestic, then over time she would settle down into the old routines and we all might make the best of it.' He turned again to glance over his shoulder. 'Please understand that I'm not asking you to be responsible for our domestic affairs. I thought you might be a go-between, a friendly face to speed up the healing.'

'It would be a very sporadic arrangement. I'm due to return to Cambridge at the weekend, and we haven't yet discussed whether I would need to return to Salvation Hall. And even then, my visits may be short and irregular.'

'I know nothing of your life outside of the work we have done together this week. But I have a proposal which I would like you to consider.' Richard shook out the orchid's roots and set about topping up the pot with fresh bark. 'I would like you to consider conducting the remainder of your work here with us, at Salvation Hall. I know that you had planned to do the bulk of your work at home, but we would be pleased to make you at home here. Now that Marcus has decided to move out, there is a most pleasant room on the first floor in need of a guest.' The old man lifted another handful of bark and scattered it into the pot. 'We could thrash out the details tomorrow, perhaps, when we have a better idea of what is to become of Becca.'

'And if Becca is charged with the murders? I wouldn't be needed then.'

He put down the orchid pot and turned to look at her with kindly eyes. 'My dear, it makes no odds what happens with Becca. You will always be needed here.' He cleared his throat. 'There are so few people who understand us. And David is considering my proposals to take over the estate.' He smiled, an almost self-conscious curl of the thin lips. 'I very much doubt that would have happened, had you not spent some time with him this morning. As a result of your influence, Kathryn, even I am beginning to realise that things have to change.' He turned back to the potting bench. 'Philip's death didn't just rob me of an excellent plantsman. It robbed me of a counsellor. Philip was my sounding board in matters of the family and the estate. It was an unlikely friendship, but somehow it worked.' He took the orchid pot in both hands and tapped it soundly on the bench, settling the bark down between the plant's roots. 'I am asking you, albeit clumsily, to step into the breach.'

The proposal hung between them in the warm, damp air. A lump was beginning to form in the back of Kathryn's throat, an unexpected rising of emotion that she couldn't swallow down. 'I haven't done anything to deserve such an offer.'

'You have been yourself. Whatever has happened to our unfortunate family over the last few days, you haven't wavered, or judged us, or taken flight to abandon us.' He stretched across the potting bench to retrieve a small watering can. 'There is no need to answer me now. I would like you to think about it and give me your answer tomorrow. But in the meantime' – he turned again to look at her – 'I have a particular dilemma, and I have no one else to discuss it with, no one to give me an unbiased opinion.'

'Of course, if you think that I can help.'

He put down the watering can, pulled a small stool from under the bench, and dropped down onto it, facing her. 'If you believed that someone very dear to you had committed a terrible crime, what would you do?'

'I would hope that I would do the right thing.'

'Yes, I see that.' He smiled to himself, amused by the simplicity of her response. 'But how would you arrive at the right thing? You see, I feel guilty for even holding the suspicion. I may very well be wrong, but I have no way of knowing unless I ask. And I cannot ask.'

Was he speaking of Philip McKeith? Kathryn considered for a moment, and then asked, 'Is it possible for you to think about the living, rather than the dead? To balance out the consequences of what you believe for someone who has already gone, against the consequences for those who are still living?' She was thinking of Becca and Francesca and wondering if somehow Richard had learned that Philip was to blame for his own and Lucy's violent deaths.

Richard was considering her now with an intense gaze. He studied her face, then smiled and nodded. 'We should always pay heed to the living. I think had I asked Philip that question when he was alive, he would have given me the same answer.'

*

DCI Price slid his mobile phone back into his pocket and slipped quietly out of his car. It was a lucky thing that the wrought iron gates at the entrance to Salvation Hall closed slowly on a timer. He didn't think that Drake had seen him trailing a couple of hundred metres behind his BMW for that last half a mile through Penwithen village, or that he'd noticed the policeman's coupe tailgate through the entrance at a safe distance. And an element of surprise was a useful thing when you'd spent the day trying to catch up with a suspect who was doing his very best to stay elusive.

He trod, soft-footed, around the side of Salvation Hall, following in Drake's footsteps, and paused outside the kitchen's exterior door. He could hear voices inside, low but chatty, Marcus for sure and a softer, sweeter voice that sounded distinctly like Nancy's. He lifted his hand and rapped on the door, then applied the policeman's prerogative and let himself in without waiting for an invitation.

Nancy was leaning against the kitchen counter and she shot a startled glance in his direction. 'Chief Inspector Price? Is something wrong?'

He gave her a nonchalant smile as he edged the door shut behind him. 'I hope not.' He extended the smile to Marcus and added a nod of recognition. 'And I hope I'm not disturbing you both. The house seemed very quiet at the front, so I thought I'd come round to the tradesmen's entrance. There was a time, you know, when policemen were considered tradesmen and asked not to clutter up the smarter parts of a house.'

'And perhaps a time when policemen, like tradesmen, had the good manners to wait until they were invited into someone's home?' Marcus muttered the question under his breath, but loud enough for the policeman to hear.

'I would think so. But luckily for me, Richard has given me permission to come and go in his home as I please, providing it's for the purpose of finding his granddaughter's killer.' Price broadened his smile, and turned it in the direction of Nancy. 'I'm sorry if I'm disturbing you. I've come to see Richard about Becca Smith.'

At the mention of Becca's name, Nancy's voice softened. 'Poor Becca. How is she bearing up?'

'I think she's doing very well, all things considered.' He turned his attention to Marcus. 'I hear you were very supportive to her last night. When she tried to gatecrash the family dinner.'

'Not particularly. I just took her back to the cottage. She was overwrought.'

'I'm sure she was. But you had good reason to sympathise with how she was feeling, didn't you?' Price snuffled a self-deprecating laugh. 'Even I know what that feels like, believe it or not. It's not something I like to talk about, but my wife had an affair behind my back for nearly eighteen months before I found out about it. And I don't mind admitting, it was a blow I could have done without. It's not an easy thing to find out you've been deceived by someone you love. But I should think it's a whole lot trickier to know that it's going on and to have to keep looking the other way.' He pulled a chair away from the kitchen table and lowered himself onto it. 'You knew about Lucy and Philip's infidelity. And so did Becca. And that's an odd thing to have in common, isn't it? It must have created a curious kind of bond, knowing that you were both in the same boat, each of you tethered to Lucy and Philip's deception.'

Marcus met the policeman's gaze without blinking. 'Perhaps it did. But unlike Becca, I didn't feel the need to take my anger out on Lucy and Philip.'

'How do you know that Becca did?'

Marcus blushed. 'Isn't that why she murdered them?'

'Now who said that she murdered them?' Price feigned an air of surprise. 'I'll admit that she doesn't have an alibi. She was alone in the cottage, apart from Francesca, and we can't base our case on the word of a toddler. But we can't presume her guilty just because she lacks an alibi.' He pouted. 'Any more than we can assume someone to be innocent just because they appear to have a convenient alibi.' He looked from Marcus to Nancy, and then back again. Marcus was studying his fingers, and Nancy was staring at the floor.

Eventually Nancy said, 'We all assumed that Becca would be charged with Philip's and Lucy's murders.'

'Ah, well, assumptions are dangerous things. As it stands, we don't have enough evidence to charge her. That's what I've come to see Richard about. To let him know that we've released her without charge.'

'But what about the murders?' Marcus looked up at him now with distrusting eyes. 'You can't just let her go free. Surely she's still a suspect?'

'Everyone is a suspect until we find the killer. And the only way we're going to do that is by casting the net wider and then digging deeper into everyone's actions and motives.' Price pushed himself to his feet. 'Perhaps you'd be good enough to tell me where I can find Richard?' He directed the question at Nancy.

'I believe he's in the orchid house, Chief Inspector. Would you like me to walk over there with you?'

'No, I think I can find my own way to it. I'm becoming quite familiar with the estate.' He cast a final glance at Marcus. 'It's taken me a long time to track you down today, Mr Drake. I'd be grateful if you would stay here until I come back. There are a few gaps in Becca Smith's account of the last few days, and I'm hoping that you're going to be able to fill in the blanks.'

31

'I don't know why you're driving me back to Salvation Hall.' Becca fidgeted in the passenger seat of DS Parkinson's Audi. 'What does it matter to you where I'm going and what I'm doing now that I've been released?'

Parkinson considered the question. "Because DCI Price asked me to keep tabs on you" was the obvious catch-all answer. That would cover monitoring whether she contacted Marcus Drake, and making sure that she didn't resume her harassment of the Lancefield family the minute her feet touched down on Salvation Hall's soil. But plumping for the personal touch was a much safer option. 'I might be a detective, but I'm still a human being. I know it's not going to be easy for you going back, I just thought…'

'You just thought you'd come with me to stop me from confronting Richard Lancefield again.'

He grinned. 'It's a fair cop, guv.' He took his attention away from the road to glance at her, but she was gazing out of the window at the passing Cornish countryside, her lips firmly pursed to keep in her anger. 'Look, my boss doesn't trust you not to go straight back there and start harassing the family again. And we can't let you do that.'

'So it's not me that you're worried about. It's the Lancefields.'

'DCI Price is worried about the Lancefields. He doesn't want you bothering them again. But I'm worried about you. I don't want you arrested just because you can't learn to curb your temper. Richard Lancefield is willing for you to go back to work as if nothing has happened. You don't have to lose your home and your job. He's happy to let it all drop. It's water under the bridge.'

'Well, it isn't for me.' She hissed out the words. 'The old man is alright. But what about the rest of them? If it wasn't me who murdered Lucy and Philip – and whatever you all think of me, *I* know I'm not guilty – then it must be one of them. Would you want to go back to a house and job where someone is a murderer? And what about my baby? You've got a child. Would you take her back to a place like that?'

'I would if I knew that we weren't at risk. You're forgetting that there has to be a motive for murder, Becca. No one is going to harm you and Frankie. You say the old man's alright, and you've already told me that Nancy treats you kindly. David and Stella Lancefield will be going back to Scotland in a few days. And Marcus Drake has moved out.'

She leaned her head back against the car's leather headrest. 'And what about that storeroom? It's not right having things like that on the estate where anyone can find them. If they'd left those things in St Felix, my Philip's body wouldn't have been at the bottom of the lake.' She sniffed her disapproval. 'Philip didn't like it, either. He told me that Richard asked him to help unpack the things that Nancy brought back this time. He didn't want anything to do with it, but he said he couldn't leave the old man to do it on his own.' She looked suddenly forlorn. 'He liked Richard. He said Richard never spoke down to him, not like the rest of them. And Richard has been good to Frankie. He's her godfather.' She tilted her head to look at the policeman. 'He's talking about sending her to a fancy school so that she gets a good start in life.'

'And you think he'll still do that if you don't go back to work?' Out of the corner of his eye, he could see the disappointment register on her face. 'Did you know that Richard sent Philip a text to ask him to come home?'

'Did he?' The thought seemed to please her. 'Even though everyone thought that Philip had murdered Lucy?'

'Richard Lancefield didn't think it, even when the initial evidence suggested it was true.' He had almost won her over. 'We think that might have been the last text that was sent to Philip's phone.' He gave a casual sniff. 'I don't think he got any reply.'

'Well, it wasn't Philip sending the texts, was it? I told you that I didn't get any more texts after Wednesday lunchtime.' She frowned, then thought for a moment. 'Have you found out yet who was sending them?'

'No, but we will.'

A glimmer of hostility returned to her eyes. 'Someone in the family who was trying to discredit Philip.'

'Maybe.' Tom smiled. 'Or maybe someone who was trying to protect themselves by diverting suspicion to Philip.'

Or, he thought with an inward grin, possibly someone who was trying to do both.

*

Ennor Price found Kathryn in the library, sitting in her usual place at the desk. She was gathering documents into neat, shallow piles, but her efforts appeared to lack concentration. He watched her for a moment from the doorway and then tapped gently on the door to attract her attention. 'Am I disturbing you?'

'I certainly hope so.' She peered at a document over the top of her reading glasses. 'I can't concentrate this afternoon. I'm sure I've filed these papers all wrong. I'll have to sort them again.' She flopped back in her seat and turned to look at him with a faint smile. 'Have you ever started something, and then halfway through the task wondered what the hell possessed you to even think you could tackle it?'

'Just about every time I begin an investigation.' He let go of the door and crossed to the desk. 'May I?' He pointed to the empty chair next to Kathryn's but didn't wait for an answer before sitting down. 'I've just told Richard that Becca has been released. He seems pretty happy about it.' Price lifted a document from the pile closest to him and ran his eyes over it. 'A bill of purchase for...' He stopped reading and looked up at her. 'A bill of purchase for seventeen slaves?' He dropped the document back on the pile with a look of disgust.

'It's dated 1771, Ennor. These documents are invaluable for academic research.'

'Still?'

'The way you're talking, anyone would think that Richard Lancefield was responsible. He didn't buy those slaves himself.' She paused, and then regarded the policeman with an awkward smile. 'I know. I'm on my soapbox again. I'm sorry.' She took off her reading glasses and placed them down on the desk. 'Have you discounted Becca from your enquiries?'

'Not completely. But we've released her for the time being. I can't really say any more than that at this stage.' There was something he was finding difficult to say. 'For what it's worth, Kathryn, I didn't take Becca in for questioning last night just because you sent me a text. It was always going to happen at some point.'

'It still gave me a sleepless night. I don't want the wrong person to be hung out to dry for those murders. Becca is a convenient scapegoat.'

'Becca is a suspect. Like the rest of the household.' His eyes softened into a smile. 'Present company excepted, of course.' He watched her face closely but she didn't react. Eventually, he said 'Richard said something about you staying on at Salvation Hall. To help Becca?'

'Did he?' She lifted her gaze heavenward. 'I haven't given him an answer yet. He's asked me to stay here as a guest for a few weeks while I continue my work. For some reason, he thinks I could help him to settle Becca back into Salvation Hall. He wants her back here, but Nancy isn't so sure it would work. I think he's hoping that my presence would defuse any tension.'

'And what do you think?'

Kathryn laughed. 'I'm a genealogist and a writer. What do I know about smoothing domestic tensions?' She pointed at the piles of documents in front of her. 'This is my field of expertise. Facts. Not feelings.'

'Would it be easier to make the decision if Richard asked you to stick to the facts, and not get involved with the household?'

'Of course. It would be a no-brainer. I'd be delighted to stay on and work on the history here. Richard is a joy to work with, and he has so much of his family's history rolling around in his head. And Nancy is interested too.' She looked unexpectedly crestfallen. 'But Becca? I'm not the right person to help out there. And it feels like the offer to stay here is dependent on being willing to help with the bigger picture.'

'On being willing to become a part of the Lancefield family.'

A deep blush suffused Kathryn's pale cheek. 'We've had this conversation before. And that's not why you came to speak to me.'

'No.' Price smiled. 'I want to know about those facts that you're so attached to.' He pointed at the documents on the desk. 'I want to ask if there was any possibility that the estate could have been a motive for the murders. Whether you've come across anyone during your research into the family who might stand to benefit now that Lucy has been removed from the landscape.'

There was an unmistakeable flicker of recognition in Kathryn's clear, brown eyes. And then she shook her head dismissively. 'I've been following the family tree methodically up the line because Richard wants me to find an extended family to support David. But so far, I've drawn a blank, at least as far as the relatively recent past is concerned. Richard had a spinster aunt, Leonora Lancefield, and an Uncle Charles who married but left no family. There was a great uncle, Benedict Moses Lancefield, who never married and died during the Great War. And a great aunt, Alice, who married and had a son, but he also died during the war. The previous generation was equally ill-fated. I can rustle you up another bachelor who lived a long life but left no issue, and four small girls who died within a year of each other from an epidemic of whooping cough. That's as far as I've gone. There may be lines of descent in the previous generation to that – there are six children there to be researched – but I can't see any way that their descendants, assuming there are any, would stand to benefit from Lucy's death.'

'And there's nothing else?'

She hesitated, and then looked away from him. 'Not that I've seen.'

'So why don't I believe you? This is a murder investigation, Kathryn. If you've found something important, then I need you to tell me.'

She turned back to him with an unconvincing smile. 'If I had seen concrete evidence that anyone else existed in Richard Lancefield's family who might have a legitimate claim on his estate, then I promise you, Ennor, I would tell you.'

Was it his imagination, or had she gently stressed the word "legitimate"? If there was a confidence, a secret lurking in the Lancefield family cupboard, then he had the measure of Kathryn Clifton sufficiently by now to know that she wasn't going to breach that confidence any time soon. At least, not in so many words. 'So you won't help me.'

'I can answer one small question for you. But it doesn't relate to the estate. And it might tie off one of the loose ends in your enquiry.' She folded her arms onto the desk. 'The print of Dido Elizabeth Belle, the one that hangs in Lucy's room, it was given to her as a gift.' She hesitated again, then added, 'It was given to her by Nancy.'

'Nancy? But Nancy told me herself that she had no idea

how it came to be there.'

'I asked David Lancefield.' Kathryn lowered her voice. 'You see, it bothered me too, that it was on the wall of Lucy's room when she supposedly had an aversion to the family's heritage. According to David, she didn't really want it, but he suggested she should hang it on the wall so as not to hurt Nancy's feelings.'

'So Nancy lied to me.'

'Perhaps she was embarrassed to tell you. Perhaps it was just too personal. Especially if the gift hadn't been received with the appreciation that she'd hoped for.'

Perhaps that was the case. And then again, he thought, perhaps it wasn't. Either way, in his book, a lie was a lie. If Nancy Woodlands could lie to him about something as insignificant as the origin of a print hanging in Lucy Lancefield's room, then what else could she have lied about?

*

David Lancefield stared at the mobile phone in Nancy's outstretched hand with uncomprehending eyes. 'You're absolutely certain that it's Philip's?'

'Without a doubt. The screensaver is a photograph of Frankie.'

He took the phone from her with tentative fingers and studied it for a moment, turning it back and forth before tapping at the screen. A vibrant image of a little girl playing on the beach filled the glass to its edges. 'It isn't locked.' He looked up at her, questioningly. 'There's no password on it.'

'I know.' She nodded. 'I suppose that would be like Philip. He wouldn't see the need.' She licked her lips nervously. 'David, where is Stella?'

'Stella? She's upstairs in our room.' He was still trying to fathom the implications of Nancy presenting him with a phone that looked like Philip McKeith's. 'You say that Mrs

Peel found this? Just now?'

'She was cleaning Marcus's room. Richard has asked Kathryn to come and stay with us for a while, and we thought that would be the best room for her to use. So I asked Mrs Peel if she could make a start on it. No one has been in there since Marcus moved out.'

'And the phone?'

'She was vacuuming under the bed. The phone was hidden under there.' Nancy's voice was beginning to waver. 'David, we have to tell someone. We have to tell Chief Inspector Price. You do understand what this means? It must have been Marcus who sent the fake texts to Becca.'

David was still staring at the phone, twisting it around in his hand, as if looking for a sign, a suggestion, anything that might confirm that Nancy had been wrong. That this was someone else's phone. 'Have you gone into the text folder? Or the contacts folder?'

'No.'

'We have to ask Marcus about this. He has a right to be asked, to have an opportunity to explain. Has he left for Penzance yet?'

'No, he's still here. He went over to see Richard. I took them some coffee over to the Dower House about half an hour ago.'

'Then we have to find him. And we have to keep this from Stella.'

'David, I don't agree with you. I'm sorry, but we have to tell the police.' Her voice had ceased to tremble, and begun to gain strength. 'Can't you see what this means? If Marcus sent the texts, then Marcus must have…'

'Must have what?' David was growing angry with her now. 'Must have what, Nancy? What is it that you're not telling me?' She snatched out a hand towards him, and he flinched away, lifting his arm so that she couldn't reach the phone. 'You know Marcus didn't do it, Nancy. Marcus was with you on Tuesday evening. That's what you told the police. You're his alibi.'

'You know that I wasn't with him for the whole evening.' She let out a sob. 'You already know that. And so do the police.'

'But at the relevant times, at the times that mattered?'

She heaved in a breath. 'I told the police that he came in at seven thirty. But I lied. He didn't come in until nearly eight thirty. And then later, after he'd eaten supper, there was a whole hour that I didn't see him.' She was crying softly now. 'I thought I was doing the right thing. I thought I was helping the family by saying he was with me for most of the evening.' She sniffed and then brightened. 'But it doesn't mean that he murdered them, does it?' She pointed at the phone, still held aloft in David's hand. 'He could have found the phone anywhere. He might not even have sent the texts. He might have found the phone afterwards and not known what to do with it.'

'Which is why we need to ask him directly.' David lowered his hand and slipped the phone into his trouser pocket. 'We'll have to go over to the Dower House and talk to him now. And then when we have a better idea of just what's going on here, only then can we talk to the police.'

'I should go back and speak to Mrs Peel. What if she finds something else in the room? Something else belonging to Philip?'

'We'll go together. Mrs Peel needs to know that she can go home for the day. And Nancy' – David put out a hand and took a firm hold of her wrist – 'if there is anything else I need to know about this alibi that you gave to Marcus, you had better start telling me now.'

32

Kathryn rounded the last bend in the path and paused to catch her breath. She was heading for the bench at the other side of the ravine, the spot between the lilac hydrangeas which had somehow become her private sanctuary. The walk from the house was mostly uphill, an exertion on a warm afternoon, and she stood for a moment staring out across the ravine to the ornamental lake. Beyond the water, Salvation Hall glimmered like a transient mirage, its leaded windows reflecting beams of late afternoon sunlight to bounce amongst the water lilies on the lake. She turned reluctantly away, lowering her gaze to the path, and began to stride the last few steps of the uphill path towards the bench.

'I like this spot. You get such a good view of the house and garden from here.'

Kathryn started and lifted her head. Marcus was sitting on the right-hand side of the bench, staring out towards the house. He looked exhausted, his soft, handsome features pale and drawn, his eyes dull and glazed. She hesitated for a moment and then stepped forward to sit down quietly next to him. 'I didn't expect to find anyone here.'

'I used to come and sit here a lot when I lived at Salvation Hall. I used to look at it all and wonder what I was doing here.' He turned to look at her. 'I wasn't born to it, you know? I was born in the Midlands, in a market town. It was my mother who… she always wanted a different way of life. But I think I would have been happier if we'd stayed where we were.'

Kathryn turned to look at him. 'Will you go back there now?'

He pushed his lips forward into a pout. 'I doubt it. We lived with my grandfather, and he's gone now. My mother has committed herself to a life in Edinburgh, and I have no friends there. Ian is the nearest thing I have to a family apart from my mother, and he's not even a relative.' He laughed. 'And to think that I was almost a fully-fledged member of the Lancefield family.'

'You're still David's stepson. That makes you a part of the family, even if you do prefer to think of yourself as a friend.'

He frowned, considering the suggestion. 'David and I have never been particularly close. And Richard barely noticed me when I was engaged to Lucy. Yet now he's made me a proposition for the future.' He looked down at his fingers. 'It would mean moving to St Felix and living over there for a while.'

'That sounds like heaven to me, to live and work in the Caribbean. Would you be working at Woodlands Park?'

'That's the idea.' He was still looking at his hands. 'But it wouldn't be an immediate move. There's something I would have to do first.' There was an odd quality in the young man's voice that Kathryn couldn't quite place, the hesitation perhaps of a question that was struggling to make its way to his lips. 'Kathryn, have you ever had the feeling that you've trusted the wrong person?'

Kathryn let out a gentle laugh. 'Oh, Marcus, I'm the wrong person to ask about that. If anything, that's why I'm here at Salvation Hall, to remember who I was before I trusted the wrong person.'

He looked up at her now with a quizzical tilt of the head. 'A love affair?'

'My marriage. My husband, Callum. We'd only been married for seven months when I found out that he'd been having an affair. She was an old girlfriend. And she was pregnant.' She drew in a deep breath and blew it out again through her lips. 'Callum hadn't wanted children, but he called time on our marriage to be with her. We didn't even make it to our first wedding anniversary.' She gave a wistful smile. 'Can you come up with a bigger betrayal than that?'

He looked away from her with a snuffled laugh. 'It makes Lucy's roll in the grass with Philip sound like a picnic.'

'But you weren't talking about Lucy, were you?'

'No.'

They fell silent for a moment, and then Kathryn said, 'I heard you yesterday evening. When I passed by the open window in the hallway. You were on the terrace with Nancy.'

'And what did you hear?'

'Something about a secret. About it being important that no one should know. And it sounded like she meant it. That when she said no one, she meant no one.' She shifted a little closer to him on the bench. 'If it's keeping Nancy's secret that is making you unhappy, then you need to let it out.'

He turned his eyes towards her now. They looked leaden, almost other-worldly. 'I didn't know that the police would be here this afternoon. I came back because Richard wanted to talk to me. About St Felix.' He looked down at his hands. 'I wouldn't have come if I'd known that Chief Inspector Price would be here.'

'Why would that make any difference?'

'Because I've done something dreadful.' He blinked hard. 'I've done something unspeakable. But I want you to know,' he said quietly, 'that I did it for Lucy.'

*

'You lied to me, Nancy. About the picture in Lucy's room.' DCI Price leaned on the kitchen door frame. 'You told me that you didn't know how it came to be there.'

Nancy pulled open a drawer and lifted out a tablespoon. 'I'm just about to make some coffee, Chief Inspector. Would you care for one?' She tilted her head towards him with a smile.

'No, I wouldn't care for one. But I would care for an explanation.'

She set about spooning coffee into a cafetiere. 'You will have to forgive me if I don't understand the relevance. I thought you were here to investigate Lucy's and Philip's deaths?'

'The relevance, Nancy, is that you lied to me. I've been told that it was you who gave that picture to Lucy Lancefield. And while I don't really care why you lied to me about the picture, I have to ask myself what else you might have lied about.'

She lifted the kettle from its stand and cascaded hot water onto the coffee. 'I was embarrassed to tell you about the picture. It was a personal matter between me and Lucy.' She stirred at the coffee with the tablespoon. 'As to what else I may have lied about, I am presently lying to you about something I believe to be very relevant indeed to your investigation. David Lancefield doesn't want me to reveal an important piece of information to you until he's taken steps to procure further information about it himself.' She clattered the spoon onto the draining board and turned to him with raised eyebrows. 'Are you sure you won't have a coffee?'

Price clenched his teeth. He stepped away from the doorframe, pulled a chair out from under the kitchen table, and lowered himself onto it. 'And where is the mysterious, disappearing Mr Drake? I thought I made it clear that he was to stay here until he'd answered my questions?'

'We don't know where he is. David is looking for him now.' Nancy had poured herself a cup of coffee, and she carried it over to the table and sat down in the chair next to Price. 'We don't know where Marcus is. But we have found Philip McKeith's mobile phone.' She stared down into the coffee and took a sip. 'It was found under the bed in Marcus's room.'

'When the hell did this happen?' Price could hardly contain his frustration. 'Why wasn't I told?'

'Because David wants to give Marcus the opportunity to explain himself.' She kept her eyes averted, away from the policeman's gaze. 'The phone was found about half an hour ago. I wanted to hand it straight to you. But David didn't agree. Marcus is his stepson, after all. But we don't know where he is. He'd been with Richard at the Dower House earlier, to discuss a family matter. We thought he might still be there. But by the time we arrived, he'd gone. Richard thought he had gone for a walk in the garden to mull over their conversation.'

'And David?'

'I imagine he's scouring the garden looking for Marcus.' She sipped again on her coffee and then raised dark eyes to look directly into the policeman's face. 'I'm afraid I also lied to you about the time I spent with Marcus on Tuesday evening. I couldn't for one minute imagine that Marcus was responsible for the murders, and I wanted to save the family from any more pain. I didn't want anyone in the family to be under suspicion. It was bad enough dealing with the loss of people we loved.' She lowered her gaze back to her cup. 'But I have to admit that I can't vouch for Marcus for the whole evening. Now that I know he had Philip's phone, I can see how wrong it was of me to defend him in the first place. I should have told you the truth, instead of believing the story Marcus gave to me.'

'And what exactly is the truth?'

'That I didn't see him come in until around eight thirty, and that he was missing later that evening for around an hour.' She looked away for a moment and then turned sharply back to DCI Price. 'And he was agitated when he came back. As if he had something troubling on his mind.'

Price gave an irascible shake of the head. He pulled his mobile phone from his jacket pocket and jabbed at it with his finger, then pressed it to his ear. His call was answered within seconds. 'Tom? We're looking for Marcus Drake. Have someone immobilise his car and check all the points from which anyone can leave the grounds of Salvation Hall. We don't know where he is, probably somewhere within the gardens. We need the house and grounds searching now. He could be anywhere.' He disconnected the call and pushed the mobile phone back into his pocket. 'Where is everyone else in the household?'

'I think Richard is in the Dower House. David is looking for Marcus, and Stella is up in her room.'

'And Kathryn?'

'If she's not in the library, then she's probably gone for a walk. She sometimes walks up to the bench at the other side of the ravine. She seems to like it there, looking back over the garden to the house.'

'The other side of the ravine?' Price had a sudden remembrance of a bench at the top of a steep and sloping path, and blowsy lilac hydrangeas that all but hid anyone sitting beneath their branches. For a fleeting moment, the hairs across the back of his neck began to prickle. And then he pulled the mobile phone back out of his pocket, and frantically began to scroll through the contact list in search of Kathryn's number.

*

Kathryn pulled the ringing mobile phone from the pocket of her tunic and glanced at the display. She rejected Ennor's call with a flick of her thumb and smiled nonchalantly back at Marcus as she turned off the phone's power supply and slipped it back into her pocket. 'It's nothing that can't wait.' She leaned back against the rough dry timber of the bench. 'This terrible thing that you've done, will it stop you from going to St Felix?'

'Not forever.' He was looking at her with curious eyes now. 'Aren't you afraid to be with me?'

'Why should I be? You haven't told me yet what the terrible thing was.'

He blinked, a disbelieving flick of the lids. 'Can't you guess?'

'I'd rather you told me.' She leaned a little closer to him. 'I'm not afraid of you, Marcus. But if you can't tell me what you did, then I'm more than happy to have a stab at the story myself.' She searched his face with her eyes and saw only the pain of remorse. 'I think the story begins with you finding Lucy's body.'

He caught his breath and turned his head away sharply. 'I was driving up to the house on my way home from work. And I saw something by the lake. I thought it was Lucy and Philip together. Outside in the moonlight, for everyone to see.' He lowered his head. 'I pulled up at the side of the drive and got out of the car. There was this queer sound, like someone gasping.' He pursed his lips to stifle a sob. 'I thought they were screwing. Out there, on the grass. And I couldn't take it any more.'

Kathryn put out a hand and laid it on his arm. 'It's okay, Marcus. Take your time.'

He cleared his throat, and swallowed hard. 'I walked across the grass and McKeith was kneeling over her. He was… he was crying.' Marcus looked bewildered now. 'He didn't see me at first. He bent down and put his arms around her shoulders, and tried to lift her up. But she looked like a dead weight. It was only when I was almost on top of him that he looked round at me. He looked terrified. I think he said something about her not breathing. But I couldn't hear him. The blood was pounding in my ears, and I just lost it.' Marcus closed his eyes. 'There were some tools on the grass beside him, I don't know… stuff he must have been carrying across the garden when he met up with her. There was a spade, a heavy thing. I picked it up and I hit him across the back of the head with it.' His face crumpled at the thought. 'There was a terrible cracking sound, and he just fell forward.

Across Lucy's body.'

Kathryn squeezed his arm. 'It's okay, Marcus. It's okay. It's out now. The terrible thing you did, it's out.'

He licked his lips and exhaled a deep, relieving breath. 'I didn't know what to do. If I hadn't lost my temper, if I hadn't attacked him, I could have run back to the house and raised the alarm. He might have got away, but everyone would have known he was guilty. But how could I tell everyone what had happened when I'd killed him?' Marcus sighed again. 'I didn't have a choice. I had to dispose of Philip's body, so I dragged it to the far end of the lake. Everyone knew that the lake was deeper there. We'd all seen Philip wading in the lower part of the waters, but at that far end he had to swim out if he wanted to tend to the water lilies.'

'And the leg irons?'

Marcus pulled his arm away from her touch and turned away. 'That was a bad bit. But I was really panicking by then. I had to make it look as though Philip had run away, as if he was trying to avoid facing the crime. I knew about the leg irons because I'd been into the storeroom with Lucy.' Marcus was fighting back tears. 'She hated all that stuff so much. She wanted to show me what was in there so that I would understand why she wanted to wipe out her family's history.' He blew out another breath. 'As if it needed any explaining.'

'I suppose you took his mobile phone to send texts to Becca, so that everyone would think he was still alive. And Lucy's body…'

'Please don't ask me that, Kathryn. I can't bear to think about it.'

She stretched out her hand again and wrapped it around his own. 'It must have been a blow when Philip's body was found. But Nancy had given you an alibi. Is that what she meant yesterday evening when she said that no one must ever know?'

'She really believed that I was innocent. She said that

we would both be under suspicion if we didn't have an alibi, so we had to be each other's alibis, as best we could. She said that we believed in each other's innocence, so we weren't really doing anything wrong. All we had to do was keep the truth to ourselves.' His face clouded. 'But it seems that only one of us kept to the bargain.'

Only one of us kept to the bargain? Then Nancy must have revealed her secret to someone else. Had she revealed that secret to Richard? Did Richard know that Marcus didn't have an alibi? 'What is it that you have to do before you can go to St Felix?'

Marcus turned to look at her and then turned his gaze back towards Salvation Hall. 'There is something that I have to do for Richard. And for the family.'

Kathryn followed his gaze. In the distance, Ennor Price and Tom Parkinson were striding out across the lawn, speeding towards the path that would lead them up through the gardens and around the ravine to the bench beneath the blue hydrangea. She gave Marcus's hand a final squeeze. 'You don't have to do anything that you don't want to do, Marcus.'

'I know. But this is something that I *have* to do.' He smiled at her, his face more peaceful now. 'Before I can go to St Felix, I have to put things right.'

*

'What's going on?' Stella Drake Lancefield emerged through the oak front door and put up a hand to shield her eyes from the sun. 'Why is Marcus getting into that car?'

Richard turned towards her. 'Nothing to worry about, Stella.' He nodded at his son, an unspoken command to step up to the plate. 'David will take you inside and pour you a drink.'

'I don't want a drink.' She shook herself free of David's attempt to shepherd her back into the house, and walked towards DS Parkinson's Audi. 'Marcus? Where are you going?' She was standing beside Richard now. 'Will someone please tell me what is going on here?'

'Marcus has kindly agreed to assist Chief Inspector Price with his investigation. There is no reason for you to be alarmed. It's all perfectly straightforward.' Richard stretched out his arm and rested it around Stella's waist. 'He will have the best possible legal advice. And he'll be home before you know it.'

'Legal advice?' Her thin face contorted as she tried to understand what was happening. 'Legal advice?' Her eyes widened. 'No.' She shook her head. 'Oh no, you are not blaming my boy for what happened here.' She tried to free herself from Richard's embrace, but he tightened his arm around her waist.

'No one is blaming Marcus for anything. But Marcus has something he needs to do.' Richard used his free hand to pull a crisp white handkerchief from his pocket. 'Now this is for the tears, Stella. I know there are going to be tears in a minute.'

'He has an alibi. Nancy is his alibi.' Stella craned her neck around until she found the errant Nancy. 'Tell them. Tell them it's a mistake.' She watched as Nancy turned her head away. 'You miserable, lying, little bitch.' She spat out the words and tried to lunge at Nancy, but Richard was holding on to her tightly.

'Now don't make a scene, there's a good girl.' He waved the handkerchief at her a second time, wafting it in the air like an impotent flag of surrender. 'Marcus and I have an understanding. Your son isn't a child any more, Stella. And I think he has qualities that you don't see or appreciate. But he will have the best legal advice that money can buy. I promise you that.'

'Why do you suddenly care?' She flung her head around to glare at her father-in-law. 'Why have you changed towards him?'

'Because I underestimated him.' He looked curiously ashamed at the thought. 'I underestimated your son, Stella.

And I'm sorry for that.'

A single tear escaped from her right eye and made its way slowly down her cheek, leaving a trail of muddy mascara in its wake. 'But they think he killed Lucy and Philip.' Her voice was beginning to break with emotion.

Richard pulled in his arm, hugging her to him. 'Not Lucy, my dear. He would never hurt Lucy, not if his life depended on it. And as for Philip, well, perhaps I didn't know my boy Philip as well as I thought. If Marcus raised his hand to Philip, then he did it for Lucy. Let's not forget that.'

Stella's tears were flowing freely now and she took the handkerchief from him, dabbing it to her face. 'Is this my fault, Richard? Is this because of me?'

'Good heavens, no. Of course not. No parent is ever perfect, my dear. If you need proof of that, just take a look at me.'

33

'You ignored my call.' Ennor Price looked at Kathryn over the top of his glass with reproving eyes. 'You cut me off, and you sat on that bench with a murderer. On your own.' He gave an exasperated shake of the head. 'Whatever were you thinking?'

Kathryn met his gaze with an impish smile. 'Is that why you invited me out to a wine bar? To give me a ticking off?' She could hardly suppress her amusement. 'Anyway, I thought you were of the opinion that a murderer needed a motive? What motive did Marcus have to harm me?' She sipped her glass of Chablis. 'In any case, if he was telling me the truth, it wasn't murder. It was manslaughter. A crime of passion.'

'Do you believe that he didn't murder Lucy?'

'Funnily enough, yes, I do. I think he genuinely cared about her. Although I'm not sure that he was really avenging her by murdering Philip McKeith. I think he saw her body on the ground, and the red mist just came down. I think he snapped. All that pent-up anger, all the feelings of betrayal, all bottled up inside him.' Kathryn placed her glass on the table and ran a finger absently around the rim. 'What will happen to Marcus now?'

'We're waiting for his legal representative to arrive. Some hotshot that Richard Lancefield is flying down from London to represent him.'

'I thought Ian Mitchell would do that?'

'So did he. But it looks as though his services are not required.' Ennor screwed up his face. 'I don't have a good feeling about this case, Kathryn. I still feel there's something that we're missing.'

She smiled at him, an inscrutable curl of the lips. 'You can't let it go, can you? You can't accept that it was a simple crime of passion?'

'I can't stop thinking about that damn picture. Of Dido Belle. I see it in my sleep.' He gave a self-deprecating laugh. 'And when I see it, I see Lucy and Nancy. I see their faces, instead of the girls in the picture. It'll haunt me now, for the rest of my days.'

'I should think there are worse things to be haunted by. At least now you know how it came to be hanging in Lucy's room.'

'I suppose so.' He didn't look convinced. 'Anyway, I'm pleased we had a chance to talk before you head off for home. I'm sorry it's only a drink and not dinner, but I have to be on standby. To question Marcus.' He leaned his forearms on the table. 'Are you driving back to Cambridge tomorrow?'

'Yes, tomorrow morning.' Kathryn nodded. 'And then back again on Sunday evening.'

'Back again?' He gave a low whistle. 'I didn't see that one coming.'

'I'm going back to Salvation Hall later this evening, to talk it through with Richard. There are a few things we need to discuss, but I'm going to propose we take it week by week until we find the right time for me to bow out.'

'Do you think there will ever be a time for you to bow out?' Ennor smiled into his glass. 'It seems to me that you want to be seduced by the Lancefield family as much as they want to seduce you.'

'It isn't the family that's seducing me. It's the family's history.' She smiled again, but this time to herself. There was no way to explain, no way to make a practical man like Ennor Price understand the attraction of all that undiscovered history. 'When you were asking me about the estate this afternoon, I mentioned to you that there were six children in a distant generation that I hadn't yet begun to investigate. I've been taking a cursory look at those six children and I think there's a possible link to some living family for Richard and David. When I return next week, I expect to begin work on those lines of enquiry.'

'So you'll be moving into Salvation Hall and becoming a part of the family after all.'

'If Richard wants me to return, I'll be staying at The Zoological Hotel and maintaining a healthy boundary between myself and the Lancefield family.' She regarded him now through serious eyes. 'As you said, I can care without getting involved. I don't need to live there to do my job. But I do need to maintain a professional boundary.' An unbidden smile began to play around her lips, and she fought to suppress it. 'Of course, that means I'll have plenty of free time to kill in the evenings. I don't suppose you know anyone local who might show me the best of Penzance?'

Ennor Price raised an eyebrow at the unexpected invitation. 'As it happens, I know someone very local who would be only too happy to oblige. The thing is, right now he's stuck in the middle of a murder enquiry, and there's a risk of a conflict of interest.'

34

Richard Lancefield leaned back in his shabby armchair and considered Kathryn with little short of admiration. 'If those are the terms on which you will return, then of course I will honour your wishes. I know that Nancy will be disappointed to hear that you'll be staying at The Zoological. She was looking forward to your company in the evenings. And we will have to discuss at some point whether you will still be able to assist us with Becca's return to the family. But for myself, I am delighted that you will be returning to Penzance so that we can work together more closely.' He leaned forward a little, bringing his head closer to hers. 'Of course, you may have some company of your own in the hotel. You may not yet have heard that Stella has decided to move in there for a while.'

'Stella?'

'She is refusing to stay here with Nancy.' He gave a dismissive shake of the head. 'It will blow over. These things always do. Once Marcus has been released everything will get back to normal.' He spoke as if it were a foregone conclusion. 'I will suggest that he spends a couple of weeks to recover from his ordeal, and then we'll make arrangements for him to travel out to St Felix.'

'Marcus has confessed to killing Philip McKeith. Whether it's murder or manslaughter, I can't see any way that he's not going to prison for the offence.'

'Marcus will be going to St Felix, Kathryn. He is innocent until proven guilty. And who has he confessed to? He is under strict instructions not to admit to anything.'

'He confessed it to me. In the gardens, this afternoon.'

'And what did he confess to? Did he tell you that it was premeditated? That he planned it? Did he tell you there was no provocation? And in any case, where is your evidence? The burden of proof will be on the prosecution.' His eyes were steely, but his voice was kind. 'Centuries ago, the Caribbean was a place for a young man to start his life over again. Marcus has lost Lucy, lost his expected future and, to some extent, he has lost himself. The case against him, even if it collapses as we hope it will, will damage his reputation. It's my hope that St Felix will be a new start for him. However long it takes for us to get him there.'

It was an argument she wasn't going to win. And there were other things to be discussed before she made the trip back home to Cambridge. 'When I return next week, I'd like to speak to you about the family tree. I've been looking at the descendants of Thomas Moses Lancefield and Lysbeth Quintard.'

'Indeed.' Richard brightened at the suggestion. 'Now that is a most interesting line of enquiry. The point at which the nuclear family began to divide. There are letters, of course, between their four surviving children. You will have found them amongst the documents in the boxes?'

'I did. It appears that the family divided not only geographically, but along specific lines of the sugar trading business.' Kathryn bent down to the soft leather bag at her feet and pulled out a handful of papers. She peered at the uppermost sheet. 'If I've understood correctly, your direct ancestor Benedict Lancefield divided his time between Woodlands Park and Salvation Hall, to run the estates, while his younger brother Richard remained in England and moved into shipping?'

'Yes, he settled in Liverpool.' Richard frowned. 'It made business sense for the family to procure their own ship.' The frown became a smile. 'The sisters married out, of course. Charlotte to a medical man from Edinburgh, and Maria to a London merchant. But the links with the family – and the trade – were maintained. Charlotte's husband had provided medical services to workers at Woodlands Park, and Maria's husband was the son of a neighbouring plantation owner on St Felix.' Richard smiled to himself. 'Sensible marriages, both of them.' He pointed towards the papers in her hand. 'There is a possibility, I suppose, that one of these lines of enquiry may lead us to an extended family to support David when he takes over the estate?'

'I was wondering whether that was going to be absolutely necessary.' For a moment Kathryn held Richard's gaze, and then she leaned down again to the soft leather bag and drew out the large, vellum envelope that was tied with crimson ribbon. She loosened the ribbon without looking at him and pulled out another sheet of paper. 'I found a certificate of baptism this afternoon, in the box that contained the Woodlands Park family Bible. But I didn't have time to look at it properly until I returned to my hotel this evening.' She looked directly into his face, and for the first time in their acquaintance she caught an unmistakable glimpse of regret. 'Did you want me to find it, Richard? Did you want me to know?'

The old man looked away, his eyes beginning to fill with tears. 'You know what the certificate means then?'

'I know about Honeysuckle Woodlands. I know about your daughter.' She placed the certificate gently down in her lap. 'And I know that your daughter had a child of her own. This certificate of baptism is evidence of that.' She reached out a hand towards him, in the hope that he would take it, but the gesture seemed to escape him. 'I'm guessing that David doesn't know that he has a half-sister. And I'm guessing that Lucy didn't know that she wasn't your only grandchild.'

'I've kept it from him, from both of them, for all these years.' There was genuine sorrow in his voice. 'I simply didn't know where to begin.'

Kathryn lowered her gaze back to the certificate of

baptism and ran her finder along the name of the child baptised. There was one more question that she had to ask, the most difficult question of all. She lifted her eyes back to Richard's face and whispered the question as gently as she could.

'And what about Nancy, Richard? Does Nancy have any idea at all that she is your granddaughter?'

*

ABOUT THE AUTHOR

Mariah Kingdom was born in Hull and grew up in the East Riding of Yorkshire. After taking a degree in History at Edinburgh University she wandered into a career in information technology and business change, and worked for almost thirty years as a consultant in the British retail and banking sectors.

She began writing crime fiction during the banking crisis of 2008, drawing on past experience to create Rose Bennett, a private investigator engaged by a fictional British bank.

Salvation Hall is the first Lancefield Mystery.

www.mariahkingdom.co.uk

Printed in Great Britain
by Amazon